THE SPIDER'S BRIDE

THE SPIDER'S BRIDE

Debbie Gallagher

PRIME BOOKS

THE SPIDER'S BRIDE

———

Prime Books
www.prime-books.com

ISBN: 978-0-8095-7211-3

ANNO 1670 not far from Cirencester, was an apparition; being demanded whether a good spirit or a bad? Returned no answer, but disappeared with a curious perfume and a most melodious twang. Mr. W. Lilly believes it was a fairy.

John Aubrey (1626 - 97) Miscellanies

BOOK ONE: A GIFT IN WINTER

CHAPTER ONE
A POISONOUS PROPOSAL

———

LAST NIGHT THE DOORBELL RANG. IT WAS VERY LATE, FAR past midnight, and I walked down and opened the door to see a finger on the front step. I bent down for a closer look. It was clean cut and dry, no blood or decomposition. I looked up.

The night was clear, a pale full moon and stars everywhere. The craters on the moon's surface shone at me and directly below, not far from where Church Lane joins the park footpath, stood a hedge I had not seen before. It sparkled slightly with what I first thought was dew—"So dawn will be soon," I told myself—but dawn felt a long way away. I went to look at the hedge.

It was stiff with frost crystallised on the web of a spider, reflecting the light, intricate and symmetrical. I stepped back a little to notice that the whole hedge was a maze of jewels and sugar phantoms, iridescent webs of differing shapes and sizes, studded by the corpses of insects. Some webs were big enough to trap small birds and these did not shine, tiny bones and remnants of feather pinched between the wire and the wood.

I realised that the roots and twigs of the hedge were held together by myriads of webs, that the hedge had not grown at all but had somehow been placed there, built piece by piece by the spiders.

At this point I saw them moving in their multitudes through, around, over, beneath the hedge, so many of them patterned and checkered, many dull, many bright. It was then I noticed a pale plump spider on a branch very close to my face, and I jumped back. I had forgotten the finger until that moment.

The spider gestured elegantly down at the foot of the hedge which was full of old cans and fast food cartons, bits of bicycle, sweet wrappers and cigarettes, broken toys and lost dolls. I wondered if the finger was part of a lost doll, but I touched it, and it was real enough, though hard and dead. The spider looked at me apologetically.

"We cannot help it," the spider said. "We do as our fathers did. They built this hedge."

I wanted to say, "What fathers? Weren't they eaten by your mothers? And if they built this hedge, why isn't it here in the day?" But the main question was the finger.

"You must leave me alone, all of you," I said, not knowing if I meant it. What I meant was, *you are not to steal bits of me or mine.* The spider didn't say anything, but I could tell it was thinking of the finger and I held it out to him. He reached up and took it between his two front legs. I noticed light patterns etched under his skin, between the blonde hairs on his back and belly and legs. I didn't know if he was beautiful or ugly.

"I could show you all of the hedge," said the spider, climbing towards me in an abrupt, decided manner. "If you want. I could ride on your shoulder." Too close to my face, I thought, though his voice was gentle, noble even. A prince among spiders.

So I stood there while the moon shone and my breath mingled with the rising mist through the air, over the hedge and the fields and all the night world, held together by cobwebs, spider gilt in frost and shadow.

I agreed, because I could think of nothing else to do. And I felt guilty about the finger. Someone's hand might be in the hedge, being used for . . . for . . . used for what? Being eaten, it would be eaten, of course. So I should do something.

The Spider sat and waited with great patience. I looked over at him and said, "I will come with you,"—his eyes brightened almost alarmingly—"in return for *that*," I added. He seemed to give a little shrug, and without a word, handed back the finger. It was all very easy and I panicked, guessing at last, how much, how desperately, he wanted me to enter his world. He looked at me, and if he thought I was inconsistent, he never let it show. Polite to the last.

Then he was on my shoulder, and I fought the urge to throw up or scream, for he was too close and he moved too quickly and bit my ear. It felt warm and thick and moist, a tongue with a barb at its end, no spider then, no spider at all, but it caught me well, the barb hooking for a second from the base to the lobe, and I could smell my own blood and another scent, which I know very well, when I am not dreaming.

I fell, and he fell with me, beside me, heavy on the grass like a body, a weight of my own size, heavier. Larger.

When I tried to stand, the glitter of his eyes, all his eyes, filled my horizons. Beside him the hollows of the hedge shone like great caverns and corridors leading inward, the labyrinth awake for me, playing music. I could not go to them, though. My head was turned towards him, now huge in bulk with eyes unreadable even yet, though the stiffness moving along my spine, the heaviness in my arms and legs, the clench of my fists and jaws told all the story I needed.

"You will see the kingdom," he told me, "but you cannot

enter dressed like that. And you will not kick." And he set to spinning, as I knew he would, while I lay on my back like a tin soldier fallen out of its box, facing the moon, mapping those grey seas in my head, unable to turn right or left.

The cold melted through my limbs as he wrapped them. I wondered when I would begin to feel the dissolution within. Would it be painful, turning to liquid? Suppose he began to devour me before? Suppose my arms snapped off with the frost and the poison? But he wrapped my body tenderly in silk from the core of him, warm and smooth on my skin. I presumed it was unbreakable, but it didn't matter. Strong or weak, I could not command a single fibre of the silk or of myself. How could I have mistaken him so?

The work was soon finished. He did not cover my face as I expected. Eyes faced forward, I could barely see him but I could feel his breath on my hair as he daubed my hair with frost or dew or whatever he had to hand. I might be food for his table, a corpse apparent, but I was dying in the hands of an artist. He stopped to gaze at me for a moment, the light refracted in his eyes. Even the warmth of the silk, the stillness of my muscles couldn't spare me the desire to look further. Do the torches of the deep gleam so wild and wise? He wanted someone to breathe on the mirrors, to examine what lies behind them, the light in the brilliant mind of a spider. "I would do it, if you hadn't tied my hands so!" I wanted to tell him. But I couldn't move, and in any case, we both knew I would never have noticed had I not been bound.

And then we entered the hedge.

CHAPTER TWO
WEB TALK

————

"YOU NEED TO CHANGE YOUR WAYS," SAID THE HUNTER TO the moon. "You are threadbare from the kisses of moths and other vagrants." She took no heed of him and danced on, smiling high over the rathe. It should have been beautiful, this landscape of sugar and night but . . . he shook his head, admitting the damage to himself. All art of light on snow was ruined, lost in a miasma of blue-grey down. He was not pleased, but he knew no better way to prepare.

Like many of the Hedge royalty, he understood form better than essence, and felt it was worth destroying a little scenery to seem so real, to be himself. So it was that his magnificent pelt gave way to a fine navy frockcoat with white and silver embroidery and matching breeches. His hair was black and thick as the dreams of corvix, his eyes the colour of lemon rind, his tricorn a glory of rapscallion elegance and his boots were ever his boots, and everything a hunter's boots should be. He had given them extra thought. To have this was worth the effort of the great change, removing all that fuzz from his body and face. He couldn't mourn it: he was well aware that no-one found it attractive.

His step had changed once (though he put that from his mind) and now it changed again, from the lope of a forest ghost to the stride of a bravado. He approached the tavern all the while practising his sardonic smile. Time enough in the wilds and he had been hunting so very long that many of his bon mots were in terrible need of rehearsal but he really felt he could wait no longer. He needed fire, and a drink and, though he would never admit it to himself, company. The tavern would be full of ready companions, and they respected him there. Or at least, he could make them respect him.

The tavern never changed but welcomed all by the light of firefly and glow-worm. Here under toadstools or wrapped in onion skins sat the hedgefolk whose blessing every witch asks in the stirring of her cauldron, and here too were brews to be found of another sort, wines of hazel and damson, fine mead and metheglin for the gentry, ales for the rougher of taste, milk and water for the pure folk who can abide nought else.

He, of course, avoided such people. Ever he cried, "Let none so refined come between me and a fine flagon!" And he would sit and stretch his long legs, all booted and buttoned to the thighs, right across the great roots between the huge blackening chestnuts, daring any to come and make him move his feet. Now there were those not so afeared as to forgo his challenge, but the innkeep always bade them give way, for though the Hunters' eyes were wild, he was of noble blood, had hunted long and could drink deep: and therefore it was best to let him have his way.

He never knew the landlord persuaded others to stay away. He concluded that they were cravens or lacking in affability, faults never calculated to ease his temper. And so fights would break out and heads would be broken for all the innkeep's efforts; a lesson, surely, in minding one's business, and letting others settle theirs.

On his arrival he realised instantly that the night promised naught but decorum unless he worked hard to make trouble, for Phynthoblin was there, all goggle-eyes and unctuous bows. He had varnished a ladybird which now served as a cravat-pin; most inventive. *Bugs*, sighed the visitor from the woods, *I know not why the Hedge is so full of them, nor for that matter, why they are so fond of me. It's not as though they don't know what I do . . .*

Phynthoblin unfolded some of his legs and hopped down towards the visitor before he had even ordered a drink. He has news, thought the Hunter, and to his irritation, Phynthoblin proved him right almost immediately. From his pocket, the courtier waved what seemed like a small wafer of gold, a card whose brilliance was only broken by the carefully crafted whirls and patterns in obsidian dancing across its surface. *Writing*, the Hunter reminded himself, *it is writing. You are no savage, you know a letter when you see it. What a fool this cricket is!*

Small glittering hearts fell from the card to the floor. The card shone like light, like joy, like laughter. The Hunter, knowing who must have sent it, decided to ignore it for as long as he could.

"Your grace!" chattered Phynthoblin. "Your grace . . . I am very honoured, very honoured . . . " He waved the card in the air. "To present you with this beautiful card of finest, finest—" He wavered as the visitor plucked the card out of his fingers, dipped it in his flagon of red and sucked on it thoughtfully.

"Blonde," finished the Hunter. "My cousin has sent me a card of finest blonde."

He carried on sucking while he tried to think of something disparaging to say, but nothing clever occurred to him. Truly, he had been away too long. "Who is it this time? Can he truly be putting us all through this again?"

Phynthoblin gently rescued the card.

"Your grace hasn't even looked at it," he complained. "This one is the loveliest I have designed. And this time is very, very different."

"He is going through this whole charade again, then."

"He is getting married if that is what you mean, your grace."

The visitor finished off his tankard with a fine slovenly gulp and demanded another, which arrived on the table in quick time. Phynthoblin ordered one himself. The Hunter was never easy to humour, but he was more genial with those who did not consider themselves above the common fare. Phynthoblin waited while the silence grew.

"Why me?" the Hunter demanded abruptly. "Why must I be part of this absurd farce? Am I not busy enough? Why can he not leave me alone?"

Phynthoblin sighed. "Because you are his cousin, your grace." He smiled his bright grasshopper smile. "And because the last time, when you weren't invited for just this reason, you turned up anyway, mortally offended, and ran off with the bride. His Highness wouldn't want to make that mistake again."

"He wants to keep his eye on me."

"He wants you to bless his nuptials with your approval

rather than kidnapping the bride and devouring her when drunk."

There was a blank moment.

"I don't remember that . . . and any way . . . " The visitor shook his head, "It's all nonsense. That one was pointless. Tasteless and pointless. No artist at all."

"We shall never know," responded Phynthoblin with a rueful smile.

"And this cousin thing. How dare he?"

"Not this again surely!"

"Yes, this again! Tell me—do that rolling thing with your eyes once more and I'll sew them on my boots—tell me, do I look like him?"

"No, your grace." Phynthoblin sighed.

"Indeed not!"

"And yet," the courtier turned his grimace into a smile of sincere ingratiation, "the similarities between your physiognomies are too strong to be denied, the blood of the noble lineage you share too evident to—"

"Do not push me too far, Phynthoblin. Know better than to aggravate me. All here is built by his hand, I know that. His and his father's and his father's father's. Do I build? Do I spin? Do you see webs here cast by my hand?"

His voice grew louder. Phynthoblin resisted the temptation to close his eyes under the advancing tirade.

"Am I a weaver now? Is that what you think I am?"

"No, no, your grace, not at all."

"Not at all. What am I then?"

"A soldier. A hunter." Phynthoblin peeked up at the visitor's face to see if it was enough. Not quite. So he sang:

"You wander alone,
you make no home.
You hunt your quarry o'er cold bare stone,
and where you bite, you leave no bone."

The Hunter nodded. "So then, I weave no webs and pursue my prey, disdaining traps. What kind of spider am I? Answer me, you green and wretched strummer, you hopper at the foot of bards, you mendacious malady of my mind, what kind of spider am I?"

Phynthoblin thought, floundered, and decided the issue wasn't worth it.

"None, your grace. None."

"And so what has your master to do with me?"

"Your grace . . . " For a mad moment, the envoy considered complete honesty, looked at the strange glitter in the Hunter's eyes, and decided against it. *The truth must surely become evident when his glamours slip away from him,* he told himself, *Thus it works with us all.*

The Hunter was famed through the wars. Hordes had parted before him, armies flowing along the earth's veins had fallen to his ferocity, and he had withstood where others could not. On his return, however, it was tacitly accepted that he was one of the less stable members of the royal household. This truth, self evident before the war, was accepted and reinvented afterwards as part of the price veterans and their relatives must pay for victory. Nonetheless, for all the monarch's sympathies to the hero, he would insist on his relative's attendance. Manners were everything to the Prince of Spiders.

"This bride is very different," said Phynthoblin, ordering another brew for himself and the Hunter. "She is an artist."

The chilly light in the eyes of Phynthoblin's companion had not changed. If anything it seemed more intense than before, and the Prince's emissary almost felt sorry for those mighty soldiers who had faced the Hunter in his war frenzy. Right now (Phynthoblin rubbed his back legs together in dismay) he seemed almost to be thinking, no, not just thinking, *cogitating*. It was all going terribly wrong.

"*She* is going, of course." Phynthoblin chirruped almost without calculation. "And she is bringing her pet with her."

"The Beloved?" A shot of darkest red lit the back of the Hunter's eyes, worse, much worse, and if there had been more room, Phynthoblin would have backed away. Then the Hunter laughed, and the grasshopper relaxed. "What, bringing her human loon? My royal cousin won't be pleased."

"It may be why he got the new bride. She is human, too, you understand."

The Hunter looked at him keenly. "And an artist. You said she was an artist."

"An artist or a dreamer or a loon, you know the sort of thing. And the pet is bringing its axe, an iron axe. So you can see why—"

"My cousin has never got over that one keeping her little painting man."

"It is a great tragedy. His Highness has never possessed any such jewel of his own."

"Too quick to cut 'em up, that's his problem. I say wait until they've done something interesting before killing them. But then, I've never been married."

Phynthoblin looked scandalised. "Your grace is being most unfair, most—"

The Hunter waved him into silence, and sat among the pumpkins, thoughtful. He pushed his drink away, which Phynthoblin regarded as either a very good sign or a very bad one. The noise of the tavern had died down around them, and the pause lasted a long time. Then he stood up, straightened his tricorn and finished his drink.

"You can tell him that I will be attending," he said. Phynthoblin's shoulders relaxed perceptibly.

"Yes. I will attend. Tell them not to start without me. I come, not as his relative, which I find an impudent assertion, but to see his fair lady and wish them both well."

The Hunter left, and Phynthoblin watched as the figure shimmered, from two legs to four, from four to more, a dark grey figure scuttling among the branches.

"What manner of spider wanders alone, makes no home, hunts his quarry over cold bare stone, you who bite and leave no bone?" he murmured. "Why, a Wolf Spider, of course." And he chuckled to himself, a dry rattling little sound.

Mad though the Hunter undoubtedly was, at least the work was done. He would put in an appearance at the wedding, his deficiencies in etiquette could be kept in check, and in the meantime his fury would be more than a match for her little doll's axe. The grasshopper's head began to shimmer and change, to peel, while he wrestled with a momentary pity. *For you are sick indeed, Cousin,* he thought, *if so paltry a device as this can fool you.*

And he paid for his relative's drinks, a matter of good form. Cannibal and mutilator he might be, but the Prince of Spiders never ceased to behave like a gentleman.

CHAPTER THREE
THE AXEMAN

———

E suum cuique dunc dictum
Transupra et ecre sinistrum
Simile similibus addendum
Daemoni date debendummmm

HE KNOWS HE WROTE THAT ONCE, OR WILL WRITE IT ONE day (time plays strange tricks among the hedgefolk) and therefore he carries on chopping wood. He knows he couldn't have really heard the Bride. She will be mute by now, a raindrop under glass, helpless and transparent. Instead he looks to his duties, eighteen-forty-three splintering every log with a brutal kiss. He smiles at her spirit of industry. She hates talk without work.

Still, he can hear the mortal or feel her calling: *come unto these yellow sands, and take hands . . .* he suppresses the shudder, and tells himself, *No, that is something else, something past and to come,* and eighteen-forty-three flashes a smile at him.

They know he misses the brilliance of the Hedge in summer, so the halls are festooned with moth wing mosaics and rich patterned shells. His hosts care for him as best they can; they dress him well, though he never lets them replace his frock coat. They furnish him with folded pairs of mouse ears to warm his hands, and if the carcass of the giver blows stiff on a nearby noose, still they have done their best according to their nature. Music echoes through the rags and tapestries of winter, for him, all for him, though he barely hears it. Three hundred speckled blue eggshells have been sprinkled harle-quinade across the earth that he might crunch them underfoot by drum and dance. He is grateful for these diversions away from endless intricacies of cobweb, but of the effort involved he knows little and cares less. He brushes the dust from a lacewing and writes his name on the faded scales with his finger.

"Richard?"

For one inconceivable minute, he thinks he hears the voice of the spider's bride, desperate and human, and then almost laughs at himself. It is only the Beloved. Only the Beloved.

"You are thinking of that mortal." The voice has the barest inflexion of displeasure, but Richard, who knows better than to ignore it, rubs his hands through his hair and adapts his face to the smiles of a courtier and a lover. She is neither fooled nor appeased.

"She took a fairy gift."

"She did not know," Richard protests gently as he looks at his love, her face smooth and round and white as a plate, extraordinary bosom tapering to impossible waist. The pleats of her skirt accentuate her hips and thighs, her legs billow out at the calves, swooping down to ankles too delicate to carry all that voluptuousness above it. Curve and curve and curve again, squeeze in, squeeze out, in and out, and the scent of maythorn which no good woman brings in the house, no woman, no woman is like this, he thinks, I paint you with your moon face, your doll eyes, and I don't think you even know yourself. But you know me and that is all that matters.

And the thorns rustle in excitement, for who does not know of the spider and his bride and the banquet to follow? What a tale it will be. A mortal, Richard knows it even before they tell him, the story whistling through the hollows of their boughs. Time out of mind they have dipped their tips through the skin of the passing world, the wrists and fingers, paws and whiskers, wings and shells of wayfarers under leaf and stone, they suck up the stories of others through sapless cores until the branches shine slick and maroon. Now the leaves shiver their applause in gratitude, a fit audience for the Prince of Spiders.

"I do not understand why you are attending," says Richard, almost timidly.

"I do not understand why you care," the Beloved replies. "I thought you had done with the mortal realm." Beyond the languorous sea of her voice, beyond the yellow sands, wait dark pebbles in places where mortals keep their eyes. "You want to rescue her."

"No. Not at all. I was just . . . aware . . . just . . . I thought she called . . ."

"You wouldn't hear her call if you weren't listening."

The lantern howls grow wilder, tiny berries rocking with halloween laughter, the gleam of the night season. They too are waiting.

"She did know." The Beloved sit herself down, preening. "As you did." She smoothes her hair and looks at herself in her mirror, ignoring him. *Soothe her anger*, he thinks, and he makes himself look to the regular slow twitch of her petticoats beneath her fingers, hating himself for calculating in such a clever way, such a mortal way, the moods of the Beloved. He lets himself feel aroused and ashamed, knowing that she will be pleased.

"For me, no,"—as the blood begins to move—"but you asked for nothing more than my soul, which was yours from the first time I saw you." Richard feels her smile though she continues to survey herself in the mirror, and his confidence swells enough to return to his point. "He will devour her without a moment's poetry."

"That I do not believe," replies the Beloved. "Nothing he does lacks poetry. He says he intends to marry her in the old style."

"Then at the very least she'll lose her hands!" Too quick, too sharp, his agitation so obvious she looks away from her reflection directly at him, but he cannot help himself.

"If I lost my hands, would you keep me?"

"You are an artist."

"As she may be, indeed, must be for him to have taken all this trouble." Deep breath. "You are going because you're afraid of him." Blow thunder and ruin and storm, hurl me from this deadly silence. Seek nothing from her eyes or lips where the lightning strikes and holds.

"Dost thou forget from what a torment I did free thee?"

"No—"

"Thou dost! And thinkst it much to tread the ooze of the salt deep,

To run upon the sharp wind of the North

To do me business in the veins of the earth when it is baked with frost—"

"I do not, my lady."

"Thou liest, malignant thing! Hast thou forgot the foul witch Sycorax . . . who . . . who . . . hast thou forgot her?"

"No, my lady."

I am not the one forgetting, thinks Richard, *these words were never yours, you can't even recall where they came from, because you, my fair one, my queen, can create nothing, which is why you keep me here.*

He is shaking, astonished at his own anger. She loves him and once rescued him from . . . from . . . and yes, he has forgotten if the truth be known, the long ago, the real and ghastly dream, an image now only to be conjured with pain, effort he makes for her sake. Eyes closed, *I will try to remember*, he thinks, a reminder, a small punitive measure, *she must feel so hurt, and the sooner it is out of the way the sooner we return to the banquet. So. Repentance.*

Trying to remember the study, his father's chair, father, father, eighteen-forty-three trembles in his hand, cognac and cigars and macassar oil, father's chair. Opening his eyes to recall the deep green brocade of the wallpaper, the clock, the room, opening his eyes to see her standing in the doorway. Sylvia. Sylvia.

Sycorax.

Sylvia's mother had been sister to Richard's own, and it was thought that their children would make good nursery companions. Sylvia, however, had other ideas, and Richard remembered them all when she strode into the room as she had done long ago, her underlip pushed out in a particularly repugnant fashion. It was as well for those around her that she was ugly. Her capacity for cruelty with the help of redeeming features would have been immeasurable.

Little Sycorax. It was father's joke name for Sylvia. Richard didn't really understand it until Mrs Bell made her pupils learn speeches from *The Tempest*. Richard didn't comprehend the play at all, (*Full fathoms five thy father lies* . . .) but he knew it was about fairy tales, and that Sylvia would never be the beautiful princess waiting on the edge of the sea.

Oh, yes, Sylvia was ugly. The adults talked about it, though they tried to keep it out of her hearing. Richard, aged eight, was all eyes and ears and he heard everything. She wanted to dance, she loved the ballet, but everything about her was lumpen, and her attempts at graceful movement were disastrous. The grown-ups felt sorry for her, they didn't know what would become of her when she grew up. To him, she didn't even have the grace to look like a proper witch. She was a goblin, with her pushed-in nose and stuck-out lips, her hairy arms and bushy eyebrows and the sheer size of her. That size boded ill for Richard. Sylvia was his senior by three years, and had a ready taste for tyranny far from the eyes of their governess. What had started as a predilection for pinching and name-calling turned into full-blooded slaps and kicks the moment the two were alone together.

Sylvia's pet game was "Queen." She would hold Richard's head down to her feet and make him kiss them. Then she would play at being Queen of the imaginary land of Sylvania, and Richard would play servants, undesired admirers, evildoers and other miscreants within and around her court. He was not the only citizen of the wretched principality. Sylvania's population numbered many but only three mattered: Himself, one permanently-defecting cat, and the strange doll.

Sylvia had many dolls, to which she tended with all the passion of a mother. Without skill in anything else, she was talented with needle and thread, and her dolls were always beautifully dressed, with clothes she had cut and sewn herself. Richard found the dolls fascinating but Sylvia was fiercely possessive, so he resorted to cunning. He was good with his hands, and made the most wonderful little card-and-paste houses with rooms, stairwells, halls and kitchens all to Sylvia's delight.

His greatest creation was a doll's mansion one could fold inwards and transform into a cottage with fewer rooms, crooked doors and slanted ceilings, then fold again and change into a small plain house of much straighter lines. He even created a small garden around it out of felt and coloured ribbon, with patches of green baize as fields, and tiny twigs making up a hedgerow, or, for the purposes of story, a dark and forbidding forest.

This pleased Sylvia so much she was ready to bargain for it. He let her play with the magical house and she let him watch her dress the dolls. Under ribbons and bonnets they stared out from various corners of the nursery, all smiles and pouts, excepting one.

That doll did not have golden ringlets, or big blue eyes or china hands. It was made of painted wood, the face round and curiously flat with black hair that fell to its waist. The outlandish doll was white with huge slanted eyes and tiny lips. It was a thing of exaggerated curves; the neck was too long for the moon-like head above it, the waist and ankles absurdly narrow. The bosom and bustle were so excessive Richard dared not even regard them. The doll looked like everything he knew Sylvia wanted to be and she held it close, as though some of its magic might rub off on her. Richard wanted to hold the doll himself, to feel it and smell it and talk to it, but he never got the chance. Even when he made a little boudoir for it complete with dressing table, Sylvia said no.

In all the endless games of Queen, he poured tea and made speeches to Sylvia, playing out stories she invented about being kidnapped or courted, stories in which she was always beloved and always won. At first he resisted and told Sylvia she was stupid but he inevitably lost the fights that ensued, so he grew sly. He would address his speeches of love, desire, and repentance to the doll, glancing sidelong at her face while kissing the goblin girl's shoes. The doll never showed that she understood, but they both knew.

The day came when Richard was alone in the nursery, Sylvania's queen being forced to re-work her sums by the governess. His heart was pounding as he approached the doll. When he picked her up, he almost fainted at her whiteness, so still and smooth. Her eyes did not move like some of Sylvia's other dolls. They were just painted on. But their gaze felt real and full of intention and he did not dare look at them. His next act was beyond explanation to himself or to anyone else. He pushed her skirts up and found himself staring at the doll's extraordinary skittle-pin legs and then, still avoiding her face, he started to pull her petticoat down.

"You!" At the door, puffing up red and purple, stood poor Sylvia, ugly as a witch in a book, tears in her eyes. He dropped the doll and stammered something lost in her anger as she hurled forward and brought him crashing down under a rain of blows and bites. He tried to put his arms up over his face, but she grabbed his hair and yanked so hard his head jabbed backwards and she spat full on him. His legs gave under them both and they fell to the nursery floor, books and dolls, teacups and toys scattering as he tried to kick her and hit her, but Sylvia gave him such a punch across the jaw that he heard something crack and felt his head grow light, as noises approached from the other room. "I'll tell them,"—her eyes filled with fury, a storm on the sea—"I'll tell your papa. I'll tell your mother." And he knew that this would be a terrible thing, but the taste of salt was on his lips, and a new scent surrounded him like the woods in the park. And *she* was there, her deathly face and smile, standing so powerful where once the witch had stood, a white hand stretched out towards him.

"You can come with me if you like."

Her eyes dark, dark. She is a fairy, Richard, beware. *Come Unto These Yellow Sands*. But if you do, you will never come back. Never come back.

Scrambling towards her. Such a smile, such a scent flooding the room, washing away all the world, no Sylvia, no Sycorax, only *her* and suddenly their legs were entangled, and he kissed her like a man kisses a woman, like father kissed mother, like Sylvia wanted to be kissed, they kissed and they kissed as the room span and Mother gasped and Father roared and tried to separate them. But by then the hedge had grown wild over their bones, and they were free.

REMEMBERING. SMILING IN THE EYES OF THE BELOVED, Richard is ready, she understands, so perfect is her love, and the time has come for the banquet.

Each man then has his own unlucky fate both here and beyond—like must be added to like, and ones due paid to the appointed spirit. Mmmm.

Richard straightens his collar and grasps eighteen-forty-three who, for her own part, is grinning with delight. She hates talk without work.

CHAPTER FOUR
OF TOADS AND SCISSORS

———

HOW EXCITED THEY WERE! A WEDDING, A WEDDING! THEY
clung to the wet woolly sides of sheep like burrs and seeds,
and chattered and sang swaying with each cloven footfall.
They sucked like tics and in the rain all their finery turned
to silver. They spoke of old poetry and amethyst wines, they
praised the Prince of Spiders for his generosity; for they were
ever hungry, and knew they could do the banquet justice.
And his bride! How special she must be! But what it was that
made her special and why the Prince was so enamoured, none
dared guess. They had seen no art from her, heard no songs or
stories, but what did that matter? She was an artist through
no effort of her own; it was only the Prince's word that said so,
and that was all they ever needed.

AND THE THOUGHTS OF THE BRIDE GLEAMED INSIDE HER
head, silent though moving, like seeds hidden far beneath the
earth.

He keeps me at the centre of the Winter's web, a diamond
unfolded, a map of glass and lace. How can I be lost when I
glitter so, an earthlight, a star under a sky brimming with others
like me? But the moon is too bright and I am too little, and I
cannot see them, or they cannot see me. All I can see in the
frozen pool below is my own reflection, a white face guarded by

a gaunt and hungry pike. I heard thunder and the snow turned to raindrops, and I thought it would thaw my prison but no, no, oh Father, if, by your art, you can allay this storm . . .

I knew then that I was changing.

CHILDREN SHOULD BEWARE OF WHAT THEY MAKE AND BREAK, and most of all, what they throw away, for of such things the Prince of Spiders makes his minions.

The body of a doll lay in the hedge, long and slim and headless. Rain fell, softening all the white world until it reached me. Then it hardened into moonlight and pearl, leaving me still and locked at the centre.

"She will soon come," supplied the voice behind me. The poison was too cold in my veins, the ropes too strong, and I could neither turn nor speak. The voice was deep and rasping, but I could feel its attempt to sound gentle. Not that it mattered. Kind or cruel, I could have done nothing in response.

"You are pretty enough," it said. "Though you have no wings." Something moved against the silk on my spine, around my waist. For a moment I was numb, and then I recognised the feeling. It was warm and strong and supple, and in the sleep of the ice, I wanted to lean against it, to fall into it and let it support me.

"I should like to eat you," continued the voice softly, "but he will not allow that."

I felt it shudder in silent laughter, as the touch moved, like a thick and massive root curling its growth around my torso. The lower edge of my eyes could almost make it out, and my guess supplied the rest. Beads of sweat on my forehead froze as soon as they formed. One tumbled into the pond below and I saw the long white jaws of the pike snap it up when it touched the water. I realised that to the creatures of the Hedge I must be a confection of sugar diamonds by now, saved from their grasp only by the will of their master. Who would have thought that ice and poison would make such a prize of me?

The tongue pulled, tentative but insistent, at the web around my neck. "You . . . wouldn't . . . dare," I thought, and surprisingly, the words came out in a slow stammering whisper. I could not believe I had said them, but the mist of my breath still floated before me, and the tongue recoiled. I tried again. "He will kill you if you affront him." The sound rusted and grew cold in my throat. But still, I had said it.

I was gratified by the moment's stillness that followed. The tongue was clearly daunted. Perhaps it had not expected me to be able to speak at all. I myself was surprised by the new ache in the hinge of my jaws. My voice sounded as though I had not spoken in a thousand years. Perhaps I hadn't.

The voice tried to recover itself.

"Do not pretend you speak for him," it said. I had intended no such thing of course, but still, the voice's incredulity gave me hope. Clearly, this was a method no-one ever used.

"Why not? Is he not, not . . . " What was he? I barely knew what to call him. And then I did.

" . . . A prince, the prince of spiders?"

I could feel some kind of pause, the equivalent of an intake of breath, and we both waited under the stars. A dank living smell drifted past, and below in the water I saw frozen strands of toadspawn. Suddenly I understood the tongue and the scent, and what it was that waited behind me. I wondered how long I had been asleep, if indeed I had slept at all.

"More than spiders." The voice seemed unwilling, a grudging acceptance, and yet there was an attempt at cunning, a kind of honey to the sound.

"You know very little. Do not speak."

Softer still, beguiling.

"Do not pretend you understand or care. Innocence best becomes you."

But pretence, I realised, was all that mattered in the Hedge, the very reason the voice so earnestly forbade it. And so I started to learn. I tried to crick my head downwards, but my neck was too stiff, and this, too, made sense. After all, the neck was where the Prince had bitten me. It would always be vulnerable to him, where his power lay thickest. My eyes however, after much strain, flickered towards a new sound.

Harsh, regular. A click, something like a click.

A snip. Repeated.

Snipping.

Through the Hedge.

Scissors, not rusty like my voice, but clean and sharp and well whetted. Jammed down over one of the handles was a plastic head, which I knew must have belonged to the body of the doll. But I was not ready for what I saw. I had expected the doll's head to be blonde and new and smiling. When she turned to me, without understanding anything of the past, or of Richard, I knew exactly who she must be.

"Sycorax?"

Richard faltered a moment. "He has sent Sycorax to her?" And eighteen-forty-three swayed in his hands, as though for a moment he was the tool and she the craftsman.

"The Toad is there, too. He will keep the bride safe." The Beloved spoke with all the serenity of dunes at midnight, under a serpent moon.

"He—the Prince—didn't do this," Richard blurted out. "It would never occur to him."

"Do I choose what he does and does not do?" She sat before a dresser of ivory. Richard himself had carved it and it had a life of its own, with nymphs, cherubs and satyrs who sat, amused and still by day, and later held revelries under the light of the lady's mirror. Around her the maid fluttered, a little beaked thing in hooped petticoats, who heated tongs and curled the long midnight oakfall of the Beloved's hair.

Aware of the mortal's eyes upon her, the servant lisped somewhat wretchedly into her lady's ears. "No, no, stay," the Beloved was impatient, as well she might be. This was no time for dispute; only one side of her hair was done. "Richard, you must understand about tonight. The Hunter will be at the feast, and my idiot sister arrives on the arm of the Red Duke. If you are not there to help the Prince keep order, who knows what will happen when—"

"When what?" There is a flame in the hearts of mortals which now and then catches fire in their mouths. "When Sycorax is finished, when she has *prepared* the royal bride?" His anger rose, stinging the air. "And how will Sycorax do it, how will she create what she, what she hates—" The Beloved flickered her eyes towards her pet who looked back at her without an instant's humility. Hard, he thought, growing harder by the hour, and eighteen-forty-three almost hissed as he held her. He did not realise this until he saw that the Beloved was almost hissing back.

"Get you to your chamber, and calm yourself," she said, her eyes blank and cold. He felt the power leave his hands and stood up, ashamed. He could not meet her gaze, but he stole glimpses of her under his lashes, and he could see the sorrow of her heavy, slanted, beautiful eyelids, feel her head almost buckle under the swan delicacy of her neck; he knew he had hurt her. The pain was like a knife slipping under his ribs. It was only when alone that he remembered her eyes.

"The Prince never did this," he spoke aloud to one he saw and couldn't see, while the servants buttoned his waistcoat, adjusted his cummerbund, and warily tried to put a bow on eighteen-forty-three. "He never sent her at all. *You* did."

And despite the protests of the servants, when the Beloved sent word for him to return, the bower was empty of lover and killer alike.

When Richard moved through the woods (how they have grown! were they not once a hedge?) he had no plan. All he could feel was her calling him, the pulling at his heart, so he moved quickly before he had to respond. He had never loved her so much as when he betrayed her.

He tried to tell himself that she did not understand because she wasn't human, but he knew there was no truth in it. She knew what she was doing, she always knew. Eighteen-forty-three trembled in his hands; he had not known how Sycorax had returned (*for the life of me I swear she lies body and face apart in a ditch beyond the Foley pastures. How did she get here?*) and he blamed himself for it all, for he had heard the mortal cry out in his mind even as the Prince of Spiders took her the first time, and if he had done something then, he would not now be running through the woods under owl-light, hiding from the only thing that mattered to him. He should have disobeyed her in a small way, to avoid hurting her so deeply now. All his fault, his own fault. He moved and the woods moved with him, the Hedge dancing around him, the world getting ready for the wedding feast. He had no delusions about how Sycorax would treat another woman, a prettier woman, a creature desired and loved. But he did not know how to stop her, and listening to eighteen-forty-three was not the answer.

He didn't even know where the Bride was. He tried to still himself, to call her in a way more gentle and clear than her first urgent cry to him. He stopped and let the thoughts flow out from him like a song, for the air of the Hedge was delicate and could carry ideas as easily as sound if one only took time. He sat down. The soil beneath him was bare and brown, and though cold, he could feel a warmth deep within it, a flame in the heart of the earth, like the flame in his own heart.

"Come unto these yellow sands." He tried to see it again, the desert near a sea in his mind, a place, a beach, a warm land far from here. "And take hands."

And he knew for a certainty that he had painted it once. But how? He had left the mortal world when he was a little boy. *No*, said something in his mind, a voice like that of a mortal woman, not Sycorax, of course, no. *After all*, came that cool female touch to his mind again, *if you left the mortal world when you were a little boy, where did you get your cold iron axe?* The question floated away, unimportant compared to finding the spider's bride. "Hear me," he pleaded, the nearest to a command Richard ever managed in his entire life. "Hear me. I know you can hear me. Reach out to me, you called and I am still here, take hands, take my hand, let me help you . . . "

The air was still.

But the earth trembled beneath him. It quivered like a dancer with gathering thunder underfoot, leaping and stamping far to his left. He stood up and ran towards that tremor, a music of its own, and the bracken moved for him, and he noticed no tree roots in his way, and he ran like a hero, and eighteen-forty-three grew warm as he passed branch and twig, feather and bone, running towards the old pike pond where, high above the shorn branches shone a trapped star.

CHAPTER FIVE
HOW TO ACCEPT AN INVITATION

———

"HAVING SAID THAT, HE LEFT NO TIP," THE RED DUKE leaned back and chuckled so heartily his tankard shook. His companion, more delectable by far than Phynthoblin, had more decorum than to laugh out loud. Her pretty lips barely touched the milk, but her eyes sparkled appreciatively. "Heard it myself, out of the wheeltapper's pipe! Your turn!" The Duke was almost bursting out of his brocade at his own cleverness—a remarkable feat for one so gaunt—and did not believe for an instant in Vulpinet's ability to out-story him. She smiled, and the Duke marvelled at the differences between this charming daughter of summer and her sister, the Beloved. "Charm without devilry," he called it. Vulpinet's hair was red, her ears were pointed and white tipped, and her eyes were speckles of tangerine in her sweet shrewd little face. Most in the Hedge would have claimed her to be less alluring than her famous sibling, but it was generally agreed that her company was more charming. Fewer storms and far less stone in her character, Vulpinet could make herself popular wherever she went. But then in this, as in many other things, she had had much practice.

"Duke, you are the most incorrigible of monsters! So the Prince has talked to the poor mad Hunter, you overhear this folly from a public tavern, you rush over here and spill your tale like a bad beer you can't wait to be rid of, and I can't even drop a hint to my poor sister! And now it's my turn, you say!"

"You can at least tell me about her pet."

"I shouldn't tell you anything. You're lucky if I tell you what colour my hat will be."

"Is it not a masked ball then?"

"Masks, hats . . ." She shrugged. The truth was that everyone had received Phynthoblin's invitations, and everyone had forgotten the details clearly and beautifully outlined in them. As usual, the Duke had missed the point, but Vulpinet was too pleased with her purchase not to show him, and nudged her ladybird servant into opening the hatbox.

"Look," she said, as she placed the creation deftly between her ears. The bonnet was indisputably a masterpiece, astir as it was with flowers and the green, even in the depths of winter. Vulpinet's hats were outrageous, with cornflowers and poppies, eglantine and foxgloves, seen nowhere else after snowfall. Perhaps she had gone to the moon to pick them. Or perhaps the entirety of the seelie court just packed up its bags and moved to her hat over winter, scale being no problem for the people of the Hedge. The Duke knew what he believed, he just wondered how she ever reached her hair to comb it through all that green tangle.

All was astir on the hat now as the duke watched. A tiny white stag with hooves and antlers of gold raced along the brim of the hat, over fields of embroidered flowers, pursued by a throng of dogs and riders. The cavalcade raced down-hill through giant ribbons, off the hat and down Vulpinet's neck, away over her shoulder and outstretched arm, for all the world like some impossible flowing millipede. Far off could be heard the sounds of shrill horns and baying hounds. She graciously bowed and extended her hand to the floor, allowing the hunt to gallop off between her fingers.

"A small present for the Bride and Groom," she explained. "As a courtesy. Should the hunters prevail, the banquet may have some summer meat for the bride and groom to savour."

"Not just the bride and groom, I hope." The duke smiled, almost with relief. The last of the Prince's banquets had been based around a dubious extravaganza of brightly wrapped and wriggling hors d'oeuvres, all scented with the residue of his majesty's own silk, and the Duke had found himself compelled to stick to orange peel fungus and white horn mushroom. He had made a considerable dent in the Prince's brandy stocks that day.

"But surely some of your folk will be there?" he asked. "You summer folk are not just sending gifts?"

Vulpinet smiled and fluttered her eyelashes in a way most captivating. "Some will be there. I will certainly be attending. There are those of the summer court who do not find the Prince's celebrations to their liking."

"And these will not be attending?"

"On the contrary, these are bound to attend, simply to begin disputes of entertaining vigour. Only those wedded to peace will be staying at home."

This was almost entirely true. The Prince of Spiders had instigated many new customs, some more successful than others. Perhaps the least popular was his habit of specific invitations to specific guests, a thing hitherto unknown in the Hedge. Time out of mind whatever the feast, whoever the host, the banquets of seelie and unseelie were never selective. All who attended were welcome, provided they knew the ways and kept good manners. But the Prince of Spiders feared disagreement among his guests, and wished to suppress over-lively spirits in his court.

Not only did he limit his court to those he could trust to approve of him, he had recently added a new law, that no weapon should be carried in his sight. This ruling had an invigorating effect among the Summer Folk, normally so sluggish in the dark of the year, and they were all coming, invited or not, with brightly polished swords and lances and even the occasional arquebus. Those without invitations among the unseelie were also determined to enjoy their Prince's hospitality—he cannot have meant to insult *them*, after all—and, remembering his rule about weapons in his sight, carried thorn daggers in their cuffs and re-designed knives of remarkable inventiveness down their bootflaps. The wedding showed every sign of turning into an unforgettable occasion.

"A reckless gathering." The Duke shrugged and added with casual gallantry, "I can offer you a guard of honour, if you wish."

Vulpinet considered before answering. Though the wars were over and done, the Red Duke's people were still regarded with suspicion by many of the Hedge, and the Hunter, angry enough with the Beloved, would surely be roused to greater madness by seeing her sister on the arm of this most famed of enemy generals.

"Why, thank you, sir." She smiled. "I think I shall be glad to accept your offer. That would be very nice."

The Red Duke looked upon her demure expression with evident pleasure. How lovely she was, so like and so unlike her sister! He was ferociously loyal to his own most demanding of monarchs, and yet if he could tear himself away from politics and the demands of his position, how perfectly Vulpinet would suit him! She had everything a soldier could want in a wife. Charm without devilry, he told himself, his medals clinking with chitenous valour. It was only much later, when she had gone, that he recalled the question he had wanted to ask her: it was of course, the matter of Richard's axe.

"It is bad luck to paint fairies, they say." The maid at Foley House had polished and cleaned until no stray mote dared enter Sir Thomas's exhibition rooms, and she was pleased with her efforts, though dismayed by the subject matter of the paintings. Sir John had high hopes for his young artist friend, who strayed and fidgeted and smiled, sometimes sweetly, sometimes like a man in the grips of a nervous fever. A nice young gentleman, she thought, but peculiar, and the things he painted were odder still.

"Hark at her!" cawed one of the footmen. "Last May she was all 'flowers-is-boring, why-don't-he-paint-something-else' at us. I reckon Mary should get herself a job as art fancier, seein' as she knows so much about it."

Mary drew herself up with dignity. "I'm not saying I know about such things," she replied. "But I know Sir Thomas knows, and he was saying that Mr Dadd would do well to follow his own way and go beyond flowers and ships. It's just that—"

"I'm with Sir Thomas on that. I'd sooner see a picture of a

fairy than a flower, specially as them ladies don't bother with too many clo'es."

Both the footmen found this raucously amusing, while Mary pursed her lips. Her opinions usually echoed those of her employer, but on the subject of fairies she was a child of pasture rather than town. Fairies were bad luck. Everybody knew that.

Some fairies didn't have to be bad for you, and if he just painted the ones out of Shakespeare, Mary might have felt less concern. They were often a bit underdressed, but she prided herself on having more education than the footmen; most old paintings had people wandering around wearing clothes that looked like they might fall off any moment. That's just what painters paint, she told herself. But Mr Dadd's fairies were different. Mary couldn't quite explain her disquiet. One in particular drew her eyes again and again, and she didn't know why. It wasn't that she liked it; quite the contrary.

The portrait was of a black haired woman, from Mr Dadd's sketches of those poor souls at the Bethlehem hospital. He called the painting "Crazy Jane," and she wore enough clothes for the footmen to ignore her. Her hands were wrapped around the branches of a tree, her hair was full of wild flowers and her face . . . only a fool couldn't recognise what kind of face that was. Crazy Jane's skin was pale and her eyes were blue-grey hazel and her expression . . . centuries of instinct coursed through Mary's veins and she knew that Crazy Jane was no more a Bedlam lunatic than she was. Jane was a fairy, more of a fairy than all those Pucks and Oberons and Titanias. And there was something else too, something wrong, but Mary couldn't quite put her finger on it. Maybe it was because looking in Crazy Jane's eyes, it was clear she *was* the kind of fairy who brought bad luck.

The exhibition was Mr Dadd's first with fairies as his entire theme. Sir Thomas, kind patron that he was, had gently encouraged him to follow his muse, and never doubted for an instant. Richard doubted, and Mary, though nobody asked her, shared his misgivings, but she knew how important this was. Success here would mean greater interest from the academy, perhaps even an extension of the exhibition in London. Glasses were polished, the rooms were as clean as a pick, and Mary's diligence knew no bounds until she was bustled out by one of Mr Dadd's friends who spent the entire afternoon hanging the new paintings.

The most important painting was called, "Come Unto These Yellow Sands," though Mary could not see what the fuss was about. She knew it was based on *The Tempest* by William Shakespeare. The painting was meant to show a magical island, but all she saw was a beach with some people dancing under a shadowy cliff, so dark it was almost impossible to make out the red tints at the edge of the water. Mary was not impressed with the masterpiece; to her mind it certainly caused more bother than it was worth. So much time was taken up "setting" it that everything else got pushed back, and the house had been frantic until less than half an hour before the first guests were announced.

Mary had seen all the bustle of the arrivals. The vestibule was full of dripping umbrellas, and outside, the sun shone like gleaming glass along the park verge. The visitors murmured and drifted here and there, almost awaiting some kind of declaration to the effect that the exhibition was open, so that they could officially start looking at the paintings. Between Sir Thomas and his friends from the academy, the young artist seemed to be genial enough, until the young lady appeared, and then Mary saw the young artist grow white and red and white again.

"Now, there's someone he weren't expecting," she mused. "Nor's she so pleased to see him. Wonder what all that's about?"

Mary's observations were much keener than those of Sir Thomas. The success of his patronage filled all his heart and most of his guests' ears. Young Richard, he noted, so quiet and calm in his work, was a bag of nerves in society, and there could be no real excuse for it. Three years of demonstrating his talent to the public ought to be enough to knock the corners off of any artist. But Richard's sensitivities were delicate, all the more so because the subject matter was different to his usual, and because family and friends were attending. "Not without honour is a prophet, save in his own country," Sir Thomas remembered his own father's unqualified scoffing at his early efforts. By contrast, Richard's father was full of praise for his son's work, and seemed determined to introduce the accomplished young man to a gaggle of acquaintance old and new, including several charming young ladies. Sir Thomas barely registered Richard's discomfort at being introduced to a woman in green. While he admired and understood his protégé's talents, he had never quite grasped the extent of Richard's helplessness in the presence of the opposite sex. Even if he had, this situation was very different.

She was not beautiful. Her complexion was too brown for fashion, and her eyes were brown and her hair was brown.

Her lips were full and her chin square, and much she had that did not make for conventional beauty. But for all that, she was impressive, tall and well formed. "Like an amazon, or a queen of Ind," some would-be poet murmured. She smiled at Richard like an old friend. Richard could not speak, and it was in that moment Mary understood why she didn't like Crazy Jane. She left off serving drinks for just a moment, to go and check. Meanwhile, the lady in green did the courtesy of rescuing him from his mute terror.

"How do you do, Richard? You must be very proud today."

Proud? Richard stared at her. What was she talking about?

"Oh, I—this is Sir Thomas's doing, I could not, could not . . . I mean I did nothing . . . very little . . . my thanks of course go out to him . . . "

"He has been generous, of course. But it is your work we come to see. Are you pleased with it?"

"Oh, yes, it is fine, a fine exhibition. Sir Thomas has been—"

"—I mean your work."

"Ah well." He paused. "There, well, Sir Thomas and I must differ. There are obvious flaws, details, I am not, that is, I have not finished, or at least I have finished these paintings, of course, or they would not be here, but I have not properly explored these themes, and there is much here that, were I to paint the pictures again, I would amend or at least approach with more finesse . . . "

His words drifted on in incontinent panic. Why had Father introduced them? He had never liked her, and he must have known his son's feelings. Of what point was this agony? She let the passing crowds speak for her, and Richard pulled himself together. Talking of his work would only bore her. She wanted him to talk of herself.

"And how is your family?"

She smiled. She must know how little he cared.

"They are well, I thank you. I have no news you have not heard." She shrugged. Her inarticulacy was more practiced than his, but between them, they had a great gift for silence. It was then he noticed the ring on her hand. Rubies and diamonds. This year, he suddenly remembered, August 1843, she was to be—

"Married?" he said, loudly and abruptly. "Married? *You*?" The exclamation was loud enough to draw glances, and she looked momentarily perturbed.

"Well, yes, you do recall, do you not? When we last met I mentioned it . . . myself and Walter . . . "

"Walter? Walter Potter?"

"Well yes, you remember, we told you we were engaged, but we are bringing the wedding forward to—"

"Engaged? To Walter Potter? The taxidermist?"

Walter Potter the taxidermist. Walter, whose moustache had more personality than he did. Walter, whose idea of art was to create small stage settings where stuffed animals posed in scenarios. His latest masterpiece had been a series of tableaux based around a boxing match between two ferrets: shorts, gloves, boxing ring, no detail was missed. Dead animals in dolls' houses. And this was her groom-to-be!

"I understand if you have forgotten, I know you have had much to think about." Her voice was gentle and low, an excellent thing in a woman.

"You cannot marry," he told her flatly. *Witches lose*

their power if they marry, he almost added, and then was confused at his own dismay. No more spirits enclosed in the cloven pine. That would be a good thing, surely. *When we last met we were in a place far from here*, the thought flashed through his mind, *and had better things to do than talk in this way.*

"Richard," she said softly. "You have been a little ill . . . "

"I have not been ill. I have been away. We have both been away." He could barely contain his irritation. What a fool she was, how absurd of her to attempt this phantasy, this doll's life. It fitted her no better than her mother's petticoat had when she was small, and he could remove it now as easily as he had then. After all, he thought, there is no time, not really. These clocks are just a game. We know nothing has changed, no matter how beautiful she has become.

"Do you still keep dolls?"

Her smile grew hard.

"No, Richard. I threw them all away a long time ago."

"I made a doll of you, I remember. I called it Sycorax." She smiled in a way that brought the nursery back to his mind. He knew if they had been alone, she would have bitten his face, but there were people all around, they were grown now, and she was a lady. Her answer was just ladylike enough, despite his provocation.

"Your father, then, was right to banish such toys. He never approved of you playing with mine."

"No. He never did." Talking about Father as if he was dead.

"I remember when he made you give them to little Louise, every one of them. You cried so hard! And the little wretch was very rough on them as I recall: they all had dreadful haircuts within the week!"

She laughed, a strong sweet hearty sound, but he was not fooled. Her voice may have softened, and her body be that of a goddess, but her eyes were unchanged, bitter little knives after all these years. Sylvia, her idiot lover might call her (he would deal with Walter later) but she was still Sycorax, and if, in the world of mirrors and metal, she had turned herself into something extraordinary, still in the Hedge he would make her see her true self. Return was easy—the Hedge was never far away—but how to persuade her to come with him?

He thought quickly. This time, he needed a friend to help him. Outside, the late afternoon sun winked, and the fields of the Foley estate spread out like a patchwork before them. He spied something glinting in a yard near a barn and the woods were close by.

Mary, out along the gallery with the paintings, could not accept what she saw. She stared at Crazy Jane while Crazy Jane stared back: white skin and long slender nose, and low brows and huge eyes that Mary now recognised. Crazy Jane wasn't a lunatic, nor was she the woman in green, nor even some imagined fairy.

"It's *him*," whispered Mary to herself. "It's all *him*."

Richard turned to Sylvia again, ready for one more conversation.

"I beg your pardon, you are quite right. I have not been myself at all. The worry of the exhibition and such things, you know." He smiled ruefully. "You know better than any other, the way I am. But having you nearby is such a tonic for my nerves. I wonder, would you join me in a turn around the park?" He gestured to the view through the open windows.

She will say yes. Of course she will say yes.

And of course, she did.

CHAPTER SIX
THE RESTITCH

―――――

IT WOULD NEVER NORMALLY HAVE OCCURRED TO THE HUNTER to consider Richard's axe. Such things were the province of his valet Palawinkes, who was too familiar with his master's party-going habits to worry about much beyond getting the blood off his boots.

Tonight, however, did not bode well. Palawinkes had congratulated himself in persuading the Hunter to let him shave the stubble already reappearing on his master's jaw, next came the thorny problem of presenting him with the Prince's gift, a fine brocade frockcoat in gold filigree. Palawinkes had taken one look at the coat and known how things would proceed. The Hunter would sneer and call it ostentatious. Palawinkes might, in return, hint at how much it had cost the Prince, and how well it would behove the Hunter to wear it to the wedding out of gratitude. The Hunter would then cast the thing to the ground saying he would be damned before being beholden to anyone, still less a yellow spider who not only bought horrible coats but was base enough to remember how much they cost. If Palawinkes was quick, he would get to it before the Hunter tore it, shot it or sprayed it with wine. He sighed.

His ruminations were interrupted by a rapping at the casement door, a sound both tentative and urgent. "Phynthoblin," was his first thought, only to be proved wrong. The visitor was in fact, Phynthoblin's ladybird, clearly relieved of her duty as cravat pin. She stood there, her face jet black and radiant, with great ear-rings of sharp scarlet and black polka dots to match her wings. This time she was wearing the livery of the Beloved. A busy soul, Palawinkes told himself. Servants in the Hedge were only marginally more reliable than their masters. Tomorrow, she might be wearing the insignia of the Prince. Palawinkes offered her hospitality, breaking the stalks of winter poppies that she might suck the milk within—a bitter delicacy, approved by many among the folk—but she declined, gave her message, and ran away on what Palawinkes hoped was business, but knew was more likely to be fear of the Hunter's reputation.

The news was not good, and Palawinkes would have liked more time to think carefully before relaying it to his master. As it was, the Hunter came in with an empty carafe in one hand and an expectant look in his eyes. He sniffed the air a moment before announcing:

"Wasn't that Phynthoblin's maid?"

Palawinkes confirmed it.

"Glad to see she's back to full size. Crawling around on a gentleman's collar, unseemly way for a grown woman to behave even if she is a bug. Well?"

Palawinkes looked surprised and gave a half bow. He had no idea how to tell his master the news without incurring the very real danger that he might understand it.

"She came to say that one of the wedding guests has gone missing, my lord."

"Indeed? And were they expected to be here?"

Palawinkes tried to smother a nervous laugh.

"No, my lord. Nowhere less likely I should say."

The Hunter shot a look at him.

"Have a care, Palawinkes, that sounded almost interesting. Who's missing, then?"

Regretting the facetious moment, the servant steeled his nerves.

"Richard the mortal, my lord, has gone out without his lady's permission."

The old unpleasantness lit the back of the Hunter's eyes but he said nothing for a moment. Palawinkes busied himself polishing the buttons on the Prince's gift.

"So why tell us? He's hardly going to come to me for sanctuary, is he?"

"Exactly what I said, my lord," lied the valet. "But I think, they thought, perhaps you might . . . " He faltered as his master stared at him. "Might . . . they hoped that, as you are called the Hunter you might—"

"I am not *called* the Hunter, I *am* the Hunter, and let any who think differently inform me of their qualms. By *They* I presume you mean *She*. Speak on, Palawinkes, but make sense I pray you. We both know I am not a patient man."

"The Beloved asks if you would help her find her mortal pet, knowing that you have no equal in such matters."

"Does she call the Hunt?"

"I think she asks more for help than hunt, my lord."

"In other words, she wants me to find her lost property. The effrontery of it!"

"My lord, this may not be the appropriate time—"

"Isn't it? When was the last time she asked me for any kind of favour?" The Hunter became thoughtful for a moment, and then his eyes glinted with malicious humour.

"Are you a betting man, Palawinkes?"

The valet allowed himself a rueful smile. "We both know the answer to that, my lord, else why would I be here?"

"True, true, a poor gambler, I remember that day . . . sometimes . . . when I try. Well now, here's a wager for you, and should you win it, seven years and a day come off your service. I'll warrant her little beast has taken off with his iron axe! Hah! And I'll bet you another seven, she has no clue where it is, no way of finding it, and no hope of fending off my cousin's royal displeasure—for nothing less than avoidance of his paddling hairy fingers on her neck could make her send a plea to me!"

"I would have thought," pondered Palawinkes, "that the lack of Richard and his axe at the wedding would please rather than enrage his majesty."

"Quite right." The Hunter grinned. "He's never enjoyed her showing off her little painting pet. Ownership of a gifted mortal is something of an obsession with him, as we both know. I'll wager you—how many years do you have left?—Never mind."

He waved his hand dismissively. "Bad enough that she flaunts her gift before his envy, add to it the way her esteem among the folk has grown through controlling that thing and its axe. No great mystery!"

The Hunter could understand courtiers if he really tried. He regarded it as an unfortunate malady, only be cured by a combination of strong liquor and ferocious brawling. It was a course of medicine he had taken for so long as to be almost entirely successful, but the occasional astute judgement still seized him, and when it happened there was nothing to be done except wait for the attack to end.

"So, if her trophy is even now rampaging through the

Hedge with cold iron because she lost control of it, my cousin will take the opportunity to combine justice and malice most expediently! What say you? Do you take the bet?"

Palawinkes bowed low. "With respect my lord, I have nothing left to stake." And, he could have added, only a fool would take the Hunter's offer if they could see him smile like this, so merry and so dangerous. He was much easier to second-guess when morose, thought the servant, and instantly retracted the idea as nonsense. In all the Hedge and beyond, no man was less predictable than his master. It made for an interesting life, Palawinkes told himself, with a distinct lack of conviction.

The Hunter chuckled and poured himself a glass of the red. For no reason Palawinkes could pinpoint, he was somewhat dismayed. He had assumed that his master would do what he had always done, charge out maddened after the prey, and bring the hunt home to be applauded in blood and gilt by the court. It seemed unlike him to decline, to think so hard, or even think at all. But then, great warriors are more than the sum of their strength. The servant roused himself from his thoughts to see his master staring straight at him.

"Come, Palawinkes," he said, "anyone would think this was a funeral. Have you not seen the coat my cousin sent me? You must undo and redo the stitching, for it leaves no room for my sword belt."

"Of course, my lord. But considering his majesty's orders, with no threat from mortals or iron, are you certain his majesty expects you to take your sword?"

"I am certain his majesty has no clue what to expect."

And the Hunter looked at his valet and winked.

CHAPTER SEVEN
SYCORAX

WHEN THE BLADES SPAN, HER HEAD SPAN TOO, AND THE words dropped out of her eyes and onto her lips. In all of it, I had never been so afraid. The body of the doll was familiar, a replica of a thousand dolls in a thousand shops, but the face was not what I expected. The head had been twisted off, and I could see why. It can never have matched the body, the neck seemed too thick and the face . . . they did not match, but there was no body in the world that could have matched her face, and while her eyes were plastic I could pretend to myself that they meant me no harm, but when they moved, when they moved . . . She was dancing nearer and nearer, those eyes moving from my face to my hair and back again. All I could think was that if the Prince of Spiders had not wished the toad to eat me, he could not want the scissor-woman to hurt me, but still she span and the blades shone and her voice, curiously guttural for a doll, filled the air.

SYCORAX'S TALE

I am beautiful, though they don't see it.

I remember my mother's dresser, mahogany and the scent of lady's things, perfume and violet and a satin puff that sprinkled soft sparkling powder down her neck and over her bosom and under her arms. Her skin was already white and pink, but she powdered it anyway. I thought it was fairy dust, but she laughed and said no. I watched as the maid put up her hair, and soft curls fell forward in a way that people called so becoming. She got her maid to do my hair, which is straight and doesn't fall the same way. But when I am grown it will. And when I told her Richard called me ugly, she picked me up and put me on her lap and said that boys always thought girls were ugly when they were small, because all they wanted to do was play with mud and fight, but when we all grew up, things would be different. When I asked if Richard would see me differently, she said, yes, but by then, I would be surrounded by admirers and Richard would seem a bit poor and a bit nothing. She took a big flower out of her vase and pinned it in my hair. She said it was a camelia, which is the sign for a very beautiful woman, and I was to remember it and keep it. I tried to, but I lost it sometime after that.

And yet I remember growing up too. There was a story by the sea, one of William Shakespeare's plays, The Tempest, and I wanted to be the princess. Her name was Miranda, and she was so beautiful the fairies all wanted to protect her. I wanted them to protect me too, but that didn't happen, because they didn't really exist, Father said, and besides the world needed protecting from me, not the other way around. He told me it was because I was so fierce, and bit Richard when he tried to take my doll.

Not just take her. I know what he was doing.

I sort of know.

No, I do know. I did grow up, after all.

But if I grew up, and there are no fairies, how can I be here?

And she turned to the beautiful woman in the web of ice, all jewelled and treasured, with hair crusted in ice and pearls, and tears frozen on her cheeks. He had made her pretty, they had all worked so hard to make her pretty. Time, she thought, it is time for blades.

A TINY STAR AMONG THE LEAFLESS BRANCHES, AN EARTHLIGHT he told himself, a gem without weight, cold and blue white, it twinkled in the middle of a web so exquisite, so lacelike and brilliant, no artist could destroy it. She was the heart of it, and somehow Richard could not hate the Prince of Spiders for what he would do, for what would any lover do, thwarted by lack of time and charm? Would they not take the prize, or say rather, could they leave it behind? It was only when he looked again at the frost that he realised what the Bride's beauty, and indeed the beauty of the whole web, must be costing her, for the moon shone above them on the coldest night of the year and it would last for as long as it would last. Though he could not deny its radiance, he also knew she must be freezing.

In front of her was a thing of spinning metal, of hinges and blades. It danced close to the Bride, and he was running towards it before he could help himself. It moved by itself. "A toy then," he thought. "A mechanism, but where—" as the swivelling blade caught his hip and wrenched him upwards, as he smelt the little girl breath of sweets and sugar tea and beef broth he remembered, she knocked him back, eighteen-forty-three ready long before he was, sweeping round to splinter one of the blades, ("Her leg," he tried to remember. "This is her leg!") but metal and bone were no match for his axe and the sparks of cold iron's fury. Sycorax almost fell to one knee.

"You are being used!" he roared as the remaining sharp edge narrowed and aimed at the star. It took no notice and span away from him towards the heart. He lunged after it and fell before the feet of one he knew. Part of him wanted to slice those feet free of the burgeoning calves above them and let them sit there, compact and bloodless save for the gleaming nails of chestnut, but he knew better. He should have risen slowly and knelt before her, but instead he leapt to his feet in protection of the Bride, even as the blade slit her free from the web. She sparkled in the air as she fell forward, and a great shadow in the pond moved beneath to catch.

"If she dies." Eighteen-forty-three lashed through the air, and even the Beloved, yes, even she, moved back swiftly from him then. "If she dies . . . "

He had expected the hiss of heat and steam as the star hit the water, but the darkness closed over her as though she had never shone, and he screamed and threw his axe and the shadow moved too. Eighteen-forty-three hurtled forwards to connect, her teeth slicing into the pike's side. The ichor gushed out from under the pocket of a gill, and the monster thrashed, turned belly up and spilled itself out through its mouth into the water. Outside of poetry, the only great victories are quick ones.

Phynthoblin's men were already hauling out the Bride, a star no longer. Where the web remained it was soggy with algae and toadspawn. The diamond herself was covered in fishblood. She stank. Her mouth was slightly open and a rusty wire pierced her upper lip and right cheek. Richard could hardly bear to look at her, or the Beloved, whose eyes never left his face. Instead he looked for Sycorax, who was nowhere to be found.

The moment was not a good one for Phynthoblin—the real Phynthoblin, on this occasion—whose life had never seemed so preposterously unfortunate, nor for that matter, so close to ending.

"Oh look at her!" he wailed. "The Prince will kill me!"

The Beloved said nothing. Richard felt that inscrutable gaze upon him, and resolved not to return it for as long as he could withhold. The Bride was shivering. Phynthoblin rolled his eyes, took off his emerald jacket (only his second best, he consoled himself) and put it around her. The gravity of the situation could not be concealed from anyone.

"This was the bridal gown," he explained to the air. "And one can see, even in its vestiges, how lovely it was. Peerless. She is meant to be wearing this tonight . . . " He could not quite control the quaver of his voice at this point.

"You are indeed to be pitied." The Beloved spoke at last. Richard could hear her voice, perfectly flat. Phynthoblin's eyes rolled towards her, his impeccable manners close to breaking.

"Madam," he said, gathering up any and all remnants of his dignity. "It cannot be denied that your servant did this damage. The toad can bear witness before his majesty."

She did not reply, and he tried to draw himself up, no mean achievement against her expressionless confidence. He could feel his blood beginning to boil. Who did she think she was?

"Serve her up as she stands," said the Beloved. "Let him reveal his folly to all the realms!"

"I have no reason to embarrass my Prince," came Phyn-thoblin's stern answer. "Have you?"

An eyelid flickered at that point, and Phynthoblin read it

quickly. Deft and cunning she might be, but Phynthoblin had subtleties of his own.

"There are magics and glamours," she said in a more conciliatory tone.

"Powerful enough to deceive your Prince? I should like to know of those."

Phynthoblin watched her with interest. *Beloved, Beloved,* he thought, *do you know what a thin line you tread? Do you know that your Prince knows?* But she, of course, said nothing in response to this.

"It was your servant," he continued. "And I have no idea what he was doing here. Can you explain?"

Now for the first time, Richard's eyes met hers again. He had forgiven her before she said a word, and when she smiled, he felt it in the core of his heart. It never occurred to him to speak out.

"This is indeed my servant," she spoke like a bell in his mind, clear and beautiful. "And he tried to help me find something I had lost."

"Was he the best person to send after it?"

"I had already sent word to the best. He declined to help me."

"And what was so important that pursuit of it, by a mortal wielding cold iron, seemed a better option than mentioning it to the court?"

She hesitated at this point. Richard could tell she had run out of imagination.

He could have spoken of the being she had sent to harm the bride, but there was no need. The wild love of him in her eyes and voice told him everything of her jealousy. She was afraid of losing him: his fault for not loving her enough, not serving her, not reassuring her. He would make amends. The Bride would be all right. He had touched her hand for a moment and it was almost warm. All would be well.

"It was my fault," he stammered at the grasshopper. "All my fault."

Phynthoblin and the Beloved stood there, the one shivering in his silks, the other telling her love with no sound. Another secret for them to share. Richard shook his head. He would ever be her thrall, saving only one other. Before they could move towards him, he leapt into the pond and swam towards the great floating hulk of the pike. He pulled eighteen-forty-three out of the wound and came back, ready to face his duty.

The Beloved and the Toad must have been busy while Richard was away, for the latter had grown very still by the time he returned, and the Beloved came towards him bearing what seemed like a garland of warts and mottled skin. She may have been whispering something over it, but if so, her voice was too low and sweet, like a kiss on the wind, for any to make it out.

"Let us prepare for the Feast," she said, and embraced her lover's head in her curving white arms. He felt the punishment press against the back of his head, and he nodded in comprehension. He deserved far worse than this. Skin to skin, the texture of toadflesh pressed his nose, filled his mouth, clamped his jaw. She looked back towards the toad.

"I do not think he will tell the Prince anything," she said quietly. Then she turned to her love. "Good Richard," she said, and pressed the tip of her finger to his lips. He bowed his head, and she led him away.

Phynthoblin nodded. *Courtiers,* he thought. *If they muzzled their pets in the first place, this kind of thing wouldn't happen.* He looked back at the foul smelling vision of blood and spawn supposedly marrying the Prince this very night. Glamours and magics, he sighed. Where to find enough of them, in all the world?

CHAPTER EIGHT
A FOXY LADY

———

PERHAPS NOT IN THE WORLD, BUT CERTAINLY OUT OF IT. In such a situation as this, Vulpinet's hat had surely to be the first port of call. Phynthoblin hated to ask Vulpinet for favours. Unlike the Red Duke, he had no illusions about her 'charm without devilry." His own judgement was that for malice she was easily the equal of the Beloved. "And more, for she knows she is the plainer of the two." But he could not deny that Vulpinet was always exquisitely turned out. It was not a matter of courtly fashion, for Vulpinet, like all the great fay ladies, trusted her own ideas for that. More it was that whatever design took her fancy, she always looked the epitome of her inclination. If her intention was to be neat, not a mote of dust could be found from glove to sole. If in disarray, the opheliate weeds in her hair would be arranged in perfect fetching wantonness. The nearest time she ever came near to capturing Phynthoblin's heart was when she wore a petticoat of pure autumn with her hair coiled up in spirals of amber and pearls, and it was this memory that prompted him to seek her out.

The secret behind Vulpinet's sartorial elegance was naturally one of the most discussed topics in the Hedge. It was the hat, of course. She often claimed to have bought a new one, but he knew it was always the same milinary miracle, in changed shape or colour. Some said that the Summer people kept court there, and there may well have been truth to this. Others said that Vulpinet's hat was a doorway to the land of the moonstruck, or that the hat was the moon itself, changed shape to perch on her head. The irredeemably addle-pated claimed that Vulpinet's hat was the moon in its true shape, then flattened each night so as to roll along the skies with more ease. On the coldest of nights, they said, one could still see the moon's brim surrounding the centre of her heavenly bonnet, a thin circular veil with whisps of trailing starry ribbon. "Or a badly fried egg," thought Phynthoblin, whose whimsical moments had grown fewer of late.

He was one of the few who knew the truth about Vulpinet's hat. Vulpinet's only journeys into the world of men occurred when she needed tailors, milliners and haberdashers. She took them, shrank them and housed them on her hat where they lived alongside her own seelie servants. The combination worked excellently, and when the Summer Court came to stay on the hat throughout the winter they were inevitably well fed and entertained. The hospitality of Vulpinet was as peerless as the skill of her stolen slaves.

This then, was the first, last and only solution to occur to Phynthoblin, nor was it a bad one considering his lack of time. The only problem was the lady herself, for this was a favour best unknown to the Prince of Spiders, and therefore what benefit would she gain? Still, the grasshopper knew well the ways of fairy courtiers, especially those whose ways were closest to those of mortals. There was bound to be something she wanted. She would ask for it, he would promise it and try to pay it as soon as he could, or, if it was unreasonable, he would get someone else to pay it, and on they would go. Or something like that.

The very first thing he did on finding her was a favour vast enough, he reasoned to himself: she had been locked in a conversation with that ghastly bore, the Red Duke, and in rescuing her, Phynthoblin knew he was one up on the game. She might sigh and role her eyes at the Duke as if to say, "Court business! What a chore!" But Phynthoblin could tell that she was relieved, by the discreet little smile that almost touched her lips.

The smile grew less discreet when she heard Phynthoblin's mission. He was not expecting her to look so very pleased, and it was disturbing to see all her teeth shining so bright and ready to help. Her price was swiftly mentioned and, though Phynthoblin did not like it, he had no choice but to agree. Phynthoblin would go up onto the hat and find all he needed, but the Bride would not join him. She would stay with Vulpinet until such time as Phynthoblin brought appropriate servants back.

"You need not worry," cooed Vulpinet, at the grasshopper. "She will be quite safe with me." Phynthoblin looked at her and one of his antennae twitched expressively. Time was of the essence, or there was much he could have said. As it was, he gave a bow and leapt upwards onto her bonnet, shrinking as he jumped. One moment he was an alarming distribution of green limbs and cravat flailing through the air, the next he was no bigger than a speck of pollen, disappearing into the jungle on Vulpinet's head. The sound of his chirruping back legs lasted a moment longer.

When it was gone, Vulpinet settled herself down on a

chaise-longue, smoothed a cushion beside her, and ordered a little warmed honey and black poppy from her velveteen clad mouse butler. The drink came in a glittering container, gilded with strange letters. The scent was rich, and filled the air, while, in front of her, stood the Bride, a phantom of drowned lace and spider venom. Vulpinet stared at the creature for a long time, before she beckoned it to come sit. The mortal did not move.

"Of course," thought Vulpinet, "his venom is still thick within her veins." It made her first plan hopeless: she could offer neither food nor drink nor any other fairy gift that might make the mortal beholden, for the latter could neither accept nor refuse. "This is why the old ways are such a bore," thought the fay lady, with a momentary frustration. Vulpinet couldn't even claim she was helping to save the Bride's life, because both knew full well that in helping Phynthoblin prepare her for the feast, Vulpinet was doing just the opposite.

Vulpinet's chambers were somewhat different to those of most lords and ladies. She lived in the hollow under the roots of a cunning old elder bush, where owlets had fallen spring after spring and provided the fay lady with many a meal. The very walls were covered in a flutter of feathers, white, tawny and twilight grey, pinned by moonstones to the walls, dragonfly wings veiling the doorways. In summer, violets and monkshoods provided soft and pleasurable seating for guests. Now she was forced to recourse to silver-edged eggshells with tiny purple cushions. It was a poor substitute.

When sparkling at the centre of the Prince's web, the Bride would have shone like a winter sun, and Vulpinet's parlour would have been whitewashed, its subtle colours blanched in the beauty of the bride and the brilliance of her Prince. Now of course, was a different story. Vulpinet could have enjoyed the fall of this prized creature had it not smelt so terrible, and had she not been facing the conundrum of how to make this situation useful. Vulpinet knew well what she wanted, but how to get there was a puzzle, indeed.

The first thing needed was a bath. Vulpinet herself cut the bride free of the dripping remnants of the Prince's web, and bid her servants fill a huge conch shell, brought from the sea at very great expense. They stuffed it full of holly berries and pine cones and the petals of a strange sweet flower from the east, filled it to the brim with hot water and then emptied it over the Bride. Then they took beeswax and sugar forced from beets, and coated her skin and hair in it, which they scraped off with the fibrulae of moths. Then, they drenched her again, this time in the pressings of winter roses and apples, and dried her down with petals of that same strange eastern flower. By the end of it, Vulpinet was impressed. It was clean, sweet smelling, naked, and still almost entirely paralysed.

"His poison is strong," she mused, looking at her guest. "He put effort and power into you. Can you be worth it, I wonder?" But as all the guest did was gape and shiver, no answer was forthcoming. Vulpinet touched its hand. It was warm, no surprise perhaps after the hot water, but still . . .

"Where he bites must always be cold," mused Vulpinet. She stared at the mortal who stared back. Vulpinet walked around it slowly, and touched its shoulders and its neck. Around the neck wound the muscle was frozen white. But elsewhere, the mortal was regaining its natural colour.

Vulpinet smiled. "His touch is unkind, is it not? If you are still in its thrall by the banquet, I cannot help you. No-one can." She leaned forwards. "You realise what will happen then, don't you?" She was holding its wrist as a sudden slow throb answered her question, and her smile grew ever wider in delight, "Ah-hah! So you *can*—" She brushed her lips with her fingers in a gentle mockery of discovery and discretion.

"The heart's blood never lies. I know you feel. And soon you will be able to move." She grabbed its head suddenly and twisted the face to the side, to observe the hole made by the wire. From a hedgehog's back she took a pin, threaded it, and pushed it into the skin beneath the gap, sewing upwards with invisible stitches.

"I am your friend, if you will have it so. If not . . . " She let her nails gently scrape down over its eyes. "If not, I will let him do as he pleases. Do you know what that is?" She could not help a little laugh. "He will cut off your hands for the root of the Hedge, and then he will do other things. Unless you get away."

There was response then. Though the lids were stiff, the eyeballs beneath them swivelled towards her.

Vulpinet laughed.

"Good," her voice was gentle, though the chime of her laughter echoed off the walls. "You want to get away! Of course you do. You understand. Now,"—her eyes deepened—"here is my offering. We shall make you a dress. We will mend your ruined face. The face will be the one the Prince desired. The dress will look for all the world like the one the Prince made, as though you are still in his bonds. But you will not be. You will be as free of movement as I can make you, and when the time is right, you may run."

It tried to nod its head.

"Run as far as you like. Run as far as you can for as long as you can. Get away forever if you can."

The attempted nod was more vehement.

"In return, you will try to take one away with you, back to the world you both share. You remember the man with the axe?" The mortal nodded again. *Teach them one trick and they repeat it forever,* floated the thought through Vulpinet's head. "That man is not one of us but a mortal. He will be sent to pursue you, with that axe. I want them both removed from the Hedge forever."

The thing seemed to try to shrug, and Vulpinet finally revealed her smile, all of it, front teeth, canines and molars, all sharp and hooked as thorns in her wide old mouth.

"If you attempt betrayal, I shall twist out your eyes that the Prince may lay his eggs in the warm gaps they waste. I will sew the lids shut and your children will turn inwards for nourishment. Do you understand me?"

Vulpinet had to conceal her mirth at the frozen horror on the mortal's face. Absurd, she thought, almost farcical. It was not the threat to its eyes that forced the silent scream but the phrase, "your children."

CHAPTER NINE
OLUF THE HEND AND OTHER DISASTERS

THE MOON HAD CHANGED SPECIALLY FOR THE EVENT. How could she shine over the nuptials in her old shabby veils? So she borrowed cloth from the sunset and wrapped herself in beauty like blood. It must have worked, for even those from beyond the Hedge pointed, and the land's thaw was a ruby river swirling around the pavements and drains. The ravens knew that crossing the river was a sure way into the true realms, but the mortals had long forgotten and so the ways were safe. The ravens wondered at the Prince of Spiders and his blindness to the signs. How could he not notice that the day was less wont to fade, that the sun waited to garb his sister in glory before retiring?

The Prince knew nothing, so enamoured was he of his bride, and when he looked up, all he saw was a sky full of jewels. When his eyes noticed the earth at all, he touched the thaw and it frosted over at his desire, and as the guests approached the Great Hall, snow fell and the warnings of ravens found no heed from him.

His majesty's raptures had not overwhelmed him totally beyond usefulness. He had, of course, decorated the halls himself, though all more mundane matters were left to Phynthoblin, who was glad to pack the Prince off to his royal apartments for personal preparation: his majesty's complacency was easily jarred by trivialities and it was better not to bother him.

For once, to Phynthoblin's satisfaction, his instructions had received the attentions they deserved. All the guests wore masks, hooked, barbed, feathered, furred, sparkling, criss-crossed, coloured. Some wore masks of their own faces. They gathered and swarmed with the vivacity of bees, and after all, apart from the early arrival of the entirety of the armed, drunk, and cheerfully aggressive summer court, everything was going very well. Ivy leaves and holly berries mingled under candlelight. The Prince had sought to gild the windows with exquisite yellow netting of silk which even now was being despoiled by those seelie most aggravated by the prohibition on weapons. Ribbon met boot and tassels fared badly, though the tablecloth remained untouched, for even in the depths of winter, no seelie would destroy true beauty. The Prince had excelled himself.

The tapestry woven for them all to dine upon was plain as frost or starlight. Through its delicate strands floated half remembered songs and long lost poems to inspire minstrels and tellers of tales. There was such pathos in its humility, so much room for the brilliant mind to weave a wish, a melody, a picture. It was elegant and captivating. *Dream*, it said, *I am the emptiness of dreams. Give me form, give me thought, it is your shaping, the maps and flowers of your mind I await.* No complexity of pattern could have taken its place as the perfect tablecloth over the most impressive of tables. Alas, then, alas for the candelabra.

Phynthoblin had been suspicious of the candelabra all

along. It was a foolish thing, a memory of ancient times when the Prince's father's father's fathers were seen as enemies in the Hedge, and yet an heirloom no son of the blood could deny. Phynthoblin's every instinct had been to leave it somewhere cherished and private, somewhere the summer's sons wouldn't be tempted to scrawl graffiti all over it.

Only a sycophant far beyond Phynthoblin's abilities could have called the candelabra "Art." It sat at the centre of the table, wrought out of a thousand spiders, some huge, some small, some tiny, some colossal. They clambered over one another, their eyes clustered rubies around crowns on their heads in which small holes dimpled for the placing of tallow candles. No amount of polishing could make the candelabra shine, for it was cold coarse iron. Only the gem eye-sockets glittered, when the candles were lit and the smoke rose. Then the eyes seemed to gleam like those of living things. The candelabra was worse than crude, it was ugly.

And yet there it sat, ready for some bold warrior to smite it or some cunning thief to steal it. Phynthoblin was baffled. It was a diplomat's nightmare waiting to happen. Nothing could occur that would not be an offence: they would kick it or punch it, run away with it or urinate on it. But in no world would they ever admire it.

Still, the Prince of Spiders had insisted on its presence. It was his father's and his father's father's, and its presence was required at the perfect moment of union with the Bride. Phynthoblin did not understand, and both his mind and his heart mistrusted it, but he was a worthy servant and having registered his misgivings, did not mention them again. Instead, he tried to make the candelabra look more seasonal by draping it in berries and leaves, cinnamon sticks and cheerful pieces of dried fruit. By the end of his machinations it looked like a singularly terrifying great-aunt submerged under an Easter bonnet.

He had also attempted to lift the rest of the décor within the banqueting hall: fireflies adorned the walls, their creations all sparks and floating globes, tremulous snowdrops and purple fritillaries softening their emerald fire. Phynthoblin wondered at his own daring for using the harbingers of spring, so sweet and unsurpassable, but he could think of no purer enchantment for the halls and frankly, if the Prince wanted more imagination, he could supply it for himself.

More guests arrived, drunk. It would be no wedding otherwise. Ready for the inevitable, the guards requested that the guests hand over all weapons as stipulated on the invitations, while to make matters worse, the minstrels started playing the Prince's favourite song:

> "Sir Oluf the hend has ridden sae wide,
> All unto his bridal feast to bide.
> And lightly the elves, sae fit and free,
> They dance all under the greenwood tree.
> And there danced five, and there danced ten;
> The Elf-King's daughter spied the man,
> And gave her hand so fair and free:
> Singing " Come Sir Oluf, dance wi' me!

"Oluf the Hend!" Had Phynthoblin sat in a chair, he would now have slumped forward. The guests would never stand for it. A fight was unavoidable; the song had surely sealed the fate of the decorations. The unseelie sighed and handed over every weapon clear to view (*"I will ne dance," Sir Oluf did say, "For the morn it is my bridal day,"*) while the seelie smiled, quoted riddles, questioned the musical choices of their host and became roisterous with those foolish enough to test them (*"You will not dance, thou dunce, Sir wi' me? Then pain and hurt shall follow thee!"*) Now, it must not be supposed that the unseelie have any less skill at bad behaviour than their Summer kin (*"They skinked the mead, and they skinked the wine, "O where is that eeejit prince of mine?"*) which they proved by skinking voluminous draughts of wine themselves, and hurling previously hidden daggers at seelie and servants alike, claiming innocence in that they were only trying to kill the bards.

And lightly the elves sae feat and free,
dance all under the greenwood tree!

Mighty and thunderous was the fight at the door of the great hall, and Phynthoblin let it continue a while, for he thought it best to get the fisticuffs out of the way before the ceremony. After all, these were high spirited knights of the realm, he reasoned, and their exuberance was surely just their way of showing joy for their monarch. But even he was surprised when the first window was broken by the Prince's younger brother flying through it, courtesy of a seelie knight's boot. It was an impressive display, and the cheers and applause that followed his exit turned to boos on his return. The younger brother, whose somewhat underdeveloped mandibles were concealed by a superlative moustache, came back through the window waving his forelegs in defiance. Such a challenge could not be ignored for all he was such a spindly bunched-up spider, and his foes drove him into a frenzy by spitting white-flies at him and chanting. "Swallow more, tiny choppers! Swallow more!" Then he challenged their own swallowing capacities by hurtling the great soup tureen amongst them, spattering Vulpinet and many other notable guests.

The Red Duke, already confused by the presence of enmity at the wedding's gate, grabbed the tureen, and slammed it down on his own head, despite the protests of his companion. A helmet by any other name would do for him. His consort, however, seemed concerned, and not least by the fact that her escort could no longer see where he was going: a triplicity of wounded waiters proved his blindness and ferocity before she took the matter in hand and stopped him from decapitating said moustachioed relative of the Prince. All this before the first toast to bride and groom. Phynthoblin could feel one of his headaches coming on.

There was a momentary lull while a servant cleaned up the soup and glass. Phynthoblin could hear them all pausing to catch breath, and to work up some new excuse for the next fight. Waiters were processing into the room now, with trays full of appetising morsels, thick glutinous royal jelly, fragrant truffles and brandy soaked dumplings, spikes of winter savoury stuffed with rich meat and stipled eggs from the Red Duke's own lands. Phynthoblin was not worried about the likelihood of affront, for the Red Duke's people were utter cannibals. The Duke, indeed, was one of the first to reach the tray, and seemed more interested in showing others how to correctly eat his tribe's children than worry about decorum. Phynthoblin smiled. Ceasefire was imminent. Any moment now the Duke would take off the tureen and all would be peace. Then the Hunter walked in.

The first thing Phynthoblin noticed was that the Hunter was shaved, handsomely turned out and wearing the Prince's gift. *He's up to something*, thought Phynthoblin, just as the Hunter roared to the hall. "Greetings!"

"Greetings!" they all cried out in return.

"I see you are stuffing your faces at my cousin's table," he smiled affably. "Which is why you are all grown fat and pox hearted, without a warrior among you to offer him a decent fight. What manner of welcome is this for a Prince? Have at thee!"

And he punched backwards over his shoulder, bloodying the nose of the sergeant-at-arms. Every guard drew sword and almost every guest whooped for joy and attacked, while the Hunter laughed, heartily knocking fists into heads and bellowing for drink all the while. The Red Duke was most anxious to join in, but Vulpinet was discouraging him. Vulpinet was not pleased with the state of events. She had expected fighting of course, but not so early and besides, as Phynthoblin noted with quiet pleasure, her dress was badly stained, so her pleasure in the evening—and readiness to make mischief—was considerably dampened. For his own part, none other could have persuaded the Duke to forgo an attack on the famous Hunter. "I must truly be in love," he told himself, "to let her talk me out of it." For he was certain he could deal with the famous warrior and told his lady so.

"Of course, of course," she whispered hurriedly. "But a state occasion is not the place to prove it."

"Hah!" came the happy roar of the Hunter from a corner of whirling fists and bloody noses. "What is that I see before me? Two maids and one of them most unfortunate plain!"

"He tries to goad you," Vulpinet told the Red Duke, who was beginning to snarl under his tureen. "Do not let your control be dashed by so foolish a ploy."

"If this is your wish, my lady." He bowed.

"Indeed," came the familiar shout, "one sorely lacks grace of visage, or grace in any aspect come to that—"

"He is a ruffian," Vulpinet said. "Pay him no heed."

"And the other is the sad Red Duke. Sir, why have you brought your dog to table?"

"Kill that barbarian!" snarled Vulpinet. Unusual for her perhaps, but her dress was stained, her consort was wearing a soup tureen and the insult was just too much, even for charm without devilry. The Duke translated it as a sign of her infinite generosity.

"Thank you my lady," he said, and waded in.

Among his foes it was often whispered that the Duke's prowess lay, not so much in his own fighting ability, but in controlling his monarch's vast armies. This base calumny could be discounted by any who had fought him in the wars. For one so lean he had great strength and he was famous for never releasing his grip until his foe was dead. Admittedly this was seldom long, as the Duke's favourite style of execution was to use that iron grip in lifting his foe to his jaws and biting the offending head off.

It had long been his regret not to have fought the Hunter face to face. His generals had told him of the Wolf's stance against the legions, and the Duke was convinced they had overplayed his prowess. They were afraid of the Hunter, that was plain, and under such circumstances it is easy to create legends.

He did not mean necessarily to harm the Hunter—this was a wedding after all—but it was such a relief not to have to think about tactics, attack, retreat and the subtle manoeuvres of armies. This was a brawl and he relished it with simple delight.

The Hunter, for his part, began to feel the heat of battle moving within, and had to concentrate a moment to keep his courtly shape. *Tonight is not just a fight*, he told himself, *there is a plan, do not forget the plan*. His fists and teeth were bloody, his heart was pumping fast and he moved towards the chitenous soldier ready to pound his tureened head straight through his thorax.

The Duke knew he should stand his ground, but was too excited and ran to meet his enemy, greeting him with a slashing blow that cut right through the Prince's gift and sent two of the buttons bouncing to the floor. The Hunter looked down at the ruin, smiled, and slammed the Duke's chin up into his helmet. The Duke grabbed the Hunter and let himself fall, wrestling the Hunter onto the floor where they both flailed among dropped dumplings and curiously carved winter vegetables. The Duke, remembering that Vulpinet was not best pleased with the Hunter, decided to bite his head off anyway and deal with the political ramifications afterwards. He pulled the Hunter close until their eyes were level, at which point the Hunter jolted forward and ricocheted his head off that of the Duke, almost stunning the general, who had to let go. Ears ringing, the Duke narrowly surveyed the Hunter. *He must have felt that,* he told himself, looking at the bloodied brow and yellow eyes, but there was no way to be sure. The Hunter was thinking very little. He had forgotten the plan. He kicked one of his legs forwards just in time for the Duke to bite into it ferociously, pinning the limb in his jaws and shaking it back and forth. The Hunter did not resist as his body drew close to the Duke's champing teeth, but waited until he was nigh and booted the Duke's ear, at which point the Duke let go and the scent of hawthorn and chestnut, mingled with a colder, harsher smell, flooded their senses. Above them stood the Beloved's mortal, muzzled in toadskin, his cold iron axe ready. Her voice was, of course, not far behind.

"Cease your clamours," the sound of her voice was calm and regal. "They are an offence to our realm, and you know that we have the power to punish." Phynthoblin winced. It was as well the Prince was nowhere nearby, to hear her use the royal "we" and phrases like "our realm." *Controlling that mortal she puts on the most outrageous airs,* thought the courtier.

There was a long silence, as her pet stood over the two of them. The Duke was beginning to recover his composure, but the Hunter's eyes were wild, and though he never took his gaze from the mortal, one could almost taste his attention moving towards her voice. When he spoke, his voice was calm and very formal.

"By whose authority do you halt our duel?"

"By that of your Prince, who has given us this right previously."

"And has he given you this authority tonight?"

A slight pause.

"He will do so when he arrives."

How do you know that? thought Phynthoblin, as he watched the two warriors stand up. On her last words, they exchanged glances with one another.

"I see," said the Hunter.

Again there was a pause. The moment flashed into life as a great sword whirled from beneath the Hunter's gold coat directly onto the cold iron axe. Eighteen-forty-three snarled with joy as the sparks between them flew, and the Duke's ceremonial blade homed itself in on the mortal's heart.

It was then Phynthoblin stepped in. "Gentlemen." He let himself laugh, a little chittering cricket laugh. "Well done, well done!" His smile lilted across the room. "Has your Prince not pleased you with his first gift? Has your banquet battle not been fine, as in the old days?"

He looked at them all panting, exhausted and ready to sit down to a fine feast. They nodded and laughed, including the Hunter, though his smile was rather wry, and he clapped his hands slowly and silently at Phynthoblin's efforts. *So he should*, thought Phynthoblin, who felt he had done a good job all considering. The Prince's enemies were constantly talking about how far from the old days the Hedge had come. Well, this was as traditional a banquet battle as had ever been known in the true realms, be they seelie or unseelie, plus (Phynthoblin almost wanted to rub his hands at his cleverness) none of this had pandered to the Beloved's delusions of grandeur. All had been sorted with no recourse to her axe wielding scion; if anything her interference had nearly made things worse. He hadn't been needed, which meant that she hadn't been needed and all this had been made very clear in front of both courts. Yes, it must have taken her down a peg or two, though she showed no signs of it. She sat, elegant and impenetrable as ever, her pet hovering behind her.

The fire seemed to have left the Hunter's eyes and he made himself comfortable, ruefully surveying his tattered coat. He had remembered the plan. Phynthoblin had no comprehension of the Hunter's ruminations, only that he looked unusually thoughtful, never a good sign. The Duke, pausing only to dust himself off and nibble on some rather flavourless pupae, returned to his lady. The bards began to play a march, a theme of princes and courtly love and high nobility. It rang like gold and the folk stood to attention. Phynthoblin smiled. Courtier though he was, there was still enough naivety in his heart to believe the wedding's troubles were over.

CHAPTER TEN
THE WEDDING

———

When the doors opened, they lifted their lights for him, lanterns and torches and fireberries and many fragments of crystal, all the better to light his way. The music was pristine and he, well, handsome he would never be, but his servants had etched the fine harlequin markings of black and gold upon him, and he was indeed impressive. When he looked upwards beyond the Hedge, he saw the moon in scarlet, and he marvelled at her. He was never really sure whether she cared for him or not, for unlike many of the hedgefolk, he had never found time to study her face. But she had donned fine clothes for him, and she shone ruby light over the thorns for him and that was enough.

The music and their awestruck eyes fed him well. He knew all the words they were singing, all the words of the wedding, for he had done it before. But this time, this time . . .

On the table sat the cold iron candelabra, now flickering with dull light, and the eyes of his fathers and his fathers' fathers gleamed out along the great hall. He picked it up and carried it through the banqueting hall and out of the doors beyond. Across chequered carpets he walked, across floors of stone turning to root, of root turning to ice, of ice that led down to the edge of a river near freezing.

They parted for him there, as the twilight darkened the ice, and only the torches of the seelie sparkled between the earth and the stars. The flames from the candleabra sputtered, but did not die; and down the river floated a swan.

It was white, of course and sang the song of greeting down the river. The reeds returned the melody, and the wind rose. Nothing else could be heard despite the crowds.

> Go and catch a falling star,
> Get with child a mandrake root,
> Tell me where all past years are,
> Or who cleft the Devil's foot,
> Teach me to hear mermaids singing,
> Or to keep off envy's stinging,
> And find
> What wind
> Serves to advance an honest mind.
>
> If thou be'st born to strange sights,
> Things invisible to see,
> Ride ten thousand days and nights,
> Till age snow white hairs on thee;
> Thou, when thou return'st, wilt tell me
> All strange wonders that befell thee,
> And swear
> No where
> Lives a woman true, and fair.
>
> If thou find'st one, let me know,
> Such a pilgrimage were sweet;
> Yet do not, I would not go,

Though at next door we might meet:
Though she were true, when you met her,
And last, till you write your letter,
Yet she
Will be
False, ere I come, to two or three.

"Twee *and* morbid," said the Hunter in Phynthoblin's ear. 'You've outdone yourself this time."

The grasshopper shrugged. "I didn't choose it," he replied. It was true. He preferred the shorter one about snakes and spiders coming not near, though he understood why it would hardly be appropriate in this case. The Prince had decided on this melody and despite Phynthoblin's protests about it being macabre, the Prince knew it was the right one. It felt less like a deception, and she would understand more of her fate if she listened. Not that he was giving her the choice of denial. He had worked his poison too well for that. Resistance could occur even in the face of poetry; yet more experience gained from his previous adventures in matrimony. Small wonder he took no chances, he sighed to himself. Had ever the Prince known such heartache before?

As the song rose from the river and the swan approached the banks, the chaplain waited, her little speckled snout quivering with excitement. The Prince appraised her with a speculative eye before he began his own stately march towards her. Last time she had not been dressed well, in a hooped petticoat which she had somehow managed to hitch over her tail most inappropriately. It was only one of the many disastrous aspects to that whole affair. This time, her skirts were subdued, an elegant gold ring linked her nostrils and her trotters were painted in gold and black. She matched his scheme perfectly, and apart from her uncontrollable nose, was the epitome of reverential calm.

There was silence from the musicians and then they began anew, a sweet piping sound quickly erupted by a signal drum. Then the notes softened, amid the white clockwork of snowflakes, fading into silence as the swan reached the water's edge. Leaf and lantern shone as the hedgefolk made their way over the shallows towards the bird, for the Prince had no desire to see the swan's spell broken by the revelation of waddling feet, and the bride of course, needed to be hoisted down.

He stood there, magnificent and hopeful in the eyes of seelie and unseelie, as the moon span her own webs above him, and the torches glowed and the minstrels sang, and he waited.

Phynthoblin held his breath as the bride appeared, and when she did, he could only nod across at Vulpinet approvingly. One could see no difference at all in the creature. She was still the sugar candy of the Prince's dreams, and somehow she was moving more fluidly too; yes, there was definitely more grace to her. He presumed she was being pulled along by the small gem-studded lacewings acting as her maids, but the impression of free movement was really not bad. She was pale, of course, but the Prince had kept her in the toad's larder from frostfall to moonrise so presumably he liked her that way.

IT WAS THE FIRST TIME I HAD SEEN HIM SINCE HE BIT ME. He had clothed me, of course, but I couldn't follow his movements then. The poison had locked my eyes rigid, staring forward. Since then it had seemed like a dream, only a matter of time before I woke up. But I knew when she spoke to me and touched me that it was real, and even now, though I felt dreamy and soft after the cricket fed me some bitter white drink, "to get me through the business," I knew I had to make my move soon.

I had never looked at the people of the Hedge properly before, and they stared at me, the beaked and cat-eyed, feathered and scaled, the winged and the webbed and the hooved: and some were people and some were flowers and some were insects or beasts or toys, but most were part of all and all of none, and I didn't know them, but I understood them or thought I did. And there were two who stared at me in a way I could not forget.

One was a pale dark headed man with an axe in his hands, and at first I thought he was one of the hedgefolk because of a thick dark green criss-crossing on his face. But then I saw it was some kind of muzzle or harness, and it occurred to me that I had seen him before, in a dream when I was held captive high above a pike pond. I could not remember properly but I knew he was there, and it was odd, now that I looked at him, that he wore the loose shirt and trews worn by many in the Hedge, only with a Victorian frock coat on top. It was then I knew he was human, like me.

The other was dressed like some kind of cavalier, with long thick black curls and a tricorn and boots. He paced around like a tiger, and his eyes were tigerish too, tawny and streaked until the light shone on them, and when they blazed yellow. I had no idea whether he was human or not, but there was something about the way he looked at me, as though he didn't really see me at all at first, and then suddenly did. I knew from the moment he snapped me into focus and a part of me grew still and expectant, that he was no human but a predatory creature. I did not know if I was his prey. I don't think he knew.

Singing floated around me, and carved snowflakes were on the air, tiny astrolabes of ice, patterns of worlds undiscovered. I could see the great squat body of the Prince waiting, the eyes at the back of his head closed. I let the lacewings move me so slowly, their bride on a pulley, and for one terrible moment I could feel laughter rising in my throat. I closed my eyes and when I opened them, the yellow-eyed man and the muzzled human were staring at me. I gazed past them, trying to remember the grip of the poison, and let myself be pulled along to the music. A star hung low over the mouth of the river, between the stark trees. It made the snow underfoot sparkle. The groom held some strange iron thing in one of his hands; dull little flames throbbed across it. He of course, could not quite stop himself from turning sideways on to me, doubtless to admire his handiwork. I stared ahead.

AND THE WIND MOVED, AND THE CANDLES FLICKERED, AND the eyes of the Prince filled with tears.

The chaplain held up a cup, silver and small, and she smiled at the Bride, and nodded to the Prince. She cleared her throat. She took a small shining thing, a cut-throat razor of the kind Palawinkes had used upon the Hunter earlier that day, and at the nod from her Prince, slit one of his hands gently, and pressed it against the edge of the cup. Dark liquid ran down both sides. The smell of peaches filled the air, and soft curls of steam rose from the brim.

Then she turned to the Bride, whose eyes, to Phynthoblin's judgement, seemed a little wider than before. The Prince held up her right hand. The knife seemed to hesitate a second, and then slash downwards. A hoarse noise sounded—Phynthoblin expected it to come from the Bride, but its direction was from somewhere in the crowd, and the seelie there looked very grim—and then the hand itself, dangling from a single slice of skin, was snipped off entirely, and popped into the cup. Her dress was bespattered and swiftly darkening down the front. Only her face grew more and more white by the second, and her pupils were dilated. He could thank the poppy milk for that.

The cup seemed to be hissing.

"And now," squeaked the chaplain, "by the old ways and the undying lands. Will you be joined by the three roads, by blood and bone, by sun and moon and shadow?"

THE PRINCE SAID, "WE SHALL," AND THE PEOPLE RUSTLED like leaves, sighing, "They shall."

Only two voices were silent, and Phynthoblin noticed them both. The chaplain raised the cup to the Prince and he drank deep, returning the cup. Then, the chaplain turned her attention to the Bride, and nodded to the lacewings who obligingly clustered around and squeezed the Bride's face, until her jaws hung open, tongue somewhat slack. It was not a flattering moment, but a moment was all it would be.

Then the cup was tilted and the blood filled her mouth.

Her eyes snapped awake, and Vulpinet bit her lip anxiously; *She shouldn't be able to do that! If he notices . . .*

But he did not notice. His face was shining with joy.

"Will you be joined by ash and elder, by oak and apple, by green and gold and shadow?"

The Prince said, "We shall," and the unseelie said, "They shall," and the seelie said nothing at all. And the drink was shared again.

The blood poured from her hands out on to the snow, and the ravens came to feed, drinking it before it seeped into the earth. One looked at the stump curiously. The Prince frowned, fearing lest the ravens' feast prevent her blood from soaking through to the earth below, but the chaplain reassured him that it was a very good sign, like in the old days. "Let her lips be red as blood, her skin as white as snow, her hair as black as the raven's wing."

She nodded.

"And will you be joined by endless sea and eternal star, by oath-in-keeping and ageless shadow?"

The Prince said, "We shall," and the crowd stirred to speak, as a voice roared, "No!" and the Hunter strode forward. The Prince turned to watch him, almost disbelieving, his mouth working in silence, his eyes gleaming as red as his lips.

"See, the Bride is a dribbling thing!" roared the Hunter. "We were promised an artist! What can she do? What does she create? Is her blood puissant? Of what use is it? Let me hear her speak!" He looked at her but she said nothing back, cradling the stump of her right hand. The unseelie gathered around him and the shadows and the night came with them. He gazed at them all, and stared at his Prince and smiled at the pleading whisper, "Don't do it, cousin . . . please don't . . . " Without looking across at the chaplain, the Hunter's hand lashed out and grabbed the cup, which he then emptied, hand and all into his own mouth. The bones took a moment for him to chew, and then he swallowed and grinned.

"Better," he said. "I was starving!"

And the silence was filled slowly by the growing roar.

The unseelie poured forward and the Duke, under-standing for once the diplomatic possibilities of the situa-tion, cast the magic of his own people, and watched as the unseelie grew long and strong with huge jagged jaws. The Hunter nodded and Phynthoblin hid his head in his hands. There was wisdom in the Duke's giving the form of his own soldiers to the unseelie, for his folk were strong and terrible in battle, but there was folly too, for they were all of a same-ness; the Hunter had fought such legions before and with-stood them.

He did not take his shape, but waited until the first ones surrounded him, swarming towards his sword. The first kill went to the Hunter, whose blade swept through the onslaught as the air grew thick with the reek of blood and acid drooling from the mouths of dying soldiers. The Hunter paused only to dip his blade into that ugly reek, and attack again. It took no skill to pierce his foes for they were many and crowding in on him (Palawinkes watched with dismay as they began to crush him from behind) and even as they could not avoid his sword, so he could not avoid their mouths and weight. Some, when they bit, fell back to let the poison do its work, others held on. Several just found points along his back from neck to hips, sunk their jaws in through the ruins of that fine coat (*Why*, thought Palawinkes, *didn't he wear armour under the dratted thing?*) The Hunter was too busy to pull them off, and the poison was starting to do its work. He began to look a little grey blue around the edges. Soon, he would have to revert to his true shape, a potentially short-lived indignity due to the ever-growing imminence of certain death.

And the seelie watched in silence, as the Prince wept and the earth grew dark, and the candles he upheld sputtered on, dark blue flames, dark red flames, flames that gave no heat and little light.

The fine little ladybird, whose day had been so busy, bent down to fluff the meringue of petticoats under her skirts. When she stood up again, she held in her hands an arquebus which she aimed at the Duke's head as he waded in to join his soldiers; the shot exploded and the powder decoction of fennel seeds and carpet tacks knocked the Duke sideways, dented his helmet, ruined his spell and provided the signal for the seelie folk who charged down into the fray, every weapon glinting under their banners.

The Prince, understanding what was happening for the first time, came out of his shock and called to his fathers and his father's fathers, and the cold iron of the ugly candelabra began to soften like wax. The red gems in the spiders' eyes gleamed and his fathers and his fathers' fathers heard him, cold iron unfolding in legs and eyes and abdomens. They coiled away from the tallow and flames, dropping to the ground like ugly scrunched fruit, and then swelling to a size beyond the power of sword or arquebus to affect. They advanced now onto the field of battle, down onto the swords and screams of the seelie. One turned towards the most errant son of the royal house, and the Hunter looked up to see it. The bodies of soldiers pinning him down, the acid eating his clothes, the blood clotting on his face, were small fry indeed compared to the bulbous form now waiting above him, its abdomen too high for him to reach with his sword.

"Tis nothing," he laughed to himself. "You must come down to hit me, and then I shall have you." When he tasted the blood, he remembered the plan.

"Damn!" he told himself. "I knew there was something!" The Bride, of course, he had forgotten the Bride. He had meant to take her and go. "But she will have bled to death by now," he told himself. "So there is no need to leave. Might as well enjoy the—" His neck opened at the back and he could not help but admit the puissance of the sting. It made him reel, made him sick, and he thought it must be the bite of one of the fathers' fathers. When he turned around, he saw eighteen-forty-three smiling at him, and Richard above her, not smiling.

"Rescue her, you dolt," said the mortal. "I will deal with your parent."

"You?" smiled the Hunter. "Who the hell are you?"

And he leapt straight at Richard, his sword meeting eighteen forty-three again, sparks flying again, and the mortal knocked off its feet, the Hunter's free hand clasped firmly around its neck. He began to squeeze.

"You, it appears," said the Hunter calmly, "are trying to steal my kill. Obviously, I must need your help. Because some milksop mortal whose life is hidden behind my lady's petticoat, doing what he is told like a craven, knows more about killing than I do. Or so you tell me."

And his mouth smiled, and his eyes were very bright.

"Not so, not so," gasped the mortal. "But I have the axe. I can wield it, and it will hurt them. It hurt you, didn't it? Let go of me."

"Why?" The pressure grew.

"Take the Bride . . . her hand . . . she will die if you don't . . . "

"Again,"—more pressure—"why?"

This time, Richard wheezed, and the shadow above them lowered itself. Had the Hunter been looking, it was well within striking range. Richard could see it. The Hunter only saw him, and his smile suddenly grew rich and merry.

"Well now," he whispered. "Would this be *betrayal*, you sorry wretch?" Their eyes met, and the Hunter laughed. "Why don't you take her, if you feel so much? I could stay here and enjoy the party."

The shadow was almost upon them now, its underbelly close to the Hunter's head. His eyes deepened with amusement, and he nodded almost imperceptibly at Richard, whose hand tightened on eighteen-forty-three. The moment was silent, except for Richard hearing his heart beat, one . . . two . . .

"Three!" he shouted and they both rolled, the Hunter to the earth, Richard upwards, eighteen-forty-three leaping into flesh, the Hunter rolling, earwig-like down the bank towards the figure in red and white. He barrelled into his prey, knocking her over, then he grabbed her and dived into the water.

The blood was still gouting from her wound, and bubbles were rising from her frozen face. "These things break too easily," thought the Hunter, and cast about for the sight of giant webbed feet anchored among the reeds. They were not hard to find. The swan was contenting itself by serenely watching the carnage, when it felt a sharp tugging, almost like a bite, on its leg. It drew the leg up and investigated its feet, giving the Hunter and the Bride the opportunity to clamber up its wing feathers and onto its back. "No nonsense now," said the Hunter. "You must take us from here to a doctor. You'll be paid well for your pains," he added, for the swan was examining him curiously. It was by no means the most intelligent of birds, and was having problems telling the difference between passengers and snacks.

It surveyed the remnants of the wedding, and deduced that there was no real point in staying. So, with a look blank enough to exonerate it from blame if the Prince ever asked, it turned itself around to face the mouth of the river rippling far below the star that shines at twilight, and sailed away.

THE END OF BOOK ONE

THE END OF BOOK ONE

BETWEEN THE WORLDS

The Barge she sat in, like a burnish'd throne
Burned on the water: the poop was beaten gold:
Purple the sails, and so perfumed that
The winds were love-sick with them;
the oars were silver
which to the tunes of flutes kept stroke and made
the water, which they beat to follow faster . . .

"I SEE YOU HAVE FOUND YOUR VOICE," SAID THE HUNTER to the swan. "A pity there seems no way to beat you into following faster. There now." He patted the Bride consolingly. "This will do for now. Better, yes?"

But the Bride did not speak. Her eyes swivelled down to the stump where her right hand had been, now stuffed with five feathers of different size bound together by waterlily roots. The Hunter's experience was all to do with the killing of foes; he managed to stop her bleeding, and his sympathies were strong enough for him to make a false hand for her, but under no sky could he claim the ability to do either well.

"Follow faster, follow follow . . . " The swan continued singing. "Follow where? You have nowhere to go!"

"Yes, thank you, very helpful." The Hunter scowled at the bird. "Swans sing before they die, twere no bad thing, should certain of them die before they sing."

The swan subsided into offended silence.

The Hunter could not help glowering as his joyful rage

faded, and discontent rose in his breast. Firstly he had been forced to leave the best battle ever seen in the Hedge, and secondly, in the clear light of hindsight he had to acknowledge that eating the Bride's hand had not helped in any way.

She was looking at him now. He did not know what to say to her. Still, he observed her to be comely enough—presumably more so, when not covered in filth—and as pale as the snow itself. Because he knew his shape was agreeable to mortals, he allowed his observation of her beauty to be obvious. His eyes met hers with a bold deliberate gaze calculated to make the blood rush to her cheeks. Her pallor remained unchanged and he realised that she had very little blood left in her to rush anywhere.

He turned back to his umbrageful mount. "We need blood for her, and very swiftly," he said. "Did I not tell you to find us a doctor? Less of this ambling, you fool. Take to the air!"

The swan turned its great yellow beak down towards him. "I could take you back to the Prince of Spiders and get a great reward for you," it said.

"Aye, you could try that," the Hunter smiled up at the bird affably, for he saw there might yet be slaughter in the affair, and was cheered by the hope. "And before you got there, I would have bitten deeper into your white throat than the puny iron axe did mine." He felt the sting and throb of eighteen-forty-three's wound at the back of his neck. Not bad, he thought, not bad at all, but no reflection of the strength she has. For all her deadly nature, she is wielded by a fool, and her kisses cannot reflect her passion.

"And then you will match the Bride in white and red, save

only that she will live and you will die. Or do you think me not capable of it?"

The swan twisted its neck forwards, lifted its wings, and slowly flapped away over the banks of the river and above the trees.

BOOK 2: THE GATES OF SUMMER

CHAPTER ONE:
TEA AND STUFFING

———

WALTER'S COTTAGE, HOWEVER DELIGHTFUL FOR AN ARTIST, could not possibly do for a married man.

It wasn't that his fiancee disapproved; on the contrary, she had been delighted with its predictable sweetness of clambering rose and surrounding hedgerow. But for all its charm, everything about the house was small and a little crooked, and to his eye, she looked like a giantess as she wandered through the rooms. Nor could Walter really believe that nearby Cobham would divert her for long. No, London was the place to please her, for all her protestations to the contrary.

And yet, he did not want to leave either. Potter's cottage was full of his little creations, worlds of unspoken stories kept safe in glass cases. It irked him somewhat that the Royal Academy could not see the merit in his work. True, he had begun in humble fashion as an ordinary taxidermist but he felt that his expression of that craft had developed into something unique.

Others in his trade stuffed birds and beasts and fish, stuck them in glass cases or mounted them on plaques, and that was it. Walter admired the skill of his peers, but despaired at their lack of imagination. His mind was more whimsical. The house had its fair share of lepidopteral display cases and more than a few heads on walls, mainly antelope and deer. In the dark, when the fire was on, they seemed to glower at him like enraged fauns and satyrs. But once mastered, mere depiction of dead beasts could not satisfy his artistic instincts. Not for him teal ducks set against a backdrop of dried reeds. No, his creations ranged more to the fantastical; Walter created tableaux, wonderful little three-dimensional panoramas behind glass, populated by well dressed animals. In one corner sat a vixen cub trying on a voluminously flowered and be-ribboned bonnet in front of a mirror; in another, two weasels with pipes and smoking jackets sat around a roaring fire. In a third, a hedgehog laundress pegged her linen out to dry whilst a flat-capped mole trundled past on a tiny penny farthing. Here was a gentleman's club full of fine looking red squirrels reading newspapers; there was the rats' den, a sleazy establishment of cards and bad behaviour. Ferrets boxed, toads fenced, guinea pigs played cricket, kittens picnicked on the village green. A night at the opera, thronged by birds deriding a feline performer took up the entire window space at the front of the cottage, and even now Walter was working on his latest offering, *The Mouse Wedding*. With delicate care he put together the church interior he had been working on all evening. The tiny chapel looked spick and span. Walter's parlour was a mess.

He knew his home arrangements would have to change completely after the wedding. It would not do for her to live here as it was now. The parlour table was covered in the tools of his trade, scalpels and needles and skin scrapers and shears, claw hammers and files and scissors and saws, brushes and paint and scraps of clothing. The actual beasts to be used were hanging outside in his workshop. It would not do for her to see that aspect of his work; the stuffing was far from the most attractive part of the process.

He could not help but smiling as she walked in, stooping her head just a little to get through the impossible doorway. She smiled back, and Walter's heart skipped somewhat, as it always did when he saw her.

"Dearest,"—how her voice sang in his ears!—"you have not eaten a bite of dinner."

"No, I confess, I have not. I never felt less hungry."

She looked at the tray of cold tea left untouched on the dresser. The table was full of miniature pews and tiny prayer books, no bigger than stamps. She picked one up, and to her delight, found that it could flick open. A magnifying glass would reveal the perfect legibility of the order of service and a tiny Anglican hymn written within. The child in her heart still thrilled to such detail. "Better than anything *he* ever built," she told herself, and as if on cue, Walter turned the subject to Mr Dadd, the artist. He was uncomfortable with the subject, but could barely define why, even to himself. Sylvia tried to explain.

"We grew up together. He was a strange child . . . but then, I suspect all children are strange."

Walter looked at her with a somewhat surprised expression which she swore was mirrored in the eyes of his pipe-smoking weasels. "Not I, my dear. I was unremarkable and ordinary."

She laughed. "Far from ordinary, my love. But you have such a gentle way about you. You are at ease with the real world and people can talk to you. It was never so with Richard. He cannot understand the world, and the world cannot understand him."

"I was not pleased—that is to say, I was worried, slightly, to see you walking with him. I know yours is an old acquaintance but some say very odd things of the gentleman."

"Richard is very highly strung, my love. He was delicate as a little boy, somewhat prone to malaise. Sometimes he would just . . . go away . . . " She shrugged. Walter smiled as she warmed the teapot close to the fire. She knew he liked his tea rather steeped.

"Good heavens. You mean he wandered off?" Walter was surprised but inclined to approve; wandering off showed an adventurous, healthy turn of mind to be encouraged in a lad.

"Quite the reverse, I fear. He would just lie there in a kind of sleep, though his eyes were open. It could last for days. The doctors called it a sort of coma." She poured the tea into his cup, added milk, placed it on the saucer and passed it to him.

"Did they now? I'd call it a sort of malingering. Amazed Robert didn't do anything about it. Not good to indulge children in that sort of fancy."

"Well, no. And when he awoke—"

"Got bored with his play-acting, you mean."

"He would tell us all the most astonishing things he had dreamt. Some of his best paintings come from those old fancies, strange though they were."

Walter drank his tea. It had an odd smell, almost reminiscent of beef broth, but he barely noticed it. The oddities of Richard Dadd were rather engrossing, and he encouraged his love to tell him more, but even as she spoke, Sylvia knew the whole of it could never be explained.

"Richard doesn't believe in time, you see. He thinks that

our childhood together, and his exhibition, and my marriage to you, are all happening in the same moment."

Walter could not help but state the obvious.

"But that is arrant nonsense! It is obvious that things occur in sequence . . . that one thing follows on from another . . . He is a man of rationality, a man approved by the academy. This is just a poetic fancy of his, I daresay."

Sylvia could not help but smile at Walter's faith in the academy.

"I assure you, my dear," her voice was light, but matter-of-fact, "Richard is clever at a great many things but poetry is quite beyond him. No, he has had this idea since we were young. He thinks everything that happens occurs in the same moment and place. He would say that our lovely home, his father's house, the academy, the asylum, these are all one place folding always inwards . . . "

Walter was unimpressed. "And so if all space is one space and all moments are one moment, how is it that we are not all here together in a great confused huddle?"

She smiled. "Well, Richard would say that ideas—our ideas of time and place—are stacked on top of each other—"

"Stacked? Like chairs you mean?"

"Well, yes . . . invisible chairs . . . "

"*Invisible* chairs!" Walter couldn't resist it. "Well, that is different. How could I have missed it? It all makes perfect sense if the chairs are invisible!" By now, they were both laughing. "And this is the man you say is not mad! May I voice my inclination to agree with Sir John's servants?" When she kept silent, he felt he must show sympathy. "It must be hard to disapprove of an old playmate, however foolish their behaviour."

"Yes." She nodded. "And he is doing so well at the academy, one doesn't like to make much of these things."

"And yet you know," Walter felt he had to press his point, almost lost in this discussion of his friend's frailties, "I find his interest in you more than that of an old playmate."

Sylvia laughed again, but there was a different ring to it this time.

"I am sure that I have nothing in this world to fear from Richard."

She was so definite that Walter could not help but ask more. She hesitated for a moment and looked at her betrothed with a strange expression in her eyes, almost . . . he hesitated to name it . . . almost a harshness.

"I have nothing to fear from Richard because he is convinced he has killed me already, and that I lie head and body apart in a ditch beyond Foley Fields. It is a crime for which he has already apologised on a number of occasions, and tells me that if we look for my head, we are sure to find it somewhere around here, in the garden perhaps or down by the river. He is also certain that he has killed his father and you, my dear, and insists that the fairies made him do it."

Walter fell back in his chair in shock. She said it as though she was reading something out of a parish circular.

"This man is a dangerous lunatic!"

"My love, I—"

"This is . . . this is unthinkable! That he has talent one cannot deny, but the academy and Sir John cannot be aware—and for you, my sweet one, to make compassionate excuses, to defend him when he could—"

"—but he thinks he has. So he will not."

"That makes no sense at all!" Walter was beginning to feel really incensed. "He should be put away! Highly strung indeed! And how, if he is convinced that he has killed us all, does he think we communicate with him, and live out our lives, talking, eating and working?"

She looked at him now, and it was strange to see how, as twilight had fallen beyond the hedge, her hair seemed to have grown wilder and her eyes become smouldering lamps under the gaze of stuffed birds and beasts. Even her mouth seemed larger. Could it be that she was bigger than before?

"He thinks we are ghosts," she said. "Living out our dreams in his memories or in fairyland, for he is not sure which is which, or indeed, if they are at all separate. I am part of your dream here, because this is where you died, but my own dream happens elsewhere."

And she reached across the room now, her giant hands growing ever larger, glinting nails like blades, her lips pushed out and the smell of beef broth and tea filling the room, her face growing purple with rage, and her mouth opening to show clockwork teeth and a tongue rasped with rusted wire. Behind him, poor tiny Walter heard the glass cases shattering . . .

And he woke, with relief, to the knocking of the front door. Checking around him, there was no broken glass and no monstrous Sylvia, just his tea untouched, and the clock on the dresser ticking, and his back stiff from falling asleep in his chair. Walter pulled himself together under the watchful eyes of his masterpieces. Dead and stuffed they might be, but he never felt alone when they were around him. He went to answer the door.

CHAPTER TWO
A MASTER OF SPIN

THE NIGHT LAY BROKEN IN THE ARMS OF THE RIVER, AND snowfall began to conceal the shards of cold iron now scattered all over the bare earth. But nothing could hide that smell.

"He might as well have salted it," murmured the river trout, pausing only to gulp down a floating limb or two.

The Prince of Spiders was silent.

His forces had won the battle; the banners of summer had fallen, and the strongest of the seelie slain. Yet no trumpets sounded.

He had lost fewer of his own, but the cost had been high. The magic of his fathers and his fathers' fathers had been used, never to return. All that was left was iron splinters everywhere, anathema to all the hedge folk seelie and unseelie alike. He had lost the Bride, and all the marks of kingship would soon leave him. His magic had gone, he had lit no spark, and, far from fertility through the blood of mortals, the realm was barren and iron crossed. What greater sign of ill favour could the ancients bestow upon him?

Still, one does not give up kingship; only the oldest of the old ways suggested that, and the Prince of Spiders was not traditional. After all, who was more suited to rule than he? Mortal blood and dreaming threaded this tapestry; it was the monarch's place to wield these powers, to weave the story of the land in perfection. No-one else could do it as he could. And yet there were always those who would assume.

The Prince's eyes darted almost instantly to the Beloved, who sat among the mushrooms, talking in low tones to her pet. Her face was impassive, but her eyes glowed with a growing confidence he did not like. He noticed the courtiers sitting close to her, laughing deferentially whenever she spoke to them. It was obvious, and it would never come to pass. He would indeed salt the land before he let her have it. Art he had loved, but power had been the blood in his veins and if one had fled, the other would stay by force or favour. Her painter and his iron axe were all she had to offer. She had no greater skill than the love of looking in her mirror. Besides, he thought, they do not know that the magic of my ancestors has gone for ever. Oh, they can surmise but they do not know and they will take no risks. He knew he need fear no sudden courage. If they were brave, they would be dead by now.

He looked across at two who could yet prove him wrong: the Red Duke was very wounded, and yet still rallied troops and gave orders; and Vulpinet, who was surrounded by dead bodies, her mouth foaming with rage and her hat distinctly rumpled. Truly, the wedding had not gone as she had expected. The Prince looked at them. Strong allies, and yet not ultimately strong; they had no mortal blood nor were they linked to any with such an advantage, so neither could aspire to the elevated treachery of a royal rival. He called Phynthoblin, and felt a deep sense of relief as the courtier came hopping towards him quickly. If he still had Phynthoblin, the ambitions of the

Beloved could not be too advanced. He commanded Phyn-thoblin to invite the two over, and the grasshopper bowed and did as he was bid.

The Duke and Vulpinet cleaned themselves up somewhat, and by the time they approached his Highness, looked calm and presentable. The Prince took out a sword of gold bound with obsidian, made the Duke a knight of the realm, and spoke to Vulpinet regarding her place between himself and the Seelie folk, as diplomat and emissary of peace, harbinger of stability, power and status of equal kind between seelie and unseelie, perhaps, even (though he barely hinted at this) a return to summer and the cycles of time. Among her own folk, her standing would grow higher, nay, of necessity she would be equal to a queen . . .

He also promised to repair her hat.

Both seemed pleased at their new found rank, and both walked with him as he went to speak to the Beloved, whose smiles seemed to fade as her sister's grew brighter. Richard stood, his face twitching as he gazed upwards at the stars that touched the tips of the river reeds, his axe covered with blood. The Prince shuddered, but concealed his disgust at the mortal's blade, covered with the blood of his fathers and his father's fathers. Leniency could easily be perceived as weakness. That axe had been permitted too long in his kingdom.

He smiled at the Beloved, who, under long and heavy lids, allowed herself a little smile back. She was inclined to treat the moment like a victory; it was only the sharp laughter in her sister's eyes that made her careful.

The Prince sat down beside her.

"I am glad to see you are not hurt," he said, his voice a blend of regal condescension and a hint, a gentle hint, of deeper feeling.

"Your majesty is too kind," and her round face lifted to his with a perfect simulation of concern. "But alack for the kingdom, alack!" A tear glimmered in the corner of each eye. "All these loyal and noble soldiers!" She stifled an elegant little sob.

Two of the royal hands, gauntleted in cloth of gold, covered hers. "Out of this battle, new life shall rise for us," he said, raising his voice slightly so that the nearby courtiers heard his words. "The field of scarlet brings rewards of gold for those who want it. See our new found allies!" He gestured at the Red Duke.

"This glorious knight of the realm will bring us powerful armies. And your own kin,"—he smiled across at Vulpinet—"will be our emissary to the Summer Court, in search of peace once more. So you see," three of his eyes gazed down at her, "what seems like an end is in fact, a beginning, and what seems like disaster is victory."

"Noble is your majesty," she began after a second's hesitation and glance at her sister. "But permit me to wish you no more victories of this ilk. And the Bride has been lost to you, also! How strong of you to think of the kingdom, when the treasure irreplaceable is taken from you!"

"Irreplaceable? In this land of beauties?" The Prince allowed his gaze to travel down the Beloved's face and back to her eyes. "There speaks modesty itself. The old ways require mortal blood and mortal dreaming but there are many ways a true king can bring that to pass, especially if he has a fitting consort beside him." And her face changed, as he knew it would, and Vulpinet's with it, and every face there excepting the the that of the mortal. But then, the Prince got the impression the creature wasn't listening, anyway. He continued. "Beauty and enchantment I see so close, in the very blink of an eye. But loyalty and strength and the power to do and have done, these are the marks of a true queen. And in the end, a true queen to help me use mortals, is what I want. It is my quest for so rare a creature that has brought me such pain . . . "

"Perhaps you seek too far from home," smiled the Beloved.

"Indeed, I have given my hopes to the unproven." He nodded. "But how should such a thing be proved?"

The Red Duke (who indeed, was beginning to understand the business of court very well) spoke out:

"If the advice of a rough soldier be worth anything, may I suggest his majesty pauses before choosing a queen from among his own? For the monarch I serve is beautiful and unwed; her battle rage is legend, and she has few equals in fertility."

A lie, spat the thought through the Beloved's mind, *the Queen of the Red Folk has neither rage nor beauty, she is so fat she cannot leave her chamber. She needs the Duke to do everything for her. Which is, of course, very good for the Duke, should she be given dominion here. Very good for the Duke and whoever he loves.* And under her eyelids she watched her smiling sister, who, much to her surprise, added:

"Well, if we are to look at neighbouring potentates, doubt-less the Black Queen would not want to be discounted." The

Beloved stifled her frown, and coughed gently before the talk of royal brides wandered too far from home again.

"And yet, these ladies are so intensely busy with their relatives and whatever it is they actually do (your grace will forgive me, but I have no idea of their work beyond egg-laying)"—she bowed to the Duke—"can they really give over time and love and effort to the governance, or rather," —she corrected herself silkily—"can they bend their hearts in service to the King of the Hedge and place his ancient and blessed charge before their own duties? For we had best be sure before we begin."

"You spoke a word wisely, a word I will repeat and keep in my heart," said the Prince of Spiders, delighted with the conversation. "Proof, proof is the thing I shall look for, in friendship and in love." He gazed at them all. "And I begin now. The renegade Hunter has flouted our sacred ways once too often. Let the Hunt be called upon him and his mortal pawn! They that bring back the head of the outlaw shall have proven their worth indeed and whatever they wish shall be theirs." And some of his eyes turned so tenderly towards the Beloved that she could almost see the royal gown he would spin her, reflected in his gaze.

"Let the Hunt be called across the lands of the Hedge, seelie, unseelie and all that lies between!" he proclaimed. "Let the head of the Hunter pay the price for the damage he has wrought."

"And the mortal?"

He shrugged. "Kill it. It is of no more use here." He did not notice who asked the question, but Phynthoblin did. He had paid attention to the change in the mortal slave, Richard, whose eyes had moved from reed to river, to Beloved, to Prince, to Beloved again. As if in response, the Beloved stroked his hair and smiled.

AND ALL THAT LIES BETWEEN.

And they shuddered and fluttered, did the dark things of the Hedge, and the shadows whispered in glee. For it had been a while, a very long while, and the prize was sweet and they were hungry. The people of Summer turned away, but all others gave chase. To be sure, some balked at the thought of the Hunter's strength and ferocity, but this did not put them off for long; He who fought without care for himself now guarded a mortal; and he would find it tiring, as all who do who play that game too long. So they sang and sharpened their teeth and claws as the wind rose under the moon. "For he has nowhere to go," they laughed to each other. "Nowhere to go . . . "

CHAPTER THREE
HOSPITALITY

———

WHEN WALTER ANSWERED THE DOOR, HE FOUND HIMSELF instantly wishing he had kept the "No Hawkers, Peddlers or Tinkers" sign up at the window. He almost wondered if he was still asleep, for his visitors looked like something to be induced by an excess of laudanum. The gentleman's tattered apparel might have looked impressive on a stage in an earlier century, and the length of his hair was wonderfully barbarous, but Walter hardly had a moment to judge the bizarre apparition; his gaze flew instantly to the lady in white linen, for she was very ill indeed. She was clad in nothing but a blood spattered shift and her hand—"My God! My God, sir!" gasped Walter. "Bring her here, bring her in!"

And almost as though she knew she was safe to do so, the woman fainted. The madman (as Walter reckoned he must be) lifted her with prodigious ease. *Clearly a fellow of great strength,* thought Walter uneasily, though his attention could not leave the poor woman for long. Her right hand was a mere dark stump with feathers and weeds in it, and she was soaked and shaking. Walter placed his hand to her head, though he knew what to expect even before he touched her. Her skin was clammy and her temperature was very high.

"What in the devil's name is this? She is ill, sir, she has been—what has happened?"

The madman propped her on the sofa.

"I have nowhere else to go. You, you fellow, what is your name?" The man looked at Walter as though he was a servant.

"I am Mr Walter Potter, and you are?"

"You are a doctor, yes, you can heal her?"

"Heal her? She has no hand, sir! What is there to heal?" But the pallor of her face, her burning forehead and shuddering limbs touched his heart, and he added, "I will give you all the help I can. The doctor must be sent for at once."

Walter's housekeeper had been watching from outside in the chicken yard. Vigilance over the coop was a matter of principle with her; chickens disappeared regularly and she was convinced that tinkers, foxes or foreigners were responsible. Despite her suspicions, she was very ready to help, and accompanied one of her boys down into Cobham to bring assistance. In the meantime, Walter wrung clean cotton hankies in a basin of cold water and placed them to the victim's head. The madman paced hither and thither, occasionally checking through the window. Walter was no fool; he knew what all the caution must mean.

"If you are attempting escape, sir," he said, "may I caution against going further? The lady is at death's door, and however successful your attempts to evade, I mean, whatever your endeavours, I fear she cannot join you any further in them."

The man stared at Walter as though *he* was the lunatic. He smiled, which Walter found alarming, and then he laughed, which was most unpleasant. Walter hoped the cook's boy had possessed the presence of mind to bring back some members of the local constabulary along with the doctor. He plucked the grisly package of feathers and waterweed from out of the lady's stump.

"Ho! Stop that!" barked the madman. "What do you think you're doing?"

"Sir, there is such a thing as infection—"

"Infection? Those are royal swan feathers!"

"Birds are covered in lice, Mr—Mr—I do assure you, I have dealt with the carcasses of beasts a great deal, and they are simply not clean!"

Indeed, he wondered as he saw the swelling of the arm, and the discolouration of the veins, it would be a marvel if infection had not spread already. The thought of lice made him itch. She was bound to be covered in them. Walter stood up.

"What happened here?" he asked. "Were you attacked?"

The madman, shifted his gaze from the nightfall outside to Walter and nodded. "Yes, yes, we were."

Walter blinked in astonishment, and his first thought was *Must be from a circus . . . a travelling fair . . .* for the madman's eyes were stark yellow, like those of a bird or a cat. The hairs on the back of Walter's neck tingled for a moment. There was no denying that those extraordinary eyes gave the madman a very predatory aspect.

"See," continued the Hunter, and he loosened his unimaginably dirty collar. Hidden under a shower of hair was a huge horizontal gash just above his shoulder, almost at the neck. The rest of his back was completely covered in blood.

Walter sat down covering his eyes with his hands. "How did this happen? What has gone on?" The lady's wounds might have been caused by a dog or some such attack, but the gash was clearly made by a weapon. "We need the police. I know there are tinkers in the woods but they have never—"

"Tinkers in the woods, yes, but not the ones you know," answered the madman distantly. "Look, she needs blood and we cannot stay much longer."

Walter's look hardened. "Sir, she cannot go any further. If you fear the law's pursuit, that must be your own concern. Mine is this lady's life—"

"Mine also or I wouldn't be here!" There was a note of exasperation to the stranger's voice. "But I do not know why you bother with the unnecessary. Why care if it was tinkers or dogs or the devil himself? She needs blood."

Walter wondered at the madman. "I am at a loss as to what you think a doctor can do for this poor—" he choked. "The most we can hope for is to save her from infection, bring down the fever, clean this wound and keep her in bed. God help us, would there was more!"

Twilight had come and gone quickly, and the night was without a moon. The Hunter's eyes moved from woman to Walter to the woods outside. "The doctor is not coming," he said, and somehow, Walter knew he was right. The boy had not returned, the housekeeper had gone home, and neither policeman nor doctor would help tonight. He was stuck here with a dying woman, and a man whom Walter was beginning to suspect of being a robber; he might even have been the one who harmed the lady, and brought her to Walter's door as a pretext for getting into the house. If the lunatic had not been so preoccupied with watching the outside, Walter could have worked himself up into a proper panic about the situation. As it was, the stranger seemed fixated on the hedgerow surrounding the cottage. Walter took matters into his own hands, hoisted the woman into his arms and took her up to the spare bedroom. It was plain but clean and he placed her on the bed with as much care as if she had been a child.

He touched the lady's dress; far from being some poor-house petticoat as he had first thought, the dress was made of very fine silk, with lace and pearls. No lack of money then, thought Walter, who could not resist trying to make sense of the folly around him. Here, doubtless, was a tragedy of the Gretna Green variety. She was clearly a lady of good family persuaded into running away with the clown downstairs. Perhaps her head was filled with the romance of life with the gypsies. Nothing else could explain her companion. Maybe his relatives and hers had met, with disastrous consequences—but Walter's imagination could not supply the scenario in which her hand was lost. It was too horrible for the civilised world. Even staring at it, he could not believe his eyes. There was a thud on the stairs behind him.

"She is safer downstairs," said the yellow-eyed man.

"She needs a bed," replied Walter. The yellow-eyed man did not reply. Walter wanted to cut her out of the dress, but feared to be immodest; the dress was unfashionably tight and reminded him of swaddling. So he began by bringing up more fresh water, and the housekeeper's lavender oil, bathing her head with a combination of both. Then he started cutting the sleeve away from the damaged arm. This was difficult, because the material was hardened with blood and resolutely stuck to her skin. Still, he focused on his work until the arm was freed and the beautiful material lay ruined, cut in little strips on the bedside dresser.

"She is beautiful, I suppose," said the voice behind him. Walter could barely believe his ears. Peculiar as the situation was, the yellow-eyed loon was the strangest thing about it.

"Surely you do not need the voice of another to tell you that," said Walter.

"I am not used to looking at them in that way," the Hunter replied. "Can you make her well?"

"I can make her comfortable I hope. Everything else we can only pray for."

The Hunter snorted at that, and walked over to the window. Walter, with the sense of regretting what he was about to do, asked him why. The Hunter gestured him over.

"Look there," he said, pointing out the back. "Do you see?"

The moon had finally risen above the clouds, so huge that her seas and mountains could be charted from Walter's little window. For a moment, he felt rather than saw the sweep of soft wings against the casement. "An owl," he told himself. Doubtless it was a good night for hunting. Clear beneath the moon lay hilltops and occasional copses of trees, separated by hedgerows. It was only when Walter looked closely that he realised they were all the same hedgerow, a long dark thread that defined the patchwork of fields, and meandered eventually, almost deliberately, to his own garden. Here it seemed wilder and higher than before, a woodland in miniature, swayed by the deepening wind. For a moment, it all held meaning. Then he turned away.

The yellow-eyed man was staring at him.

"Well?" he said. "Don't you see them?" To Walter's blank stare, he shook his head and started to walk downstairs.

"Have you barred the door to the back from the kitchen?" he asked.

"It is locked already," called out Walter, while the Hunter gazed around his new surroundings with the dawn of a smile on his face.

"Of course," he said, and called out to his host to join him. Walter followed him down into the kitchen, like a man in a dream. "Your waiting woman . . . if I am where I think I am, you may have iron here. Pots and pans and such, yes?"

"Well, yes." Walter's head was beginning to ache.

"Excellent. Now, I require one more thing of you, and I will pay you well for it."

It was the most preposterous thing Walter had ever heard, and yet, some curious voice within him, like a guiding star, inclined him to say, "I need no payment in return for my hospitality, sir," and there was something right about the way the Hunter nodded back at him, approvingly.

"Of the blood I see. Very well, then this is what we need."

And the Hunter told Walter the plan, and Walter struggled against the conviction that he was losing his mind. Yet, less than half an hour later, an impressive collection of iron pots, pans and knives were rigged up in two traps, one above the front door, one above the back, and the gentlemen rested with a brandy each.

The wind gathered, and the moon hid her face.

There was a rapping at the front door, and Walter moved to answer it.

"Don't be a fool!" said the Hunter.

"Just to see. As I have tried to explain to you, Hunter, it is locked."

They both watched as the key, still in the lock, slowly turned anti-clockwise. There was a clicking and a small quiet noise from the other side of the door. Then the key slowly pushed itself forward, out of the lock and on to the floor. The noise outside was more audible now, a distinct low sound that felt, to Walter's ear, like laughter. The door knob began to turn and with a smooth movement, the door pushed inward an inch, two inches . . .

The top of the door jolted and the crockery came crashing down in a hail of metal victory. Knives and pots bounced off the floor, and the door slammed itself abruptly. Behind it, Walter could swear he heard muttering. The Hunter nodded. "Now they will try the back," he said to Walter. "And have no better luck there, the fools!"

As if in answer to his words, there came indeed, a rapping at the back door. But this time, Walter found it harder to stay put, and went to the window, expecting to see something out of a child's nightmare. There was nothing there, but still, at the edge of his hearing, a strange guttural sound bothered him. "Did you hear that?" he asked the Hunter, whose reply was drowned by the smashing of glass all over the house.

Walter ran into the front room to find the air swarming with butterflies. They knew him; most retained the pins he had pushed through their middles and wings, and now they crowded his eyes, his mouth, his nose, his ears. All the glass cases had been shattered, and he realised, as his flat-capped little mole rode away to safety on its penny farthing, that the world had changed. The hedgehog washerwoman, with an air of stout practicality, waddled over to the kitchen debris and picked up the sharpest knife.

"What?" shouted the Hunter in response to Walter's anguished wails. "Skin and sawdust, man, nothing more! Kill her!"

But it was not so easy, Walter found, to kill one's own. For some irrational reason he wanted to talk to the laundress, to placate her, even though her eyes held his with a depth of malice he couldn't conceive. She moved and with a sudden flash of the blade, he felt his shin slice and burn. A stuffed raven looked down at him with purpose. On the wall, the head of a deer snarled. The eyes of weasels and toads, stuffed mice and birds looked at their creator. The vixen, pert in her bonnet, turned her snout to him and laughed showing all her little teeth, and everything started to move.

Walter screamed, but even he did not know whether his cries were at the killer slashing his wounded leg, or at the Hunter tearing apart his foes with teeth and hands. The yellow-eyed man moved quickly enough to be a blur to Walter, though the air was whirling with fur and feathers around him. Two glass eyes fell out of the cloud of dust at Walter's feet and he recognised them; they had belonged to the vixen.

"Upstairs!" roared the Hunter, and ran up towards the bedroom. "The Bride!" And Walter would have followed him, but for a sudden gentle knocking at the back door, a sound he could never have ignored for all the warnings in the world. It sounded like her, like Sylvia, and he rushed to the door and flung it open, grateful for her saneness, her sweetness in this terrible dream, this newly broken world.

The door swung open, and the clamour of the beasts ceased, for it was indeed his love and she smiled her calmest smile at him, scissors glinting at her side.

"Dearest," she said. "You have been dreaming. You have been working too hard, my love . . . you should finish your tea . . . "

Snip.

The Hunter heard the blades at the bottom of the stairs as he dashed into the bedroom, where the Bride was sitting up, trying to fend off the advances of Walter's creations. The larger ones had armed themselves with scalpels and needles, perfect for slashing skin and skewering eyes, while the smaller beasts, including the tiny occupants of the mouse church simply crammed themselves into the gaping hole of her wrist and drank deep. Their feast was ended by the Hunter, who ripped them out and hurled them against the walls. He scooped the bride into his arms and headed downstairs, to a sight that caused him regret. Walter had known nothing and had given a great deal; he was clearly of the blood, and now the blood was leaving him. A great hole in the side of his head told the story, and all the Hunter could do now was make his end easy and look for his enemy. He did not have to wait long, as the metal ballerina span out from under the stairs towards him, her outstretched blade aimed to pin him against the wall. One stab on target would eviscerate the Bride, he realised, as the scissorwoman sliced a wayward lock of hair from out of his eyes.

"I have no quarrel with you, Hunter," said Sycorax.

"You're here to hunt. Don't waste my time," he said, hoisting the Bride over his shoulders and freeing his sword arm.

"Yes, I am. But you are not my prey," she said gracefully stepping sideways, so that one of her limbs, perfect in repair, pointed directly at his heart. "I could have killed you then, if you were."

"You cannot have her, Sycorax. I have done her too much harm as it is."

Sycorax sighed, while he watched. His sword was no use against her. There was a better way.

"Then I will take you both," she said, and hurtled forward, her blades pushing deep beneath his waistcoat, into his chest, twisting vertically and slashing up across his collarbone. She span and flew straight towards his outstretched hands, her blade sliding across his stomach as he deftly caught her head between his two fists, and wrenched it round and off the scissor handle. There was no blood. He sent the head bouncing out through the open back door, where it rolled away into the grass. The scissors lay still. The Hunter walked over to his friend and drew his sword.

"What are you doing?" asked the Bride.

It was the first time she had spoken. Clearly, she was feeling better. The Hunter was not ready to look at her yet and he kept his eyes on Walter. "He could live," said the Hunter gruffly. "I could put his head here,"—he indicated the scissor handles—"and he could go live in the Hedge."

"And become like Sycorax?"

"Possibly. I don't know."

"He made things. Unless you can give him that choice, you should leave him alone."

She paused for a moment. "I think you need to stop lopping chunks off people," she said. He did not reply, but she could tell his breathing was uneven and when he did look at her, his eyes had changed from yellow to red.

"Come," he said, and walked out through the back door. She paused to kiss Walter's face, and pick up the remnants of her make-shift hand. Then she followed the Hunter, whose step was fast and deliberate. Behind them, the flow of blood from Walter's heart, flowed, slowed to a trickle, and stopped.

THE HEAD ROLLED OUT OF THE DOORWAY, DOWN THROUGH the puddles and along the length of the hedge until it came to a river, where it stopped, and nothing happened for a while.

The hemlock umbels grew tall and the dark haired man walked beneath them, his eyes full of stark purpose and the perfume of the Beloved still lingering on his shirt. He walked down to the river in silence, until he saw something lying in the mud. He looked at it, gasped and ran to pick it up. As he held it he began to cry.

His tears splashed into its dead eyes and overran its eyelids. He pressed the head close enough for it to reverberate like a drum to the beat of his heart.

He sat on the ground and placed it on a rock in front of him.

"I did this," he said, and looked to the head for a reply but the flooded eyes met his in silence. He waited a while longer, and when nothing happened, he got up and kicked the grass. Then, faster than the Hunter could have dreamed, he leapt forwards and knocked the head off the stone, pursuing it, rolling around in the dirt as though fighting an invisible enemy or tumbling through the grass with an old friend. This time when he caught it, he kissed its lips very gently.

Sylvia, he murmured, *Sylvia. I let them take me away for too long . . . I let them take you too, and they parted us.* And he remembered Sylvia's legs and the pretty dolls in the nursery, he remembered his first sight of the Beloved.

Never come back, she had said, and she had meant it. But she had taken Sylvia too, and made her Sycorax (*No, Richard*, came the thought, *that creation was your own, all your own work . . .*) and that had been done without Sylvia's consent. Now she was using him to hunt the Hunter and the Bride; one so that she could become queen and the other because she hated mortal rivals. Sylvia had been one such, and the Bride she saw as another.

"I will go back, I will," muttered Richard. "And I will chase this dream out of my head, I will crack it like a nut. I will paint them all and make them small and flat. I will find a place, far from home, where she has no power and I will grow strong. And then, when I am real and whole, I will chastise father and all of them for mocking you . . . " And he kissed her now in a way he had never dared kiss the enchantress. "And they will pay for what they did to us."

Eighteen-forty-three lay on the ground waiting while the lovers kissed. Nearby, the discarded torso of a doll lay naked and half hidden under the earth. The head was still on it, but eighteen-forty-three knew she could remove that small encumbrance with ease, and Richard took his cue from her. Sylvia's head was marginally too big but the fit was not so wrong as to be grotesque. They finally lay together, as Richard realised should have happened long ago ("That fool Walter!"). He laughed, and when all dreams ended and they became one, he sighed and slept in peace.

CHAPTER FOUR
HOW NOT TO REFUSE AN INVITATION

———

PALAWINKES WAS AS GOOD A SERVANT AS ONE COULD HOPE for through indenturement. He certainly did not resent his master's luck at cards and dice, though it had cost him years of service already and he could not guess how many more. But the life he had once lived never held much promise; a tanner's apprenticeship in Whitechapel smelled bad and paid worse. He had no intention of leaving the undying lands, and marvelled at those who fretted for the human world. His problem now was how to stay alive in this one. Palawinkes had known from the moment the Duke attacked, that the Hunter would forget the plan entirely. He should have slunk away then.

Now the Hedge was all alive with the Hunt, and Palawinkes was alone, clearing away the banquet. Something twisted and long toothed shuffled under the table and he threw it chicken bones to keep it happy. Perhaps he should have waited for a gift in return, but it never occurred to him. The under-table dweller hissed and gurgled, which, though disturbing, did not worry him like the long boggling stare of the grasshopper courtier.

Phynthoblin had not taken part in the battle. He had sat silently—unusual for one of his clan—and observed the whole farce, his face as stern as the stone he perched on. He watched the knighthood of the Duke, the elevation of Vulpinet and the conversation between the Prince and the

Beloved. Even then, his face did not change, but he leapt down off the stone, and wandered for a while among the ruined banners and bodies of the summer folk. Phynthoblin then approached the Hunter's servant.

"I presume that wasn't quite the way it was supposed to happen," he said. Palawinkes swore wide-eyed he had no idea what the grasshopper was talking about, which led to Phynthoblin's first genuine chuckle since the Prince had mentioned getting married again.

"Now, master Palawinkes," he smiled. "Waste my time and lose your head, or be a sensible fellow. It will not be long now before the Prince turns his thoughts towards you. He is, as you can tell, exceptionally angry."

Palawinkes couldn't tell. The Prince's expression was one of loving condescension as he gazed down on the new angel of his court, the Beloved.

"He does not expect the Hunt to be successful," said Phynthoblin. "I suspect he has called it so that some of his more dangerous rivals to the throne may be brought low."

Palawinkes continued his act of bafflement, but he was not used to this change in Phynthoblin's tenor: Phynthoblin, who seemed to become calmer and colder by the minute.

"Come now, master butler." He smiled. "You must do better than this. The Beloved swells with her own importance and sends Richard to the Hunt, so that she may woo the Prince with her success. See, he makes it clear how close he is to falling for her charms, and the end result is that she will jeopardise her one real claim to the throne, her ownership of a mortal soul, to gain the crown she hopes for. Poor simple creature! She does not know him. And for his own part, he does not expect the mortal to survive meeting the Hunter, axe or no axe. Then her potential for taking the crown from our Prince decreases from some to none."

"But the Prince has no solid claim either, without the bride," burst out Palawinkes, then remembered discretion and added, "And in any case, sir, begging your pardon, but I don't see what this has to do with me."

"Don't you? Well, I abhor ignorance, so let me explain." Phynthoblin rasped his back legs together, most distractingly. "There were three mortals in the Hedge, and the old ways require that one, an artist, lunatic or dreamer, gives blood to feed the undying land. The ruler who cannot provide this is no fit ruler and must leave the throne. One is—was—the Bride. Another is Richard. And a third,"—he leaned forwards—"is you, Master Palawinkes."

Palawinkes fell back somewhat. He was surprised, he had to admit it. "I have been in the Hedge a long time—"

"But you were born mortal."

"Saving your honour, sir, I haven't got no artistry in me, not one spark. Can't write poems, can't paint pictures, and every ear for miles will be sorry if I have to prove meself by singing . . ."

"But you gambled with the Hunter, some mortal pittance for servitude in the undying lands. Some would argue that makes you a lunatic."

"Oh, reaching, reaching, Master Phynthoblin. Don't know how blood helps anybody, but I'll wager my master's boots that mine won't do. The courts won't buy such rubbish, sir."

"The courts will buy whatever we sell them. They may not believe, but they will wait until your blood makes the case clear, and his majesty will use that delay to make himself stronger by another ruse. But by then, Palawinkes, you'll be betting no longer."

How will my blood make the case clear? Palawinkes wanted to ask, but thought better of it. The courtier obviously had something in mind, and Palawinkes reckoned to serve his master better by just listening.

"Even a plan as absurd as the one I suspect you and your owner cooked up must have had some sensible points. There will have been a rendez-vous place agreed upon, in case, well, in case of something just like this. Now where could that be?"

Palawinkes kept stoutly silent.

"Of course, the advantage you need is easily bought; the revelation of such a rendez-vous point would put you in good stead with our monarch."

No true monarch, thought Palawinkes, *as you near as damn spelled out for me in words so short even I can understand them.*

"Now," continued the courtier smoothly, "I am going to suggest that he offers you the chance to reveal that place to him. And I would suggest to you that you throw yourself on his mercy and offer to take him there, making it clear all the while that it is a dangerous place—and of course, it *is* dangerous, isn't it?"

Palawinkes almost nodded without realising it. Phynthoblin smiled again. "Of course. Nothing less could please the Prince's cousin. Who knows, it could be too dangerous for the Prince to risk his royal personage. Perhaps the Red Duke could go in his stead. And who knows what he might find there? An ambush, perhaps?"

"Well, that sounds very dangerous indeed," said the servant calmly. "As well as breaking my oath to my master, even supposing I knew what you were talking about, how does any of this help? Your ambush would not be getting rid of any false claims to the throne. You'd be getting rid of what seems to me like a rival for your own place at the high table. What are you like, Master Grasshopper?" And Palawinkes gave a little laugh, his only real mistake since coming to the Hedge all those years ago.

Phynthoblin's smile faded, or hardened, the servant could not be sure. Either way, he did not like the change in the courtier's face. "Look at you, mortal, trying to ape the fool who bought you! Well then, take your chances like the dunce you are, for I am weary of talking."

He straightened and leapt up in a kind of backward somersault towards the river bank, and Palawinkes watched, his thoughts in turmoil. It wasn't the grasshopper's gymnastics of mind or body that worried him. It was Phynthoblin's claim to be weary of talking.

"Never in a million years," thought Palawinkes, and yet, the courtier's voice had held an uncustomary ring of sincerity. For a moment, he considered fleeing, as he saw the grasshopper lean across to the Prince and speak. The many eyes of the Prince flickered over to Palawinkes. Then the servant saw the powerful geas sparkling and flashing in the hands of the Prince, and recognised that Phynthoblin's suggestion had been adopted, worse, *adapted*, by the royal imagination. He steeled himself for what was to come. After all, he had nowhere to run.

CHAPTER FIVE
INVISIBLE CHAIRS

———

THE PROBLEM WITH THE PLAN, OR AS MUCH OF IT AS THE Hunter could remember, was that it entailed getting to the rendezvous and meeting Palawinkes. This was dangerous enough to be interesting except for one small point: the Bride was close to death. She needed blood very soon, and though the Hunter had a geas or two to his credit, they were all about taking life, not giving it. She would never last to the meeting place, and for reasons the Hunter could not quite fathom, he was not ready to let her die. There was always the chance that those who guarded the place might have blood to spare, but it seemed very unlikely. Besides . . . *they will eat her,* his common-sense told him, *they will chew on her bones with even more relish than you did. Because you know, she tastes very good . . .*

He dismissed that from his mind. By now they had crossed the back yard adjoining the hedge, and he found himself frowning at the chicken run. He looked across at the Bride. They had not managed a single conversation yet, and as a gentleman, he felt the need to at least make the attempt.

"Do you see anything odd about this place?" he said to her. Her eyes widened in response, and she stared at him. Then, after a silence, her shoulders started to quiver. It took him a few moments to realise that she was laughing.

"What? What? Madam, we have no time for this!"

For now she was doubled over, her whole body shaking so deeply she was clutching her stomach. It hadn't been what he expected, and neither was the strange whistling noise she was making through her teeth, a curious "eee—eeee—eeeh" sound.

"You . . . you ate my hand . . . " She gasped indistinctly. "You ate my hand . . . and . . . the spider . . . and now you ask . . . " and she began that strange wheezing squeal that recalled to the Hunter his reasons for eating the other Bride. Not that the circumstances had been remotely similar. Totally different scenario, he told himself. In the meantime, it was crucial that this one get a grip on itself. He didn't know how to deal with hysterical humans; he had heard some tales about slapping them, but he was afraid of knocking its head off with the blow. Mortals were fragile, and he wasn't lucky with them.

"Pull yourself together and look at this chicken yard," he told her. She stopped laughing and squinted meaningfully around her, but to his irritation, she wasn't looking at the earth. Instead she was staring at the cottage.

"I know that place," she said, as it shimmered before her. At that point she stood straight, and walked round to the front. The Hunter followed, bemused.

"Tell me what you see, "she said to him.

He clicked his tongue with impatience. "Red stone, straw thatch, two chimneys, some roses, front door slightly ajar, iron rubbish in the doorway—"

"And around us?"

"Woods, the hedge, the moon, dirt track."

The dirt track he dismissed was the old park footpath, and there, where it joined Church land, was the hedge itself. The house in front of us was not red stone but red brick, and though I could see the thatching, it was superimposed on the tiled roof I remembered, like one acetate over another. The door was not slightly ajar, but fully open, and rubbish free as I had left it when I had picked up the spider's gift. Within, the light was welcoming and bright and electric. I walked straight towards it.

He grabbed her.

"What are you doing?" he said.

"That is my home," she told him. "I am going home."

"You are englamoured," the Hunter told her. "That is not your home. Your home may be built on that spot in the cycle of mortal years to come, but for now it is just a dweomer. While your blood is in the undying lands, so are you."

She smiled, most unpleasantly for a bride. "My blood isn't in the undying lands. The ravens ate some and the rest is here, inside you. So I may just use the lessons I have learnt, and with one of the knives I have in my kitchen—all of them cold iron—I'll cut my hand right out of your belly and take it back."

He laughed. "Try, by all means," he said. "My life becomes much easier if I can treat you as an enemy."

They both walked into the house together, the Hunter stepping gingerly over something in the doorway that the Bride neither saw nor felt as she walked through. She went into the bright kitchen, and looked out of the back window as she pulled open one of the cutlery draws. The Hunter was beside her, and though he seemed to be looking out of the window, she could feel his attention upon her fumbling search for a knife.

"The yard is spotlessly clean," he observed. "Remarkably so, for a place full of chickens."

"I don't keep chickens. The yard is clean because it's covered with concrete slabs."

He shook his head. "I smell chickens here. The yard is clean because some Folk must hunt here, from the time when it had chickens, or before. And I wonder, I wonder . . . "

She turned away from the absurd conversation, and walked into her front room with a knife tucked up her sleeve. There on the carpet was the biggest dolls' house she had ever seen.

In her life before the spider's bite, the Bride was no fan of dolls, and her experiences in the Hedge had not improved her opinion. But this was an enchanting if inconsistent creation: part country manor, part fairy-tale schloss, all turrets and towers and tudor chimneys. Around it someone had created a garden out of billiard table baize and bits of felt. An old cut-out moon was stuck high on a weather vane above the topmost turret, smiling down over multi-coloured banners. On the green cloth were pasted lines of little twigs that sometimes developed into clumps. Around the castle, the twigs almost formed an irregular barrier like a wooden palisade, or, depending on one's sense of scale, a hedge.

There were many make-believe windows. Some of them had small mirrors in the place of glass, reflections creating a sense of movement as the Bride pointed out with delight.

"Reflection? Don't be such a fool," he said roughly. "The reason you see movement is because something is moving."

She stared at him, convinced once again that he was the uttermost loon she had ever met. "It's a dolls' house," she spoke gently, as she might to a child. "Who are you expecting to be moving around in there?"

He stirred impatiently. "Dolls, of course," he said. "Who else? If you don't believe me, look through the windows. Some of them are open."

She peered through the windows. On an upper storey, a male doll slept in a little bed. The bedroom was bare, but it had the most wonderful floor, with an effect almost like a tiny mosaic in blue and white, which sparkled in a very textured way. The Bride reached through the window and gently pressed on the floor. Motes of blue and white stuck to her finger, which, when she touched them to her mouth, revealed themselves to be eggshell.

The bedroom next to it was clearly that of a lady. The lady wasn't there, but her dressing table was most exquisitely carved, painted white and gold and festooned with chocolate boxes and cadeaux and absolutely minute brushes and powder boxes. The Bride could almost see the talc in its shaker, snow light and glittering. On the storey beneath her was a bigger room, a nursery, where a little girl played with a dolls house of her own, and a little boy helped her.

Another window revealed a long hallway full of framed and detailed portraits. A tiny doll, dressed like a maid, stood in front of a painting, one hand holding a silver tray, the other half way to her mouth. The Bride could almost make out the look of alarm on the maid's face, and found herself curious to see what the shocking painting actually depicted. She tried to reach in, and found herself stumbling against the dolls house, accidently caving one of its side in. The Hunter shook his head and went back to the kitchen, laughing.

The Bride found herself examining the disaster more closely, for it was clear that the walls were not damaged. They folded inwards and created a very different shape to the house. New windows revealed themselves, and new rooms behind the windows, the shape of the roof changed, and very tentatively, she tried to move the other wing of the house in the same way.

The result, after much folding and careful adjustment, was a Victorian cottage. Peering in through the front window she could see rooms which must have been further on in the interior when the dolls house was a castle. Now she could see a parlour with a lady and a gentleman sitting together laughing. Crockery shone on the dresser to either side of a tiny ornate clock. The table was full of bric-a-brac so small she could not make out what it was at all, and miniature replicas of stuffed animals were everywhere. There were oak beams across the ceiling, and the door out to the corridor opened aslant to reveal a somewhat crooked stairwell.

As she touched the little walls and doors, she found herself wondering what her talent was, the art for which the Prince had chosen her to be his bride. She could barely remember. Perhaps, once upon a time, in the world of men, she had understood these little houses, and how to repair them. This one was an antique; maybe she had been reconstructing it when the Prince came to her door. It certainly looked familiar. Once again, she folded one side of the cottage backwards, as though she was creating some intricate piece of origami. Sure enough the sliding of card and paper began but this time she was more confident, and pushed the walls more swiftly back upon themselves, stacked in layers. The house was now no more than a ground floor and upper storey with very plain windows, indeed, the whole house was very plain, almost a box with a triangular roof.

She looked in the windows of the front room. There sat a female doll on a blue rug. She was dressed in white, with a dark red pattern down the front of her clothes, and she was playing with a dolls' house.

The Bride let out a cry of alarm, and fell back on the rug. The Hunter ran in, saw her face all white and ashen, and applied his boot to the dolls' house, crushing walls and paintings, stairs, dolls and windows. Then he stopped, and picked something out of the wreckage. It was the miniature clock from the dresser in the parlour.

"Put this between your breasts," he said. "See, it works." Sure enough, when she placed the clock to her ear, she could hear it ticking. "A fairy heart," continued the Hunter. "To keep time with your own. When they tick as one, you are safe in the land. Well, as safe as anybody is." He glanced out of the front window, for the wind was beginning to rise, and the house itself was creaking loud enough to have a voice. "We had better go."

They went out through the back door, the Bride following the Hunter while he watched the gathering dusk and muttered to himself.

"What are you talking about?" she asked, securing the clock in the bosom of the dress.

"The plan I made to stop that wretched cousin of mine. I forgot it in the battle. Sometimes I forget things."

"What plan?"

"This is really not the right place to discuss it."

"The plan that included eating my hand?"

He stopped in his tracks and turned to look at her. This would have to be dealt with eventually. It showed no signs of going away by itself.

"All right. Sit down." He pulled up a huge chunk of orange peel fungus for her, and she collapsed onto it.

"My cousin is clearly not a rightful king of the Hedge, of the undying land. He has held on to that kingship through many different methods, and it never really bothered me before. But he is too quick to use cold iron to enforce his rule. Because it's the rule he loves, not the land." The Hunter shrugged. "And I have an aversion to rules. My destiny is to break them. It is my geas."

"Your . . . "

"My geas, my, my—I don't really know what you would call it—each has their own . . . magic? Strength? Trick? Glamour? I don't know, for no two are alike. Some you can buy and sell, some you learn and some you are born with. One who is powerful among the folk—like the Prince—will have many a geas at their command. But every geas has its price, a forbidding or a law that rules it. Break that rule and lose the geas. Break enough of them and the Land itself will do for you. That is the law of it. The geas I keep in my blood detests laws, so that is the code I must live by."

"So you are going to break laws and eventually be killed by the Land?"

"Yes." He smiled. He really thought he had explained it well.

"So all rules have to be broken. Except yours."

His smile faded.

"Don't try to be clever. You just spoil everything."

"That is exactly what the toad said."

"Are you trying to anger me? I am not the toad and you know it."

"But you want me to be quiet, just like everybody else."

"You wanted the explanation, shall I carry on trying to give it?" *Moon give me strength,* he thought, *I should have just rolled her into the river.*

The Bride was silent.

"I'll take that as a yes. So. Your hand, symbol of your art, went into the sacred cup as did your blood. It was consecrated according to the old ways. Now. Once the contents of the cup touch the earth, you are part of the undying kingdoms forever. Is that what you want?"

"You could have just carried the cup."

"A battle was going to start, Madam! How would I carry it? Spilling the cup rather than pouring it might affront royal protocol, but the job would be done just as well!"

"You could have given it to me."

"You could not have defended it."

"You could have put it in your wineskin."

And pour out my own best red to accommodate it? Hardly. With an uncharacteristic wisdom, he refrained from saying so. "I did not think of that at the time," was his more tempered response.

"Because you did not think of me at all."

"No," he admitted and paused. "I am not used to thinking about mortals. I do not understand them." He looked at the Bride. "But I have learned something. Things change, even the Hedge changes—"

As he said it, he noticed the change the Hedge had already

undergone, with clouds covering the moon and the wind whipping towards them. A clatter rang out of the dark, and from between the thickets of the great thorn forest leapt a white hart, gold hooves and antlers shining in the dark. It stared at the two for a moment, its eyes fixed on the Bride, and then it ran, as behind it the shrill noise of horns and baying hounds grew louder and every thorn leaned forwards, shadows darting out into the open, darkness sharp and ready.

He leapt up. "Nothing changes," he snarled. "Prepare for the attack. Here they come!"

CHAPTER SIX
COUNTRY PURSUITS

———

THEY CHARGED INTO THE CLEARING, HORSES CHAMPING AT the cold air, and the pack swarmed forward. The Bride was not ready for the pack; dogs she had expected but these were naked men running on all fours. Every one of them wore a collar and they bayed and yelped and snuffled with excitement. Some had long strings of spittle, like cobweb or toadspawn, dangling from lips and noses. On the backs of horses rode the huntsmen, and for a moment the Bride thought they were foxes sat upright, until she saw that the vulpine faces were tethered to the heads of the riders, blood smearing necks and chins, blood, even now, as she stared at the leader of the Hunt, trickling down beneath his fine red jacket, seeping through his gloves, smearing the reins as he held them. Red fur, red whiskers, red blood, but the eyeholes of the mask were black and empty.

"Vulpinet's hat . . . " muttered the Hunter.

The Huntmaster smiled and the Hunt smiled in perfect unison. He took out a silver horn and blew a ringing note; his followers took out horns and did the same, and the collared men started to snarl and drool. Looking among them the Bride was sure she saw neighbours and old friends, people she had known once upon a time, before she came to the Hedge. The Hunter saw only one face he recognised; with ears serrated and eyes like dull stones, Palawinkes crouched and growled with the others. The riders watched with a kind of merry malice in their expressions. Then the Huntmaster struck downwards with his crop, and the men advanced.

The Hunter drew his sword and the Bride pulled out her kitchen knife with almost no time before the men leapt upon them. The Hunter moved straight between the Bride and a huge pink fat man she swore was the local butcher.

"Run!" roared the Hunter, and she did. But the pink man did not lose interest. Instead, as the others attacked the Hunter, he galloped towards the Bride with his tongue hanging out and a look of dog-like joy in the hunt. She ran and the trees struck her until she found one where the roots clambered over each other like adder knots. Under the roots she glimpsed the eyes watching her.

"In trouble, little gel?" whispered the old, old voice. The Bride looked behind her. The fat man was gaining.

"Yes," she nodded. "Can you help me? Please?"

She could feel the voice beneath the roots grinning, she could feel the way its teeth were brown and broken and very long.

"Gift for a gift, geas for a geas."

The Bride knew there was no time to haggle.

"Please, whatever you can do . . . what do you want?"

The eyes were looking at the house behind her.

"All the chickens in that there place. All the chickens I want, past, present and to come."

"All the—"

"Chickens. All that have been there, all that are there, all that will be there. All for me."

"Chickens? But I don't keep—no, never mind, all right, yes, a geas for all the chickens."

"Backwards and forwards, have been and to come?"

"Yes, please, the geas, the—"

A small bone tube rolled out from under the roots towards her, with a hole through it. It seemed to be laced with human hair. The Bride put it round her neck.

"Done!" the voice rasped happily. "Now run, little gel!"

THE HUNTER'S SWORD CUT THROUGH TWO ENTHUSIASTIC hounds, as he felt the rage taking over. He wanted to give in to it, but instead kept control, hacking through flesh and bone until he reached Palawinkes, and punched the poor yelping fool in the throat, yelling, "Put some clothes on, you fool!" Then he launched himself at the smiling Huntmaster who lashed him across the face with the crop. The Hunter felt the sting and the loss of his geas, as the blow drew blood and blue-grey fuzz sprang from his jaws. His hair began to change, and his jacket faded from him, and his form shrank vertically and spread horizontally, and the fur on him grew. His limbs grew too, and the Huntmaster's smile narrowed somewhat as the change became clear. To force a being back to their true shape is a mighty geas indeed, but the Hunter's true shape was far more alarming than his usual, even in the Hedge where such things are common; the Huntmaster may have expected many things, but a spider the size of his horse was not one of them. He pulled back his reins, and in the dry rasp of his people, ordered his minions to attack.

THE BRIDE REGRETTED CHOOSING TO CLIMB RATHER THAN run. Looking below her she realised that though her pursuer barked like a dog and ran like a dog, he could climb like a man. She watched as he stopped to urinate against the tree-trunk and sniff his doings. Then, smiling up at her with sharp teeth, he began his ascent.

She had indeed made a bad mistake. Two feet meant she could run; one hand meant that she couldn't climb, even with her knife between her teeth. The fat pink man caught up with her easily, cocking his head as he approached her along the branch and making friendly puppy noises. He reached a hand towards her, and his eyes smiled, and he wagged his behind in a simulation of playfulness; she shrank back. She wanted to use the geas and her hand moved up towards her throat, but the blood swam in her head as she looked between the man and the earth below, and, before she fell, she jumped.

CHAPTER SEVEN
LUNA LANDING

———

THE SOUND OF THE RUSHING AIR WAS IN HER EARS, AND SHE watched as the tiny figures below fought; one monstrous shape among them, huge and grey and many-legged, picked men up in its mandibles and bit them in half. Three of its eight eyes, baleful in the moonlight, looked upward, and the Bride wondered if she was the object of its gaze. The world came up to meet her, and she spiralled on towards it, waiting for the earth to break her fall and her neck. Then she felt a gentle touch on her back, and a tugging so smooth she wondered if this was the moment of death, if she was leaving her body for real.

She twisted her head around to see them in the moonlight, semi-transparent creatures of thistledown. They seemed to sparkle like diamonds, but this, she realised, had to be the reflection of countless frozen ponds under stars shining through them. She could not help but smile. They were so light it took a posse of them to haul her upwards, and she gazed at them with delight. Having seen so many of the fanciful shapes worn in the Hedge, her one great disappointment had been the lack of wings among them. These were winged. They also had antennae, long sweeping single ones like wires of silver and electrum or great intricate feathery combs, and the patterns on their bodies and wings were like leaves, like chequers, like pavings, like mosaics. One great one, a female, all violets and shimmering opals, swooped downwards towards the fighting shapes below. Another seemed to be rising from the fray with something limp in its arms. The Bride would have watched further, but shock and blood loss had taken its toll, and she blacked out.

When she came to, she was lying under great stems of grass, grey-blue in the twilight, like pillars above her, their tops bent with dew. It was beautiful but she was very cold. There were soft patting sounds, like whispers only richer, more velvet on the ear, and the moon was rising again. The moon never seemed far from this world. "Does daylight never come here?" she wondered aloud. One of the rescuers turned towards her, and spoke.

"Yes, but then we sleep. Most of us."

"Most of you?"

"Not all. Our cousins you would know better. They are bright."

"Thank you for . . . " But the creature just smiled and wandered away.

She looked around her, and saw many other creatures, talking to each other in a soft strange language of low clicks and flutterings. They touched antennae many times. A body, not much larger than her own, lay nearby wrapped in some kind of see-through white wisp that reminded her of all those wings. One thing she noticed was the Hunter, returned to his usual shape, talking to an extraordinary woman. Her hair and her eyes were azure, her skin was white, and shone with occasional glints of purple and blue and grey. She reminded the Bride of the gem they call moonstone, and she wore a cap of spun silver with small pairs of gossamer wings set into it. The Hunter and the lady were speaking at length. It did not surprise the Bride that he was flirting dreadfully.

When they saw she was awake, they moved over towards her. The Hunter bowed low.

"If I may have the honour of introduction," he said, his voice so courtly that the Bride was positively astonished. "Madame Adscita, this is the Bride. Lady Bride, this is Madame Adscita of the Midnight Seelie."

The lady nodded and the wings on her cap all buzzed together. "I am pleased to meet you, Lady Bride," and she smiled.

The Bride tried to remember what she had learned of the ways of the Folk. "And I am honoured to meet you, Madame Adscita. I wish you all the best on your travels."

The lady bowed. "Can I accept so wonderful a gift as your wish? Such things are precious."

"And yet,"—the Bride faltered, yet knew she was finding her way—"this night I have already been given something precious. It fills me with joy and—" She tried to find a word to take the place of *gratitude*, and thought better of it. "And it would give me more joy if you would accept my wish."

The lady thought and then replied, "If giving it pleases you, I shall gladly receive your wish."

The Hunter did not interrupt the Bride; indeed, he smiled at her words, as though she had hit on exactly the right thing to say.

"Good," he said. "Now, Madame Adscita and I have been discussing what to do next. The rendez-vous point is no longer of use to us." His face fell momentarily. "But finding help for you is still possible."

"I never understood why the rendez-vous was important in the first place."

The Hunter's face was somewhat more grim than before. "I was to meet my servant there. Well, my servant is no more." He broke off for a moment and turned his face to the shadow in white lying on the ground. "And we know what the situation is."

"I don't. Would you like to tell me?" Maybe it was the loss of his servant or the presence of Adscita, but the Bride found the Hunter far more compliant than usual, and though she felt sorry for his loss, thought it best to work with this new mood before it reverted.

"The Hunt has been called on us, dear lady. I strongly suspect your fiancé doesn't love you anymore."

"The Hunt? I thought you were the Hunter."

"I am, hence their lack of success so far. I am now also an outlaw. The Hedge is currently full of my cousin's fools trying to win favour by destroying us. Every portal is protected—"

"There are portals out of here?"

"There are portals everywhere. You would call them fairy rings."

"I thought you people danced around them."

"Did you? Well, it takes more than a circle of mushrooms to make me dance, unless I eat them, and even then it depends. The point is that all the quick ways are covered, and the land is crawling with aspiring courtiers, some better at hunting than others. Much as I would like to tour the land and teach every one of them manners, we have no time. The little clock won't last long. Madame Adscita's kin cannot help us much further, for soon they will hide from the owl—"

"I'm sorry, I'm confused. Where are we going?"

"There is a passing place between our land and yours, likely to be guarded, but not as likely as the more usual ways. It is dangerous for one and all. Still, from there is a road that leads back to your own world." Back to her own world! The Bride's heart pounded. Then she looked at his face, and was sorry to see it so grim. She went over to the shrouded corpse and pulled the linen away. The being beneath was one of the hound-men.

Without quite knowing what she did, she took the geas-bone off her neck, and looked at it carefully. It was covered with scrapings of mud and clay, and underneath were carved words.

> *"Cunning and art they do not lack,*
> *But aye these words will fetch it back*
> *Prey, take heed of a hunting hound*
> *Will harry thee all these lands around*
> *For here we come in the old ones' game,*
> *All for to bring thee home again.*
> *Oh I shall go into the shape of a hare*
> *With sorrow and sighing and too much care,*
> *And I will run in the old ones' game,*
> *All for to find my home again.*
> *Cunning and art they do not lack,*
> *But aye these words will fetch it back . . . "*

The bone shattered as she spoke, though her voice was soft. Adscita and the Hunter were looking at her in surprise. The fay lady bowed gently. "An old geas," she observed, her voice showing just a faint trace of surprise, while Hunter's attention turned to the corpse. The Bride stood there, expecting some great power to tingle through her, a feeling of magic and strength. Instead the Hunter just smiled at her a little sadly.

"Let's get some sleep," he said.

CHAPTER EIGHT
WAKING THE DEAD

———

WHEN RICHARD OPENED HIS EYES, THE SUN WAS STREAMING through the window with all the power of mid-day, and he smiled. He was well. For a moment, he did not recollect the house, for the walls were very bare and he could not get away from a sense of whitewash, like a prison or a cell, and it took him a moment to remember. Observing the inmates at Bedlam Hospital, while useful to his work, always left his nerves somewhat on edge. For a moment, he thought he could see Crazy Jane watching him, but he swept that idea out of his head. Crazy Jane, like all the other paintings, was being kept in storage by the Academy. He was neither in Bedlam nor in the Hedge. This was his father's house in Cobham, and downstairs, servants would be cooking breakfast.

He sat upright in bed, as more and more recollections crowded his mind. He had suffered a long fever such as the ones he endured as a child, and voices had plagued his thoughts, had haunted him. There had been a doll and Sylvia and Walter and other, terrible things. His father and Sir Thomas had decided between them that his artistic purposes should be directed elsewhere, to subjects less fantastical. He could not agree more, for his diary had been full of the turbulence of his dreams: *I often have lain down at night with my imagination so full of wild vagaries that I have really and truly doubted of my own sanity* . . . True, very true, these doubts were his own. If only he could remember writing them.

Forgetting fairies then, and lunatics, and all the rest of it, could only help him. And he remembered now the destination, an equally haunting dream but alive and real: Egypt. He would see its landscapes and its people, he would find a new music in his paints, in the sunsets and the deserts. He would begin again, and be clear and sane. He could not shake off the stern sense of there being something else he was meant to do before he left, but he could not recall it. All was packed, all was ready, the ship would leave on the dusk tide at Dover. He might as well get up.

So he threw back the blankets on the bed, and swung his legs to the floor, where he felt rather than heard a resounding crunch beneath his feet. When he looked down, he saw egg shells, dutifully split in half, covering the entire floor, from bed to door. As he gazed at the sight, it never occurred to him that a floor covered with eggshells was a strange thing: but he did know for an absolute certainty that there were three hundred of them.

THIS WAS DANGEROUS, SHE KNEW, AFTER BEING AWAY SO long. Never go back, never go back, but she had to now, if she was to understand, if she was to find Richard again.

It was not as though she lacked power in the mortal world; had she not brought Richard through in the first place? But for some reason he was resisting her, he was not returning, and that was ridiculous. The Hedge was where he belonged, *she* was where he belonged. She was beginning to suspect the whole hunt had been a ruse to get rid of her greatest power among the folk; one up to the clever scrabbling Prince, she thought. She had given up power too easily. She wanted it back.

And to gain what we had in the beginning, she thought, we must return to the beginning. So here she was, in the dark with them. Their dead faces glinted above petticoats and lace, their porcelain skins shone under bonnets and they waited. How terrible they smelled! (*Keeping these things near a grave-yard is so foolish*, she thought, and wondered why mortals knew nothing of any use). She thought the inhabitants of the room could not see her, but a creaking of limbs and a certain shudder in the air told her she was wrong.

How they hated her.

They had always hated her, for she was different and rare, made long ago before their makers had entered the world. And she was the thing that belonged in her shape. They had borrowed these forms, so pretty and impotent, for they had nowhere else to go.

And she had taken Richard. She looked behind them, at the ugly doll with its ruined hair and its broken neck, jambed back onto its body. The neck wound looked like a torc. The doll tilted its head to look at her, but it was not the one who spoke. That was a yellow-haired creature with bright blue eyes.

"We are going to kill you," it said.

She nodded and smiled.

"But first, you are going to help me," she replied.

"You took him," they said as one.

"I will bring him back," she promised.

The yellow-haired creature looked across at her.

"Back here?"

The Beloved wanted to dissemble, but there was some strange oiliness of the air around her as the smell rolled forwards: talcum powder and sweets, lollipops and pretty striped humbugs, and underneath it all, a cloying reek. She found she could not lie. Normally she would have called this a powerful geas, but she knew her enemies. This was something else.

"Not straight back here—we are lovers after all—but nearby."

The dolls laughed.

"There is another who will bring him back here," one of them said.

"To us," added her sister.

The Beloved knew that there was only one who could make such a promise. She was almost impressed by him.

"The Prince of Spiders lies to you," she stated boldly. "He wants Richard for himself, as sacrifice."

"Then why did he fool you into sending him home?" hissed a tiny girly voice out of the darkness, and giggled, a terrible sound.

"He was angry. He was foolish."

"The Prince of Spiders is no fool. He is our ally. He has made us strong."

That at least, the Beloved could not fault. Malicious they had always been, but never like this. From cold iron to graveyard stinkers, there was no tool disdained by the Prince of Spiders. They closed in upon her now, and she knew she had to get out; still, there was one more question:

"How? How did you become so—"

"He has stretched the old ways for season upon season,

until the web has broken on the face of mortals and folk alike. We are hungry now."

Delicate china hands reached up towards her hair, pretty pink fingers slid up her legs, and she felt a soft drip of something cold, phlegm or drool upon her neck. She would need to change her clothes. Still, they had given her information, and a gift requires a gift.

She let her present fall to the floor; it had taken much magic to keep it pumping, but there it was. They lifted their little faces, made in Paris, made in London, and sniffed it. The touch and stink of them fell away from her and turned instead, to Walter's last gift: his heart, warm and soft beneath their ripping little teeth and nails, provided the Beloved with a clear route of escape, though the sounds of them eating followed her until she was safe and sound, back in the Hedge.

THE BRIDE COULD NOT SLEEP. SHE HAD ALWAYS LOVED NIGHT time, but she began to suffer from a surfeit of moon and twilight, and found herself craving the presence of colours, dawn and sunset and the sun at mid-day, bright in a vibrant sky.

"Does the sun never shine here?" she asked one gentle fluttering creature with white fur growing between its scalp and shoulders.

It shuddered. "Why yes, yes," it said. "And I have known some say they will stay up to see it. But those that try, die painfully. They are drawn up towards its terrible light, you see, and their eyes are burned out of them, their wings catch fire. Stay awake until dawn and some say you will hear them screaming—only do not look, or the light will draw you up to join them."

"But . . . " The Bride faltered, for these were gracious folk and she did not want to seem rude. "Where is the difference between that and . . . what I mean is, I understand your people fly up towards the moon, and that is surely too high to reach as well . . . "

"High but not as high. We must get there because we belong there. That light is cooling, it would never burn us . . . Adscita can explain this better than I can."

But Adscita was busy or asleep, perhaps with the Hunter, and the Bride felt awkward about interfering. She suddenly noticed that hanging from the understems of the grass around her were large ghostly packages reminiscent of the spun corpses found in the webs of the hedge. These, however, were more lumpen and solid. "Cocoons," she realised after a moment, and found herself curious to examine them more closely. She asked the being to show her the nursery and Io, as it called itself, was most obliging.

The cocoons were the size of people—or Hedgefolk at least—and they were clearly not made of the same silk as the Prince's creations. They were hard and grey-yellow-brown, like linen soaked and dried in plaster, and the Bride was mystified. "It was a long time ago," she explained to Io, who could not see anything to be surprised at. "But I was sure there was silk involved," and even as she said it, a soft ripping noise from nearby elicited a small excited chitter from Io.

"How lucky!" the moth said. "Now you will see!"

The ripping came from a rather large cocoon dangling from under a snowdrop. Io lisped and fluttered happily, the

Bride was suddenly transfixed by her first sight of a real flower since entering the Hedge. Harsh as the snows might be, the Bride knew that this delicate being was ever a true herald of Spring, and such news could not be good for the Prince of Spiders. "We have not had Spring for a long time, it is true," concurred Io. "But look, look!"

The outer casing of the cocoon had a long thin crack down one side, where the material seemed hardest of all. Now it looked brittle, a bit like spoilt leather, slitting and breaking in half a dozen places. For the Bride, Io carefully pealed back a portion of the cocoon to reveal the silk that made up the underside of the wrapping. It looked white, but when one held it up to the starlight, one could see a rainbow of colours in it. "There are weavers and dyers who have the magic to make the cloth show one colour only, or change the cloth to whatever pattern they please," said Io. "But most think it better unchanged." By now, however, the Bride's curiosity had moved beyond the beautiful silk to that which was revealed by its removal; a shining black hand with long fingers and short, shell-like nails. She stared at it for a moment as the ripping sound grew louder. The crack down the side became a thick line with small fractures spreading out from it, like rivers on a map. The Bride's attention was drawn to the upper part of the crust, which, apart from the tiniest of fissures, seemed almost untouched by the disintegration around it. Then, the crack at the side burst, and the cocoon swung open tearing across the top to reveal a face.

The silk within had not been damp, but the being that stepped forward gleamed as though covered with some kind of dew. Its body was black and almost entirely transparent.

The Bride could see the quick fluctuation of breath and pulse, lungs and ribs and intestines like that of a human. Near the middle of the chest sat a small indigo heart pumping fast, and she watched as the blood, like ink in a pen, circuited the body and moved back over the shoulder, to the great wings still lying unfurled against the creature's back. Its face was more pointed, more human somehow, than that of Io or Adscita, and its antennae were single rather than combed. It stood there, looking at everything out of huge faceted eyes, and as it breathed, it grew wider and, to the Bride's astonishment, slightly taller. The body colour deepened to a glossy ebony, in contrast to the huge wings, which expanded like flames out of coal, very different to the usual delicate tones found among Adscita's people. The outermost tips of the wings remained black, a fringe of speckled lace to all that orange and scarlet.

"Marvelous," came a familiar voice behind her. "Nice colour under moonlight. Should save the owl a lot of inconvenience. Short hunt, less appetite, good for all mothkind. Adscita should give it a medal now." The Hunter was hungry, and that always made his humour somewhat wry.

"Be quiet, you!" The Bride was furious for no reason she could quite explain. "Just leave it alone!" For the being looked so joyful, she could not bear its first experience of speech to be the Hunter's sneers. She stepped forward and smiled at it.

"Welcome to the Hedge," she said. "I am the Bride." She did not look away as she said, "Why don't you go get some breakfast, Hunter?"

The Hunter shrugged and turned away. In another time, the new moth would have *been* his breakfast, but he judged it best not to mention that to the Bride.

Io bustled towards the arrival holding a large chequered cloth, which the Bride presumed was a picnic rug. The moth placed it on the floor, and the Bride waited for the rest of breakfast to appear. It took her a moment to realise that the rug was the breakfast. Io sat on the ground, picked up one edge of the cloth and put it into her mouth. She looked as though she was half chewing, half sucking it. The Bride was nonplussed, and the new arrival, watching her attentively, seemed hesitant. Io pulled the rug out of her mouth. Where she had been eating was a round and perfect hole.

"Are you not hungry?" she spoke to the being.

It opened its mouth and out scrolled a long, honey-coloured proboscis by way of answer.

"Then eat," said Io.

The creature looked upwards and then back to the Bride, who felt a trembling in her skin, as though she understood.

"May I try something?" The Bride went to the base of the snowdrop stem, and leant all her weight against it. The flower nodded, the stem leant forward slightly, and then sprang back. The Bride gasped, realising how weak she had become. She tried again, and slowly the snowdrop seemed to lean down and almost buckle. She pushed as hard as she could, just in time to see the scarlet-winged figure swoop upward and hurl itself straight into the centre of the flower head. Its weight made the snowdrop head bounce backwards, and the Bride fell away from the stem. Still, she could see it up there, clinging to the flower as the world rocked around it.

"You know, I think it is a cousin," said Io, and sighed.

"Do you not like your cousins?" asked the Bride, delighted with the sight above them.

Io looked worried. "Of course I like them," she said. "What is there not to like? But they need the bright light and they drink flowers, and we have few of those here. This one is too early. It is sure to die."

The Bride had no answers, but she sat and waited, while the moth ate the rug and its cousin swayed on the flower. She had managed to light a small fire by the time the Hunter returned with red wine and a deer over his shoulder; that is to say, it looked vaguely like a deer and it had horns, so she decided not to question. He skinned and gutted it swiftly, and the roasting began in time for Adscita and the others to rejoin them. Adscita did not eat as the others did; when the Hunter offered her the head, she drank the tears glistening in the fur beneath its eyes. The Bride was not hungry, but she made herself eat, and the cousin rejoined them, huge and black and scarlet with golden pollen dotted around its head. It looked happy and full.

Adscita's people had brought someone with them: a skinny leveret all feet and ears and big amber eyes. Scale being a matter of continual surprise and only occasional consistency in the hedge, the hare was giant in comparison to the Hedge Folk, and someone had enterprisingly saddled it. "So sorry," they explained to the Bride. "Normally the reins would be daisy-chains but . . . " She did not know what they had to be sorry for. Any kind of saddle would have impressed her, and the Folk had gone further. The seating arrangement on the leveret's back could best be described as a kind of howdah, a curious but very beautiful combination of multi-coloured silk and silver canopy, all fringes and tassels. The reins and straps were leather, adorned with little silver bells that rang with every movement. Best of all, the howdah had one unique addition; silken curtains that could be drawn across, to preserve privacy.

"This is too kind," said the Bride.

Adscita bowed. "Nothing is too good for the Bride, and my old friend, the Hunter." She smiled across at that gentleman in a way that irritated the Bride. *Nice people*, she thought, *but something about her just grates on me . . .*

The Hunter, for his own part, was beaming, first at the hare, then at the Bride and then at the Hare again.

"Recognise him?" he said. The Bride shook her head, to his great amusement. "Well, of course, he's a lot younger than he used to be. Meet my servant Palawinkes!" The leveret blinked one of its eyes. The Bride just stared at it, astonished.

"So that was . . . "

"The geas, yes."

"And it worked?"

"It worked well, unlike Palawinkes here." The Bride could not be certain, but the way the hare twitched a single ear had the same tone as the flip of a finger. She sat among the pebbles with Adscita and Io discussing the journey to come, while Palawinkes and his employer celebrated their reunion with a quick bout of boxing. Palawinkes was better at it than before, but the Hunter still won. The ladies applauded politely and awarded Palawinkes a cowslip, which he wore, and the Hunter a greenfly, which he ate.

"Where does long ears go?" said another voice, intruding on the discussion. She had never heard it before, but she knew who it must be. It had more clarity and music than that of any of Adscita's folk.

"Cousin," she said, as she turned to face the butterfly. With its wings spread, it was almost a giant among its kind. Admittedly, pound for pound, the Hunter looked bigger and stronger, but he was full grown. This was just a baby, its happy round face shining like jet. It fluttered its wings in response.

"Please," it said, "where does it go?"

"We are going to find someone to fix the Bride," interposed the Hunter roughly, paying attention at last. "And no, you cannot come."

The Bride stared at him indignantly. He looked at her, his expression innocent. "Well, it was obvious!"

"Not to me," she replied with an attempt at hauteur. "The cousin hasn't said that this is what it wants."

"Yes," said the cousin, "this is what it wants. Can it come?"

"It knows the answer." Again, the Hunter's voice was curt. "It cannot come."

"It cannot come?"

"No."

The cousin stood there, looking confused. The Bride felt a kind of helpless misery at the thought of it crying.

"It has a name," it said, as though this might help. "It is not just a baby . . . "

"What is your name?" asked the Bride.

"I am Danaeus," the butterfly replied, with a sweet childish attempt at sounding lordly.

"Of course you are," said the Hunter. "Shall we go?"

But she didn't move.

The Hunter looked impatiently from the Bride to the

butterfly. "Look," he tried to explain, "we go into very great danger. The cousin cannot fight because it is too young. The Bride cannot fight because it is too hurt. Only the Hunter can fight, and so—"

"But the Hunter is a great wolf?"

"Yes."

"Is the Hunter frightened?"

"No, you ignorant little oik. Listen to me. I can fight and fight and fight, and kill many without tiring. But you are just a distraction. You can't actually do anything at all, and having a name bigger than your head doesn't help. We are going through the realms of Owl and Crow—you know who they are?—and others too. They will eat you and then the Bride will make a lot of noise, and the Hunter can't bear it."

"They will eat the Hunter, too. He is only a spider."

Hunter moved forwards, his eyes aflame.

The cousin flapped backwards, and the Bride stood in front of it. "He doesn't know, Hunter, please, he doesn't know. He's just a butterfly, a baby really, he was born today and he'll die in the cold if we leave him . . . please, Hunter, just for once listen to me."

The Hunter stood very silent, but his eyes never left the butterfly. The Bride, not really knowing what she did, placed her hand over his heart, and was surprised at how slowly it beat, *ouboom . . . ouboom . . . ouboom . . .* such a slow heartbeat must mean he is calm, she told herself, but his eyes told her otherwise. His hand travelled slowly across his chest, closed itself around hers and pulled it gently away from him. Then his eyes met hers with a strange undisclosed expression in them. They were the eyes of wolf and hunter, of a strange man you should beware of meeting in the woods, far from the safety of locks and keys.

"The last lady who played fast and loose with me lost her grandmother." He smiled. *My, what big teeth you have!* she thought with dismay. He released her hand.

"Very well," he said, with an air of courtesy, "if we leave this thing here, it will die of cold, and the world will be rid of a singularly fat premature butterfly. But you are the Bride, and I have no wish to make you unhappy. It can come if it doesn't get in the way."

The butterfly did not seem to notice the sting in the Hunter's words. It fluttered straight to their mount and sat between the ears of the leveret, fanning a breeze towards the howdah, as the Bride and the Hunter climbed into it, and said their goodbyes to the midnight seelie. This would be wonderful in a hot climate, thought the Bride. A pity then, that all is Winter, and this breeze feels positively arctic!

"What did you say?" The Hunter turned to her with a look of intense ferocity. She could have sworn she had thought but not spoken.

All is Winter . . . he thought hard. There had been more to the plan than stealing the Bride and meeting up with Pala-winkes. And suddenly, there it lay in his head, like a badly drawn map of the land: the plan in its entirety, absurd, ridicu-lous, impossible to succeed in. He could not believe he had ever planned anything so stupid, and yet it had his utter loyalty.

"Are you going to tell me this plan?" she said, and he looked at her in astonishment.

He did not return her smile. She was beginning to know

the ways of the folk, to talk like them, and feel like them. Dangerous. He paused for a moment. "No," he said, and flicked the reins. The little hare leapt forward, the silver bells jingled, and the wind was left far behind.

CHAPTER NINE
PAINTING THE ISLAND

———

His notebooks were already alive with the tour. Everywhere he went, his avid heart gazed at beauty, beauty, beauty! He drew it, sketched it, painted it wherever he found it and he found it everywhere, for the world was beautiful, his starved soul knew it, his eyes touched everything, as though he had once been blind or hidden.

Ay, he told himself, I was hidden. I hid myself because it seemed so harsh.

Not *seemed*, a voice within his head seemed to rebuke him, it *was* harsh, unbearably so: Time was when you thanked me for rescuing you. Time was . . . but he heard and saw no more of the voice. He closed his ear to it. *That was in another country, and besides, the wench is dead.* Sir Thomas was astonished at the prolific creativity of his protégé. Italy had them both enthralled. Richard was working on a pastoral scene, the working title of which was "Italian Rustic Musicians." Sir Thomas well knew how music affected the young man. Poetry, ancient poetry, musical and simple filled his heart, and quotes from Theocritus appeared against sketch after sketch.

Sweeter, shepherd, and more subtle is your song
Than the tuneful splashing of that waterfall
Among the rocks. If the Muses pick the ewe

As their reward, you'll win the hand-raised lamb
If they prefer the lamb, the ewe is yours.

He was thunderstruck with Corfu, which, seemed, as he wrote to his delighted father, " . . . *A large assortment, or menagerie, of pompous ruffians, splendid savages, grubby finery, wild costume . . . I never saw such an assemblage of deliciously-villainous faces. Oh, such expression! Oh, such heads! Enough to turn the brain of an artist!*"

But not Richard's head. He was glowing with passion for life, and for the first time since his childhood, took up playing the violin again. They were old childhood tunes, but Sir Thomas could see the skill in them. More, he could see the laughter and joy in Richard's face, so different to the nervous fidgets and twitches of before. His sketches were still extraordinary if not magical: each one had that curious stillness and attention to detail that was Richard's unique gift. They were still very fine, Richard was clearly happy, and perhaps, mused Sir Thomas, one could have a surfeit of fairies. The Levant awaited, and real life held as much enchantment as any dream.

The faces of the people bewitched Richard, and he decided to try his hand at portraiture. Inevitably, he tended to prefer landscape work, but still, the dark eyes and gleaming skins, the brilliant colours of those around him, were too vivid to resist, and Sir Thomas arranged for a sitter to attend him, a woman Richard colourfully dubbed "The Gypsy Queen," having been told her name twice and promptly forgotten it.

He had a bad dream the night before she came to his room at the hotel, but the memory was hazy and he suppressed it with only one horrid detail refusing to erase itself. In the dream, he was staring at a miniature portrait of his father that he kept at his desk, when a yellow spider emerged and, wrapping its legs around the top of the frame, scuttled down over his father's face. Richard woke then, almost in a panic, but he pushed it from his mind. He was no stranger to nightmares.

A seat was prepared for her near the window, where he could work with the light upon her features. She entered the room dressed something between a shepherdess and a romany. Her teeth shone white, her hair was a jungle of black curls, her eyes were brown and flashed with a corsair's fire. She was at the very least a pirate, he decided. The profession of shepherdess could not have suited anybody less. Her English was rudimentary in the extreme, but still surpassed his Greek, and she understood more than she could speak. Richard considered that an unparalleled talent in women.

She sat in jingling finery close to the window, and Richard enjoyed trying to reproduce the shades of her olive skin in the sunlight. To be sure, all his tinctures were too pale, and however brown he thought he had mixed his pigments, on canvas they had a curiously washed-out quality. It was an effect he often favoured; out among the ruins where the light drowned the earth's colours it worked very well. Here, he wanted to capture the deeper tones of her skin, and it was harder. The colour of her eyes he captured, but the shape . . . somehow, he found himself extending them beyond their true almond shape, and once, when the lids drooped in a heavy languid sweep, he almost stopped working to stare, for he could have sworn he knew this woman, though he could not recall from where. He stared at her for a long time without movement. She looked at him questioningly, after he had gazed at her for what seemed like an hour but could not have been more than ten minutes. Abruptly, she pushed her shawl off behind her, and disrobed down to her waist, and then sat there looking at him, with no expression whatsoever on her face.

Richard was too awestruck to say a single word. Her breasts were full and voluptuous, swinging above her waist, her nipples like the undersides of big dark mushrooms. She arched her back slightly and moved her hands, giving him a questioning look as if to ask if she should stretch her arms up. Richard's eyes drank her in, and he felt, for the first time since the fight in the nursery, a desire powerful yet ordinary.

Recognising it as such, he picked up his paintbrush and tried to continue. As a gentleman he knew he should tell her to dress herself, and he dreaded the thought of somebody outside seeing her naked profile at the window, but still . . . "I am a man like any other," he told himself. "And this has eluded me for too long." So, resolving to pay her a great amount more, he let the lady sit there, and let his own thoughts wander between painting her and more intimate activities. He was beginning to enjoy the frisson of the afternoon when she spoke.

"Richard?"

His heart froze. It could not be, it could not be . . .

"Richard?"

Not you, he thought, you are just a doll in a nursery, probably thrown away years ago.

"I know you can hear me, my love."

These are just the old delusions, he told himself, *be not afeard, the island is full of noises* . . . He steadied himself and looked across at the woman, who lifted an eyebrow at him, as though she too had heard something. Black-haired and brown-eyed, her face was pleasing and her breasts were beautiful. She was magnificent.

But she was not the woman sketched on his canvas. There instead sat a white faced woman with long drooping eyelids, straight hair, an impossibly long neck and a body of exaggerated curves. Her eyes gazed straight at Richard and she smiled.

"No!" He screamed and slashed the canvas with a scapula, once, twice, again! The gypsy queen jumped up, gabbled something in Greek, and grabbed her clothes. Richard tried to calm himself, and made placatory gestures at her. He could not tell if she was angry; she was certainly not afraid. He offered her money, and she grew less tempestuous, but still she would not stay. Covering herself up, she accepted a fee much greater than that previously agreed upon with a silent hauteur. She left, and Richard found himself staring at the ruined canvas. The mind is a thing of tubes and holes, he found himself thinking, and it gets through. It trickles through, it sneaks in, it eats the day and night. But I must not recall what it is.

Memory was at the door, waiting unbidden, and Richard knew that it had to be kept out. He needed a greater magic. Corfu was too close to home.

Egypt, he told himself, the deepest magics are in Egypt. I shall ask Sir Thomas if we can bypass Damascus and go straight to the oldest land. Nothing can follow me there. I will be free.

He started packing.

CHAPTER TEN
AT THE CROSSROADS

———

THE WIND HOWLED ACROSS THE NIGHT, AND CLOUDS RAN TO keep up with the little dancing hare in its silver bridle. It was too cold for the butterfly, even nestled in the fur of the leveret, so they made room for it as best they could in the howdah, and everything was very cramped. The Hunter had the sneaking feeling that the third passenger just wanted to be near the Bride; it certainly nestled close to her, and she didn't seem to mind, despite the fact that it was full grown now. The Hunter didn't mind having to touch the Bride either, it was listening to her that did all the damage. Even now, she was talking to the butterfly, teaching it new words, which it absorbed with endless attention: *where the bee sucks, there suck I, in a cowslip's bell I lie* . . . The Hunter tried not to snigger and contented himself with holding the reins and watching out for owl-shadow above.

Palawinkes, he knew, could not serve his master much longer. Oh, the fellow would do the best he could, but he was wild now and, boxing aside, the world of grass and wind and hollow was calling him. He had paid his dues. It was time to be free. A movement beneath the trees brought the Hunter back to the moment: his eyes were keen, and just as well, he told himself. On a normal night, the bird was a silent adversary. Tonight the owl could be approaching with a brass band in tow, and he still wouldn't hear it over the nursery lesson behind him.

The hare raced across the fields like a tiny steed of silver, and the mist fell and all the world grew grey, with neither moon nor stars nor clouds. Only the grass grew along the hedge, and the road shone as though rain had fallen. It was an old road new made, and it was black with curious lights down the centre. Sometimes they seemed like lines, other times they seemed like glinting jewels, meant to reflect light. There was little enough light for them to reflect, for the mist flowed thick over the road and up to the sky. The Bride could make out the eyes of giant beasts gleaming as they lumbered through the fog. She knew they could run much faster, but dared not because they could barely see, and when they passed the hare, they smelled of metal and heat. Few came by, and neither the hare nor the Hunter took any notice of them. The purr and roar of them died away, and for a long time all was silent. Then there came the distinct sound of hooves on the road.

There were many of them, and the familiar clopping sound echoed across the empty land, but no neighing of horses could be heard, no voices of riders. The hare stopped to watch, and sat up on its hind legs, to the consternation of those sitting in the howdah, who nearly all tumbled out the back. Adscita's folk were kind, but vehicle design was not their strong point. The Bride would have had something to say about it, but her attention was quickly taken by those approaching.

They were much bigger than the people of the hedge, indeed, thought the Bride, both she and the Hunter could sit upon the palms of any one of them. They wore green and gold and purple, red and blue and silver, and their horses were white and black, dappled grey and piebald, all dressed for tourney. One lady rode in front, or at least, the Bride presumed it was a lady. It had the head of a white deer with golden antlers and wore a dress of green velvet, its long white hands feminine and human-seeming, but its feet cloven. It held a falcon out upon its wrist, and the hounds that followed were white with red tipped ears. With the queen were knights and squires, bards and jesters, some beast-headed like herself, all with wild wise eyes. To the Bride's wonder, there appeared to be three mortals in the procession. One was clearly a bard, clad in green to match the lady, and he rode next to her, strumming a harp. He winked at the Bride, singing as he passed. The words floated by like pollen on the wind:

> "Harp and carp, Thomas," she said,
> "Harp and carp along wi' me,
> And if ye dare to kiss my lips,
> Sure of your body I will be."

> Her shirt was of the grass-green silk,
> Her mantle of the velvet fyne
> At ilka tett of her horse's mane
> Hang fifty silver bells and nine.

> True Thomas, he pulled off his cap,
> And bowed low down to his knee
> "All hail, thou mighty Queen of Heaven!
> For thy peer on earth I never did see."

"O no, O no, Thomas," she said,
"That name does not belang to me;
But if ye dare to kiss my lips,
Sure of your body I will be."

"Betide me weal, betide me woe,
That threat shall never frighten me;"
And he has kissed her rosy lips,
All underneath the Eildon Tree.

"Now, ye must go wi me," she said,
"True Thomas, ye must go wi me,
And ye must serve me seven years,
Through weal or woe, as may chance to be.
"She mounted on her milk-white steed—"

"Shall we go?" interrupted the Hunter. "This warbler bores me to death." He had heard the song many times and by now, he felt that the fairest critique he could give the Rhymer would be to slice his head off just to get a different note out of him.

"I have never heard it before," said the Bride, with a look that the Hunter was beginning to identify with her interest and enthusiasm. He felt his heart sinking. The song continued:

"And they rode on and further on
Further and swifter than the wind
Until they came to a desert wide
And living land was left behind"

THE SPIDER'S BRIDE

O they rode on, and farther on,
And they waded red blood to the knee,
beyond the sun, beyond the moon,
Beyond the roaring of the sea"

Beyond the night, beyond star light,
They waded red blood to the knee;
For all the blood that's shed on earth
Runs off the shores of that country . . . "

The song faded as the troubadour went passed, and an audible sigh of relief could be heard from the Hunter.

The second mortal in the procession was, of all things, a minister of some kind. He wore a tiny white ruff above plain black garments, and he stared at the hare and its occupants and took notes down in a little book. The third was a knight in green armour with roses tethered to his horse's mane and tail, and woven thickly across his breastplate, almost as though they had grown out of him. His emerald visor was up and he was very comely to look upon, with fair skin and fair hair. His eyes seemed to be closed, and the Bride could not help but wonder why. Then, almost as though he felt her staring at him, his face turned towards her, though his horse marched onwards, and his eyelids opened. Beneath them the sockets were inlaid with wood. His horse stopped as if waiting for something to happen, and he waited a long while, until the lady in green looked back, first at the knight, and then at the point under the hedge where the hare sat. The falcon let out a cry, and the green knight moved on to join the rest. They vanished into the mist as quickly as they had appeared and an orange-red rose lay on the ground where the knight had stood.

"Leave it!" said the Hunter, for the Bride had leapt forward to pick it up. The rose was gigantic beside her and the scent from its heart was full and sweet.

"It isn't for me," she protested, and beckoned the butterfly over. It obligingly pushed its face into the wall of petals and drank very deep. The Hunter shook his head.

"Nobles," he said. "Neither the good sense of the common Folk, nor the grace of the Sidhe. If I had time I would pound in a head or two." He shook his own head with regret. The Bride would have asked more about them, but she dared not, because for all his scorn, the Hunter looked very like them; something about the eyes.

"So these are not Sidhe then?" she asked.

"These?" The Hunter laughed. "No, no, you shall know the Sidhe if ever you meet them! These, the Daoine indeed!" And he laughed heartily at a joke no-one but he understood.

"But they must be more closely related to them than most Hedgefolk; they are what I expect from fairies, they are more . . . more . . . " she floundered, trying to be polite. "More elf-like," as opposed to shape-shifting insects, stuffed animals, tiny madmen and malevolent dolls, she could have added, but the cold laughter in the Hunter's face was becoming unbearable. The silence between them was broken by the arrival of the butterfly. She could barely look at it now, for its face was beautiful and strange and swiftly becoming adult, and she felt a little shy as she heard it say, "I would like us to keep the rose." The Hunter picked it up (*any damage will have been done by now*, he told himself) and, with a barely spoken geas, shrunk the flower and put it in the buttonhole of his tattered frockcoat. When they were all rested, he chivvied the hare onwards, and sure enough they came to the crossroads, as he who had traveled these lands a long time knew they would.

"One of these roads is the way to your world," he told her. She poked her head out and tried to see if any path out of the three in front of them seemed more real, more homely than the others, but in the mist and the darkness they all looked the same.

There was a gibbet at the cross roads, and as she looked at it, the corpse hanging there seemed to swing with more deliberation than one might expect. One of its eyes had gone, and one of its hands was missing. The other, a bright blue one, seemed fixed straight on her.

"Behind the veil," murmured the Hunter, and the Bride obeyed. The corpse swung round and back, round and back, but the Hunter feared the eye of no man, dead or living. What worried him more was the company dead men keep. A murder of crows had gathered on the beam, and were enjoying a grand banquet of carrion, and that was a good sign, he thought, for they would be stuffed too full to want a battle. But crows never stay full for long. They are always hungry, and always clever, and for that reason, they make the best spies, expensive, accurate and malicious. He looked at the hand cut from the dead man and knew exactly who he was dealing with.

"Greetings, good people!" He hailed them, and pulled on the reins. The leveret chafed a little, but stopped. The crows looked at him.

"Ahh! Hunter," an old crow cawed back. "Aa! Aa! A fine mount, and new to thee! Where didst get all this silver?"

"I have grown rich," laughed the Hunter. "From a great inheritance!" And with that, he threw a wine skin at them. It was caught by a young one without thinking, and the Hunter laughed in earnest when he saw its elder glaring. A gift accepted. They knew what it meant and would stand by it; for all their malice they kept the laws as well as any, better than most.

"The bier has not passed that carries your benefactor, they say. Aa! He lives yet, Hunter, and calls you names that the Good Folk do not repeat!"

"Spare me his dreadful cursing," said the Hunter piously, and covered his ears with his hands. The long volley of crow laughter and nightshade berries spat at him told him he was doing well. He let the berries bounce off him. "Beware things you cannot see," he whispered to the Bride.

"What?" she replied, and tried to focus on the birds from behind the veils of the howdah. Something told her it was a mistake, that their eyes were better than hers, and any information she gained would be far less than they would learn about her. Still she had to look, for the wispy veils blurred the outside world, and gave the crows the strangest appearance.

To her eyes, their heads were not those of birds, but of children. She thought she must be going mad, and squinted determinedly at them. Sure enough, on staring, one or two of the heads turned back to crows, and one or two became very old women indeed, hundreds of years old, but most stayed children with hungry faces and dark cold eyes. None of them had long hair, and she could see why. They chewed on each others' feathers, strands of hair and eyelashes and even picked at each others' talons endlessly, and the more she stared, the more they seemed like stick puppets, thin in black rags, starving and lost.

There was a soft tugging on her arm from behind her.

The butterfly leaned over and said, "Beware of things we cannot see. Something we cannot see is behind us." Danaeus gesticulated to the back of the houdah.

One of the veils was twitching. They sat and watched. The Bride was growing less and less enamoured of the veils. In sumptuous lands of heat and dust, she was sure they would be delightful. Here, she was never sure what they showed, or if they moved, what it was that moved them. They parted indistinctly and she knew what had to be behind them, but the ripples of curtain were so gentle, so innocuous, she felt she must be imagining things. It was Danaeus who leapt on an invisible shape and dragged it all the way into the howdah. The butterfly child was much stronger than she imagined, and not stupid either. He shook his head, crumbling pollen motes all over the unseen visitor, to promptly reveal the outline of a little crow. In the crow's mouth was a strange object which, while impossible to make out, became clearer if the Bride held one of the silk veils up and looked through it. The shape was like a thick match, with one end flickering. She blew upon the little light, and instantly, a small crow was revealed, squirming in Danaeus' grip. Its head was that of a very young girl.

"Don't you be causing me any trouble now," it warned them. The object was a thumb. The Bride wondered if it was from her own lost hand and she picked it up to check. It was thick and broad and decaying. Someone had coated it in tallow, and a wick was sticking out of the blackened nail.

"That's off a hand of glory," said the crow. "Fresh done, too."

"Where's the rest of it?" asked the Bride, for she was toying with the idea of trying to graft a spare hand onto her own wrist. The hedge was pure magic after all, so why not?

"Aaa!" squawked the girl, and cocked her head to one side. "With our cailleach. She'll finish the Hunter, you'll see."

"Is that what you want?" The Bride wanted to pick the crow up. Some part of her believed that if she did, a huge and terrible enchantment might be broken, the feathers and bones would fall away and a pretty little girl would step forward, like Thumbelina or Vassilisa or . . . or . . . but the Bride could not remember her fairy tales. In fact, the Bride was finding it hard to remember many things she had known before the Hedge.

The little bird twisted its head towards her.

"Of course not," it said in a tone which, to Danaeus's ear, had a timbre he could not describe, for his vocabulary, though growing fast, was still young. *Practiced* might have been the word he was looking for. She certainly had a sweet little voice, and that in itself seemed odd for a crow.

"But you've done for the Hunter, haven't you? He can't go back now. The Prince will kill him."

"I'll wager the Hunter against the Prince any day or night. The Hunter need not fear his enemies, if he can trust his friends."

The little bird smiled and hopped onto the Bride's knee, and the Bride stroked its tattered head. "You remind me of children back home . . . " she finished uncertainly. The crow child looked at her with knowing eyes.

"You're forgetting," she said, "Forgetting where you came from. That's not good. You want to watch that."

"No, no, I can remember all right. But," the Bride could

not resist asking, "did you ever come from my world? Because you look so familiar, you and the others."

"We come, we go. *Tarans* they call us. Have you had a baby?"

"No. Why?"

"I can't see any other way you could have seen us. I can tell you how we move between here and there if you like. I know because I've done it. I know your world. I can tell you my memories if you like."

The Bride paused, and looked at the little girl. She listened to the raucous caws and jests still being exchanged outside.

"Yes, you tell me what you know. I would like that very much," she said.

The small crow hopped off her lap and perched between the cushions of the howdah. It cleared its throat, as one would for a recitation and began very differently to how the Bride expected, the little girl's voice that of a child from her own place and time.

CHAPTER ELEVEN
CROW TALES

———

WHEN I AWOKE IT WAS DARK, AND THERE WAS MICHAEL staring down at me as usual.

It was all too hot and the air was thick and everything itched and I couldn't move. And Michael himself was even more spindly than I remembered. His nose stuck out over the cot, and his tiny eyes moved around behind it.

"Back again then," he said.

I was, but it had changed. No bothy and no peat fire and no singing woman. A place too hot and bright and full of bunched up cloth around my throat, across my chest. I remembered her too, and wanted her to sing to me, but she was nowhere to be seen.

"Where is the road up the hill? How far are we from the well? What is that smell?" For all I could smell was sharp and new, and had nothing to do with home at all.

"No, you have come further away, not closer," Michael shook his head. "This is not the way home for you."

"But it is for you or—who is that?" I saw a woman in white. She was not the singing woman. I can't breathe in this heat, I thought, I am choking and it feels wrong and it smells wrong.

"It is only cleanness that you smell, ignorant girl," whispered Michael. "I knew you wouldn't like it. I knew."

"And where is she then?" For I wondered if the warmth would be less heavy on my chest if she was near.

"They are making her ready for you. She cannot wait to see you."

"Is it all as hot as this? I am all cramped."

"If you'd spare yourself cramp, move around. See, you can if you try."

And I tried but I was too tired. "Weak," I said. "This is stupid. I can't do anything."

And maybe because I was so tired I started to cry.

"No, you can't," said Michael. "But you can stay and get better. You can get used to it. It is much warmer here."

I looked around and saw there were others like me, almost like me. But they could not see Michael. There was a strange feeling in my stomach. I know what that is, I thought. I am hungry.

But then I will be too heavy and hot, and Michael's eyes flashed just the way I remembered them.

"If you eat the food, you will have to stay," he said. "If you eat or drink you are part of it and this will be your new home. Is that what you want?"

Well, I didn't know. As far as I could see were others lying in little cots under the glass light, some wailing, some sleeping, but none like us. None who could see like me or remember like me. None of them had Michael. He looked just awful and I asked him what had happened. He shrugged. "I am a bit hungry, too. And they named me so it's not so easy . . . "

Yes, that is something else. If you eat or drink their food or if they name you, you can get stuck. Of course, that was why Michael was here. He was more than hungry, he was famished and he was stuck.

Michael was watching me to see how much I would remember. "She named you," I said. "They named you, and then . . . " He looked all pale and trembled like a little boy made out of egg white. He was no good at this. I didn't want him to cry.

"And now you are there," he whispered. "And I am out here, all cold. And you don't even want to be there, you don't like the heat. It's not fair!"

I tried to stretch out towards him, with these funny little . . . hands . . . my finger nearly touched his nose but I was too weak and small.

"This is a stupid shape," I said.

"I liked it," said Michael.

"I never did," I said.

"No, you never did," agreed Michael. I wanted to cuddle him then, because he was so unhappy, but I didn't. I just couldn't reach. And anyway, he was shaking, burning hot like everything else under the light and the glass. And I wondered where the roads were and he said they hadn't really changed, unless I looked at them the new way.

In the new way they were much bigger and covered the sea and sky, and you didn't ride them yourself but were carried by great hard beetles and flat birds, and all your words and pictures filled the air and the colours were as flat as the birds, but there were lots of them, and there was lots to do if you liked words.

But you had to stay with the warm people. You had to sleep with them and play with them and work with them and you would forget the old things, the crowfolk and the black dog and the well, the rathe and the road, and our brothers and sisters in rags, hovering on the sticks of fences, perched on the old trees *waiting to go home. And you couldn't fly by yourself any more, unless the annis came for you.*

"Only they killed her off a long time ago," said Michael. "They put an iron bead in her heart."

For they have these beads now, and they mean a lot, it seems. And I looked at Michael and it seemed to me that for one who understood how it was too hot and too dull and too cramped and way too small, he wanted to be where I was, really badly.

Another woman in white came by. I told her to take me to the window so I could see it all. They don't always do what you want, especially if there are lots of them and they are all talking to each other, but if you get one by itself you can normally persuade it. So she took me there, and I stared out at it all, so bright and fast.

And all the time, Michael was next to me, nearly crying. So when we turned around, I asked him why.

"I'm so hungry." *He was trying not to weep.* "She's going to feed you soon, and I never . . . "

Milk. We all like milk. Poor Michael.

So they took me through to her, and her face lit up and she was beautiful. Truly. The most beautiful. She was all I could think of. And she lifted me up and I knew how much she loved me, and I just stared at her for a while, so lucky, I thought, lucky lucky me, and I almost let her feed me as she held me and smiled. I heard poor Michael whimper beside me, and water from his eyes fell onto my skin. It was salt and hot and I remembered everything.

So sad. After all, yes, it was too hot here. And he needed it, and I didn't really.

So I looked at her one more time, because she was so beau-

tiful, and then I closed my eyes and slipped away, just peeled out from under it, and it was much easier than you think before you do it, and Michael smiled and slipped in where I had been. He would have said thank you, but we both know it's rude.

The others were waiting outside, cawing and flapping anxiously, in case I changed my mind at the last minute. And the night cooled me and lifted me up, and I could breathe deep and I flew again, properly, feeling the others singing around me. They had been worried that this time I would stay and never return, but that is not my way. No, I will always come home, to the old road and the hill and the shivering wind!

I looked back just once and they were perfect together. She never even felt me leave. And for me, her face began to fade when I left and returned to the starlight and my own kin. Had I not stopped to tell you, I would have forgotten her completely.

"And that," said the little girl, "is how we become crows."

The Bride sat there very quiet, her face concealed in part by the veils all around her.

"Don't you like my story?" asked the almost little girl.

The Bride took a while to reply. "I don't know about *like*. It's a sad story I think. What would have made you stay?"

"Michael not wanting it."

"You gave up a lot for Michael."

The little crow shrugged.

"He's my brother. Besides, if you stay with them, you won't be free anymore. His problem, not mine. I'm a crow. Aa-aa!" She cawed as if to prove it.

"What happened to Michael?"

"I don't know. He's probably wandering around your world wishing he was here."

"But do you start off as humans, or Hedgefolk or just souls or—"

"That's a very big story. I would need lots of time to tell it, and you haven't said if you like the first one yet. Did I tell it well, like someone from your world?"

"Very well, very well, and I thank you for it." The words were out before she could stop them, and the little crow's face grew dark.

"Aaa! If you're thanking me for it then it must be a gift!" The crow call echoed, as she lifted her wings and half leapt, half flew out of the Howdah. "A gift, a gift, a gift!" And all her kin ruffled their feathers in joy, yelling, "A gift for a gift!" And the Hunter swore under his breath, for they were beholden no more. The flock took to the air all jeering at the same time, and at least half of them disappeared back towards the Hedgelands.

"What have you done?" The Hunter roared, though he did not turn his face from the mob. "What have you done? We had them—I had—you stupid—"

"Are they so dangerous?" fluted Danaeus in a desperate attempt to soothe between the wails of the Bride and the curses of the Hunter. "They have mostly gone now."

"Aye! Gone to tell the Prince exactly where we are! And those remaining will keep us entertained until he arrives! That woman is the most imbecilic—get her out of here, you fool!"

For those crows remaining did not attack. Rather, they

gathered round a crow old enough to have a grey head, she who had first greeted the Hunter, and she stared at him and muttered as he strode towards them. In her yellow talons she held the hand of glory, its four remaining fingers now being lit, one, two, three, four . . . and the murderer's head lolled upright and his one blue eye fixed brightly on the Hunter. Some enterprising members of the flock jabbed their beaks down into the rope around the cross beam repeatedly, cutting the noose as the dead man jumped to the ground.

The Hunter could feel the rage beginning. He was aware that it was more directed towards the idiot mortal in his charge than the crows or the dead man, and tried to make up for it by anticipating the fight. It was unlikely to be long, he reasoned, for the corpse had one eye and one hand and besides, such things were remarkably slow. The calleach smiled at him and pointed to the second lit finger on the hand. As she did so, the dead man leapt dexterously in front of him, hooked bones bubbling out of its wrist stump, grinning through rotted teeth.

Danaeus, looking at crow-filled skies, decided not to risk escape by air, grabbed the reins and held on tight as the hare ran forwards in a panic. As the butterfly could not steer and the hare could not think, they found themselves going round and round the centre of the cross roads with crows swooping down on the leveret trying to attack its eyes. In the end it screamed and stuck its head in a clump of grass and the birds settled on its neck, aiming with their beaks at eyes and head, trying to pull the howdah off its back. The Bride ran out, kitchen knife at the ready and tried to fend the birds off. Danaeus was there and then was not. Four or five birds were on the hare's back now, and the sounds of terror Palawinkes made were unbearable, so she grabbed the stirrup and cut. The shining silver and silk of the howdah fell to the ground, and the birds, interested in its sparkle, followed it. "Go!" she shouted in the leveret's ear. It didn't take much bidding and sped away fast over the land, out of sight within a moment. The Bride looked around for the Hunter, who faced his foe with a certain astonishment. The dead man was jigging.

The Hunter liked a joke as much as anyone else. For a moment, the corpse stood there, then it winked and took out some kind of penny whistle which it started playing. To complete the scenario, it then started hopping around in front of the Hunter. Clearly it was determined to enjoy itself. The Hunter, surprised to say the least, started hopping too. The cailleach was not impressed and she chastised her slave in the old language of necromancers and other workers of evil:

Quod sententia vadum accerso mihi fiends ex abyssus!
Sententia transporto lemma ut sodalitas of sol solis
Quod totus incendia coniecto of ipsum
Illud fiends vadum addo quod addo per is vox
Unto sol solis facio is rutilus cruor vomica!

"What did she say?" said the Hunter.

"Telling me to kill you, mate," came the hoarse reply. "Or fiends'll boil me blood in 'ellfire, usual stuff. Pity really, I was startin' to enjoy meself."

"The pity's in her Latin. She should stick to the curses of her own country. To yourself, man: killed thirteen or more?"

The corpse smiled. "Dark is my heart. Fed on twenty and still not sated."

"Then let's drink and have done." A wineskin passed between them, and except for the cascade of liqour down over his ribs, the dead man availed himself politely. It was all very civilised. The cailleach started to scream again, and the dead man sighed. "Sorry, mate," said he, put the penny whistle down, and launched himself at the Hunter's throat.

The Hunter leapt to meet him, fist sending half his foe's brain-pan over the road, while the dead man's bones hooked themselves deep into his shoulder and the little worms squeezed out of dead flesh with a sound of popping blisters, and burrowed into the Hunter's skin, towards his heart. The Hunter's sword whirled out at the height of the enemy's ear but didn't touch him. He sent it spinning past corpse, crows and gibbet beam, straight into the heart of the cailleach, who made no sound. Only the slit from forehead to nose told the story, the sword sticking so deep in her skull that the Hunter had to tug on it to remove it. A little blood and other matter, but still, thought the Hunter, remarkably clean. The fight had not satisfied him, and he resolved to destroy the remaining crows for the sake of the riot in his head. It was only when he realised the other birds had gone that he looked up and saw, high above him, what seemed like a dimming jewel grasped in the talons of the last of the flock. The Bride was being taken.

"Don't let me get in your way, mate," said the dead man, "but ain't we got business?"

"That depends. Do you want a fight?"

"Nah, truth be told," said the dead man. "I'd prefer a drink."

"Help yourself. There's a wineskin I gave the crows lying over there. It's full."

The dead man went towards it and then looked back, uncertain. "Ye aint gonna diddle me with no *isitaintitagift* stuff are ye?"

"Don't be a fool. Have the wine, and I'll leave the hand alight, and you can carry on as you like. How strong are you?"

"Stronger than most things in this world. Hand of glory'll do that for ye."

"Throw me at that crow and we'll call it quits. What do you say?"

The corpse smiled. "Ain't you forgetin' something?"

The pain in the Hunter's chest seized him, and he grimaced. The worms had ceased to burrow, for his blood was strong and powerful and in its flow they were growing. Already, he could make out the bulge of their coils beneath his skin, but he had no time to do anything. The corpse picked up him in its remaining hand, and with a stupendous shove, vaulted the mad man into the air. The throw was nowhere near high enough to reach the crow, but the bird's attention was well and truly caught. The return of the Bride would assure great rewards from the Prince, but for the capture of the Hunter as well, the crow knew it could name its price.

It swooped down and with a neat clack of its beak, caught the Hunter in mid-air. The pressure on the Hunter's back and gut was so powerful it nearly split the Hunter's chest, and out burst the worms, fat and writhing, the crow's last meal, but for him, a delicious one. His tongue tipped them down his throat, as the Hunter saved himself by sticking his sword up into the bird's palate and hanging on to it. The bird opened its mouth in a screech of pain, and the Hunter tumbled out, just catching the edge of the lower beak and holding on. The upper beak, serrated like a saw, would crash down any second and there would go his fingers. He swung himself like an acrobat backwards and forwards, and as the beak smashed down, he leapt to the bird's breastbone, and stabbed it through the heart. It shuddered, and in its death throes, loosened its grip on the Bride. The Hunter leapt across to her just as she slid out of the talons of the crow, and they both spiralled downwards together.

"Can you fly?" asked the Bride, hope in her voice.

"What?"

"You fly, don't you?"

"Are you mad? I don't fly."

"But you killed it!"

"We really don't have time for this, my lady—"

"You killed our only way of reaching the ground!"

"Of course we'll reach the ground!"

The wind roared and filled their ears and the words blew away like broken sticks never to return, and the earth span ever nearer. Then her view of the world was blocked by something beneath her, a flying carpet of black and red and gold, and as she fell onto it, she felt the velvet safety of Danaeus's voice telling her everything was fine. When, less than a second later, the Hunter landed beside her, she knew it to be true. Far below she could see the twinkling wreckage of the howdah in the grass, a crowd of crows in flight, a tiny hare drinking from a pool, and at the crossroads, what appeared to be a lone figure hopping to itself.

"I hid between its wings, on its back," the butterfly was explaining to the Hunter. "It was thinking of you, it never saw me." How Danaeus had grown! The rose nectar must have agreed with him, for the butterfly boy, always tall, was now gigantic, with the face of a fine and beautiful man, the facets of his eyes shimmering in endless kaleidoscope. The Hunter looked less than impressed. The Bride broke a thorn from the rose, plucked three threads from her head, threaded them through, and began stitching his wound.

"I found another flower," said Danaeus. "It grows up here."

"No my dear," said the Bride. "Flowers don't grow in the sky."

"They must do," reasoned Danaeus. "Or I couldn't have drunk from it."

The Bride looked. There was no pollen on Danaeus' head.

"Show us this flower, Danaeus," said the Bride.

"Yes," said Danaeus, "I think you should see it."

And the butterfly wheeled away from the wind towards the Great Flower.

CHAPTER TWELVE
A FAMILIAR FACE

———

Now she shuddered and barely talked. All the pallor and weakness she had suffered at the wedding was returning, for the little fairy clock had been one of the first casualties in the fight against the crows. She kept looking at her hand again, and her face was covered with a deadly grey sweat. The Hunter wiped her face as best he could, and tried to think of something to get her through the fever. He found himself looking at Danaeus and wondering if the butterfly could spin a cocoon around her and save her with the magic of the bright-winged folk. If it worked, she would stay a season or two in the cocoon, and then she would break out, new hand and all. Of course, she would be of the Folk, not mortal, but maybe that wasn't such a bad thing. Being mortal was the cause of all her problems. This might count as a lucky escape.

The only problem the Hunter could see with this plan was the possibility of the Bride waking in her cocoon, mistaking it for the Prince's imprisonment again and breaking her way out before she was fully formed, at which point she would die. But then, she looked very likely to die anyway, and a problem averted for now was a problem he could ignore.

"Danaeus," he called. "We must land now."

"The big flower is very near," said Danaeus. "I think it will help."

It must be one impressive flower, thought the Hunter. *Mind you, butterflies think all flowers are impressive.*

"It's no good, Danaeus," he said. "She just can't go any further. We must land. I have a plan . . . "

"Let me just go over this hill—"

"What hill?" The air was beginning to burn the Hunter's face and it smelt different. He almost forgot his point in the intoxication, the smell of a new place, of adventure and of . . .

He knew the word as soon as they rounded the curved horizon of the earth.

. . . Morning.

For there it was, huge and warm and golden, filling a turquoise sky. He lifted her up so that she could face it, and it touched her skin with delight after so much winter. The great flower turned its head to them, and smiled.

Its smile was the most powerful thing the Hunter had ever seen, and the joy he felt grew fierce when he felt the heart of the Bride beat, not faster, but stronger. It might not last forever, but she was better in this moment. She was happy.

"Do you see?" called out Danaeus happily. "Do you see the big flower?"

"Yes I do, you total fool!" Beamed the Hunter. "Call yourself a butterfly? That's the sun!"

"What's the difference?" said Danaeus.

"Touch a flower and it will feed you. Touch that and it will burn you. No, don't try to look directly at it!" This was to her, for she was winking and blinking as though she wanted to stare into the heart of the limitless fire. He tilted her head away.

"I want to go up to it!" said Danaeus, and to the Hunter's

express irritation, he could feel her nodding in agreement against his arm. He scowled. Then he thought about it and stopped scowling.

"Well, why not?" he said.

Because he was a Hunter and he had never visited the sun, and nothing as grand waited below. So he smiled and his eyes flashed the same colour as the great flower, and Danaeus turned his wings upwards and flew. The heat grew stronger, the blueness of the sky ever more intense, and the Hunter remembered something else from long ago. This was not just morning. This was summer.

CHAPTER THIRTEEN
AIMING A DUM-DUM

———

THE SUN MADE THE AIR SHIMMER AND MELT LIKE GLASS.
Sir Thomas held out valiantly, but Richard felt ill and looked
it, with his flushed skin and dry cough. His eyes though . . .
Sir Thomas would have called the tour a triumph just for the
spark and passion in the young man's eyes. Cairo was more
real perhaps, than either of them had expected; the streets
around Saladin's fortress bustled with life, with the smells of
onions and mint, turmeric and rose, with parrot sellers and
performing monkeys, with the mysteries of shador and street
dancers, merchants and bedouin, all selling their wares.
Without the artist's gift, the place was a treasure trove; with
it, Cairo was a gateway to paradise. Richard was frantic in his
sketching, the only drawback being the number of subjects,
and the lack of time. His sketchbooks were full of extraordinary details and profiles, his days were delighted and indus-
trious, his nights barely less so, though Sir Thomas found
it easier to draw him into conversation once the light had
faded from the streets. He judged rightly that his protégé was
finding the experience intense in its inspiration and wanted
to get him used to the heat, to calm him down, before taking
him on to Thebes and the temple of Luxor. They were to
travel there by boat, and, after much pleading from Richard,
Sir Thomas decided not to delay. Palm trees, river reeds and

Egyptian water lilies, the languor of the Nile and the gentle breeze above it . . . Sir Thomas was convinced that the boat trip would bring the young man a combination of colour and reverie preferable to enforced seclusion at the hotel. Richard was certain his nerves would stand it, and he was so seldom sure of anything, Sir Thomas wanted to capitulate just to teach him some confidence.

The boat trip was indeed serene and exquisite. Richard could not decide which part of the day he preferred. Sunrise was music, the sound of the muezzin calling the people to prayer, the flapping of sails in the wind, the occasional slap of waves where some creature turned over in the depths. (*Crocodiles,* thought Richard, *there are crocodiles in this river*). Sunset was a panorama of silhouetted palms against the black and yellow sky. Then came the moon, jasmine in its sweetness. Richard had loved the moon at home for a while, until it became tainted with other night thoughts. He felt like a traitor, preferring its enchantment here to the paler version to be found above English fields, but he could not help the way things had been.

Here everything was different. Richard never wanted to leave.

Only once on the way did he see something to shake him out of his new-found contentment. One evening he saw some travellers bringing their camels down to the river's edge. Richard found camels the most comical of beasts, and had made many sketches of them, their tasselled reins and cloth-covered saddles. One bent its head to the water and he noticed something; an enormous pale spider clinging to the poor beast's underlip. Neither camel nor rider seemed to have noticed its presence, and Richard could hardly shout across to them from the boat. Nonetheless, he asked the guide about it and was told that such spiders were common; their way of feeding was to poison the victim with its venom, which had a numbing effect on the area of the bite. The attacked beast would continue unsuspecting, while the spider ate its living flesh. Such things had been known to run towards men and leap up at their faces. Richard had terrible dreams about the thing, but Sir Thomas couldn't blame the young man's nerves for that. After he heard about it, his own sleep was far from comfortable.

The incident was forgotten the next morning, to take its place among the anecdotes of travellers returned, and the peace of the boat trip remained untouched, only to regretfully drift away when the boat reached Thebes. On first exploration of the place, Sir Thomas noticed that Richard did not take out his notebook and start sketching immediately, which had become his response so often as to be automatic in Cairo. Richard was impressed to the point of poetic awe. There was an undercurrent of agitation about him, a subdued intensity, but that was only to be expected from first sight of so extraordinary a place. Sir Thomas saw nothing to worry about, and soon became too involved in enjoying his own observations to fret about Richard.

Dust and sand and footprints crossing the ancient land; he could feel the power in the earth, he trembled at those ancient faces, he touched the stones and knew the carvings could speak. It was not the gentle countenances of Isis and Hathor, though they called to him gravely and held up their hands bidding him come, nor the jackal god who loomed on pillars in the dark of the temples, nor the ram-headed giants who stared down at him and spoke of the sun and the moon and a magic greater than he could grasp. They all spoke in the language of the dead, in the language of the ancients mastered by no living being, but he could resist them. This was some other voice, a different kind of echo. He did not know who was calling him. He needed to be in the temple by night under that gentle light. He needed to be alone with the voices, with the one voice, if he was ever to understand.

Sir Thomas held out long against this suggestion. He could think of no swifter way for his protégé to get himself mugged or even killed; it was folly. Only Richard's pleas, combined with the assurances of the guide who had brought them from Cairo, made it possible. Sir Thomas' dwelling was not far away, Richard pointed out, and the view of the midnight temple was bound to inspire him; the glow of warm sands was so different to everything he had ever painted before, and he wished to experiment. Sir Thomas eventually relented, and the night came when Richard found his wishes answered, in the place of the oldest magic, where the moon rose over the temple. The guide had been bolstered by Sir Thomas' gener-osity, but he was less than stalwart among the shadows, and it took a much smaller bribe from Richard to send him away.

Richard felt uncomfortable under the moon. Oh, the view was as captivating as he had hoped, but he knew, the moment he tried to paint it, that this was not why he had come. The light touched the stone with a soft and dappled gleam, yet still it was not what he wanted, and almost without thinking he retreated deeper into the temple. Here, the dust made it harder to breathe, and the moonbeams struck colder against dark stone. Richard found himself in a tiny chamber with just one great pillar at its centre. On it was a parade of animal-headed beings centred around a pharoah whose face was scraped with green pigment. The heads and the green face felt distantly familiar; someone else's memory, not his. The eyes regarded him and he wanted to run, but could not. Instead, recalling the myths he knew of Egypt and the green-faced god, he sank to his knees.

"Osiris . . . " he whispered. The face looked back at him, and he heard its voice indistinctly, a curious and savage muttering of syllables alien to him. He wondered if his guide was still outside, praying for safety. It did not sound like a prayer.

The Lord of the Dead watched him calmly.

I am inclined, he had written to his father, *to fall in with the views of the ancients and to regard the substitution of modern ideas thereon as not for the better . . .*

He was paying for that preference now. Though the face of Osiris did not change, Richard knew the lord of the dead was not pleased.

"Father of Egypt," he whispered. But, though the pagan within him lived through his hands, his voice was solidly Christian, and he had no thought of how to speak to a living god, indeed looking at the pillar was too much for him. He abased himself on the ground, and rested his face in the dust. He listened to the voice as it commanded him. "You ask too much of me!" he cried, and tried to get up, but could not.

He waited a long time, realising his mistake. He had not been humble, he had been too quick to try to leave. As he lay there, he felt a change, a presence nearby. Hoping the god would smile upon him, he looked up at the face on the pillar.

There, hanging on the underside of the mouth was a huge yellow spider, of the kind he had seen devouring the camel by the river. This one was bigger and nearer. Richard wanted to scream. He blinked and the spider was gone, and he instantly gazed in panic around the room and up in the corners. Osiris in the meantime, looked noble, looked like his father.

"I have heard your prayers, my son," spoke the voice of Osiris, clearer and kinder than before.

"First pharaoh . . . king . . . " croaked Richard hopelessly.

"And yet you do not serve me." The voice was smooth, without reproach and yet, the words cut a dagger's length into Richard's heart. Osiris the kind, Osiris the betrayed, Osiris, father of the underworld, king among the wraiths, god for all eternity. Richard's head throbbed and he trembled.

"How can I . . . what is thy purpose, oh lord?"

The Prince of Spiders wanted to laugh aloud from his corner, as he watched the mortal lying flat on the ground in abject fear. If he could have guaranteed the terror to have stayed this strong in Richard's heart, he would have taken him back to the Hedge for his own amusement. But mortals were hopelessly inconsistent. He couldn't guarantee that the artist would stay cowed. He might grow bold, worse, he might become the Beloved's thrall and start the whole rivalry nonsense again. No, the Prince wanted him back in the Hedge one last time for one specific task and that would be an end to it.

"Behold, my foe walks the earth. He offends me. He torments me. He will destroy all!"

Richard's face was white with terror. The voice was not the same as it had been at first. Now it was clear, a royal voice, a voice of kingship, magical, powerful. He knew it well.

"You must destroy him. He is the ruin of all that has been, all that is to come. You must find him and kill him."

"Who? What is his name, my, my . . . "

"Behold, my relation who hath attempted to slay me, who hath taken my wife to his own, who looketh boldly upon your own love! Behold him, kinsman and betrayer!"

"I know, my lord!" the mortal whimpered. "I know!"

"I ask you for you are the strongest, my son, my only friend." Magnificent though the Prince was, his hyperbole was beginning to run dry. He had never imagined it would be so easy, and the sheer brilliance of his success floundered him somewhat. Had he known Richard was such an idiot, he would never have feared him, cold iron axe or not. Which reminded him:

"Make thyself not impure in the killing of him. Rather make it a sacrifice to me, in the most sacred of places that thou knowest."

The mortal looked baffled. "Here, my lord?"

"No." The Prince had to work hard to keep the irritation out of his voice. He could see Richard would have to be led by the nose.

"No. Not here. Or if you find him here, take him homewards with thee."

Richard looked confused. *How did she keep the court in fear with this dunce?* thought the Prince, and decided to make the Beloved rue her presumption all the more later.

"Fear is what makes a place sacred, Richard Dadd. Kill him in the most fearful place you know."

Richard gaped, and even in his fear, felt he had to question; "Great one, that must be . . . I mean, I know nowhere more fearful than this place."

Then the eyes of the god gazed at him and in them was overwhelming knowledge, cold, irrevocable.

"Yes, you do, Richard."

Then the dust swirled away from Richard's mind, and for a moment he struggled to recall London and Cairo and Corfu and all the real world. But the memories flooded in, cold and bright, and the people who never were laughed at him and pulled him back to the place he had forgotten, and in his hands he felt eighteen-forty-three, who rose in delight at his return, and smashed everything he could see, everything he could touch. It had taken time, but in the end, the glass cracked once and for all, never to be whole again.

When he woke, he found himself shivering and sweating. They would say he had a fever, they would worry about malaria and mosquitoes. It would suffice as an explanation, until he needed it no longer.

He left the temple, without looking back at the pillar of Osiris. Instead he looked in his notebook, to see what Sir Thomas had never noticed. The book was full of sketches and profiles and hastily drawn landscapes but Egypt was nowhere to be found. Over and over again throughout all his travels, all Richard had drawn was the Hedge.

CHAPTER FOURTEEN
ONE FOR SORROW

———

PHYNTHOBLIN WAS SERIOUSLY CONSIDERING A WIG.

Being a grasshopper never helped his political ambitions. His kind lacked the necessary gravitas; it isn't easy to carry the burdens of state when all you can do is hop and make sounds with your leg hairs. Dignity, he told himself, he needed to cultivate an air of dignity. And he was convinced a powder wig could help with that. The one he had in mind was very tall indeed, and white, with a couple of gold and green bows to match his skin. When he tried it on, he could not help but be impressed by himself.

Yet he had to think carefully. The secret of his success had been the world's tendency to treat him as something ridiculous and then ignore him. This might be galling for a more extrovert personality, but it meant he could get things done. A wig of tallness might just make people take notice of him in the wrong way, not so much: "My, isn't Phynthoblin a fine looking figure of a fairy, give him more power at once!" More: "There goes Phynthoblin looking very pleased with himself. What do you suppose he's up to?" The latter was precisely the question he never wanted to occur to his Prince.

He had no reason to suppose the Prince would ever ask it. His Highness was brilliant but tended to focus on one thing until he had exhausted all its possibilities. Currently his overriding priority was with keeping his throne whatever the cost. Phynthoblin's wardrobe was hardly likely to draw his attention.

So far, his Highness could only be pleased. Richard Dadd had been lost in the hunt for the traitors, and Phynthoblin felt certain that he was no longer in the Hedge. The scent of cold iron was no longer faintly detectable anywhere at all, and the Beloved had stopped coming to court. That mortal was gone all right, and Phynthoblin's personal pledge was that he should never return. Palawinkes had died too, and Phynthoblin felt a little regret for that, but it was all for the best. Giving that servant over to the Hunt so they could use him to track the traitors had appealed to the Prince's humour. Phynthoblin had guessed rightly that he was too angry to be prudent. The changing of Palawinkes had made the Prince laugh but it had also robbed him of another potential sacrifice to justify his rulership. There was only one mortal left and she was with the Hunter.

Phynthoblin hoped the Hunter understood what this could mean, if he chose it to, indeed his every calculating instinct told him that surely, the plan between the Hunter and Palawinkes must have been leading to this. Why else do it? But the Hunter was mad, and Phynthoblin felt with an unnerving certainty that he had forgotten the plan completely.

"I'll bet he's trying to get her back to her own world," though Phynthoblin with a sigh, and put the wig to one side. There was a rapping at the door of his chamber. He opened it to see Mrs Pyewacket waiting, wearing a somewhat familiar bonnet.

"My dear lord Phynthoblin," she said.

"Mrs Pyewacket! Do come in!" cried Phynthoblin. "Come in, come in! Do sit down. What a marvellous surprise! How are you? Wait, first, let me get you some refreshments," and he picked up a tiny golden bell and rang it.

Mrs Pyewacket demurred at first. She wasn't used to the gentry making a fuss over her but when it came down to it, she loved food enough to overindulge. Phynthoblin's latest servant, a distinctly plain-looking field mouse with no hint of an arquebus hidden under her petticoats, brought out some grubs, bacon rind, cheese, corncobs and biscuits; all well enough but presented with neither beauty nor grace. Phynthoblin remembered the ladybird with some wistfulness and not a little resentment. Bad enough that she was a gun-toting anarchist rebel, worse that she had left without giving a month's notice. Life in the Hedge could be very trying at times.

Mrs Pyewacket didn't mind. She made happy chattering noises to herself as she picked through every single morsel of food and discarded the pieces she didn't want by throwing them to the floor. Phynthoblin rolled his eyes privately, but let his guest make herself comfortable and poured her a generous tankard of ale. By the time she was finished, her eyes were glinting with good humour and comfort.

"That bonnet seems a tiny bit familiar to me," said Phynthoblin.

"In style, my lord, but not I think, in colours. I did find it in a ruined place, sir, and thought to keep it."

"It looks like the Lady Vulpinet's famous hat," mused the grasshopper.

"Does it indeed?" For the lovely lady had disappeared

recently, just after the Hunt was called on the renegades, and no-one knew where she had gone. "Well, I couldn't comment on that, my Lord."

"No, well, you are looking very fine. That ruined place must have been a positive chancellery," for the lady had surrendered to a very harmless love of finery well known to her family; around her neck and feet she wore chains of beads, which bore a resemblance to glass eyes, and smartly set off her black and white attire.

"Fortune favours the bold," she said, and then favoured him with a cheeky smile. He shook his head and nodded. The House of Corvidae were among the oldest bloodlines in the land, but apart from the raven (whose tastes tended to alchemy) they were brigands and looters, each and every one, and none more so than his guest.

"Indeed it does," he said, and poured another drink, for her and for himself. "Now, my dear lady, what can I do for you this day?"

"Oh," she said, tipping her head back (how the light glinted off that beak!), "to be honest sir, I was wondering if there was some way I could be of use to you, my lord," and her eyes sparkled.

Phynthoblin couldn't help laughing and shaking his head. Her good humour was infectious. "Out with it, dear lady, you know you are dying to tell me!"

"By the crest of Corvus, you are quick to read what ain't written, sir. I merely observe that the days grow very interesting at Court."

"Yes, well." Phynthoblin brought out a condiment set which *should*, he sighed to himself, have been brought with the food tray by the maid. It was a beautiful little set of four jewelled spice shakers: one was gold, one was silver, one was studded with citrines and topaz, and one was plain. That last one he let no-one touch, and small wonder, for it was the salt cellar and he kept it only for emergencies. But he picked up the two nearest and sprinkled his cheese biscuit with fine glittering flakes. She, of course, was all interest then. "Indeed they have, my lady, but you haven't come here to tell me this, surely?"

"Not to tell you," she said. "To discuss it with you. For the Hedge is alive with gossip, you know . . . "

"Really? And what is it they say?"

She pushed her little platter of biscuits towards him, and he sprinkled half with gold, and half with silver, then pushed the biscuits back towards her. He was amused to see her take out a little purse of purple velvet and tap each biscuit against the open clasp so that the flakes fell inside. He laughed. "You will need a great many biscuits to make that worth your while!"

"Perhaps there is a lot of gossip!" She laughed back. "And in any case, it is just my little habit." Never a truer word spoken, Phynthoblin knew; for Mrs Pyewacket's home was famous for its collection of objets d'art, some pretty, some useless, all shining. It was just her way. She leaned forward. "You understand," she said, "I do not hold with gossip myself, nor do I believe a word of it."

"Very wise," nodded Phynthoblin. "Personally, I avoid it like the plague. Have another biscuit."

"It is said that the Beloved's pet mortal has left the Hedge forever, and she is devastated. For you know, without him, what else has she got?"

"Mmm . . . well, yes, I had heard something like that myself."

"And it is said that an attack was mounted on the Hunter and the Bride, but they got away leaving many dead behind them. Some even say," she tapped her hat, "that Lady Vulpinet got involved . . . "

"But that you would know, for if you had found her hat, you would have found her also," smiled Phynthoblin.

"Tis certainly a lovely hat. But I found no-one with it, no-one that I could recognise anyway."

And if she couldn't recognise the body of Vulpinet with her precious hat, no-one would be able to identify it now, for Mrs Pyewacket, like all her family, was a notorious eater of carrion. Phynthoblin suddenly felt uncomfortable.

"Well, my dear lady, if this is all—"

"All? Sir, I have hardly begun! You see, I have been spending time with the crows. One cannot disdain one's kin, however low they sink," she sighed prettily, "and they told me something interesting, which you will know before your Prince does . . . "

"Good, or there is no point me paying for it. Mrs Pyewacket, the point!"

"They met and fought the renegades at the far cross-roads."

"They caught them?"

"No. They got away, and there was much carnage. The flock will tell the Prince as soon as they find him. They expect to be paid well for their trouble."

Phynthoblin laughed. "He does not pay for trouble—trouble's free in the Hedge—but for results. What did they find out?"

"They were spotted not long after, too high in the sky for the flock to follow."

"What? How? The Hunter can't fly!"

"They were on a big red butterfly, but the How, begging your Lordship's pardon, is not the business."

"You are right, of course." The grasshopper collected his thoughts. "Where, my dear lady, where are they headed?"

"They are headed towards the sun, my lord. Straight towards it, with no waver of a wing turning back."

"When you say straight—"

She looked a little doubtful here. "My kin said they reckoned they were headed into the heart of it, but that cannot be, sir, surely."

Phynthoblin bit his lip. "Never say "surely" where the Hunter is concerned. Blood and moon, when it comes to stupidity, he always exceeds my expectations." There was a long pause, while Phynthoblin sat there, tapping his fingers thoughtfully. The pause had stretched into a long silence before he looked up. Mrs Pyewacket was still there, but two of the pots had gone.

"Two for two pieces of information," she said, with the sense of having been very generous.

Phynthoblin smiled slowly. "Two more and the stand they come on, for two more favours. First, give me a lift. Second, I must speak to the people of Dvalin, there are some living by the Greenburg."

"I know where they are, my lord," she said. "Salt cellar and all?"

"Salt cellar with the salt still in it, if you can do this quickly."

"In the twinkling of an eye, sir."

Her wings were uplifted before he had finished, and he jumped on to her back with no hesitation as the wind rose under her feet. Despite that earlier awkwardness, it had definitely been a constructive meeting. Neither Phynthoblin nor Mrs Pyewacket believed in the twinkling of an eye, but both believed in the twinkling of gold. Their mutual faith made partnership much easier.

TWINKLING GOLD FILLED THE CENTRE OF THE SKY NOW, AND its smiling face was freckled with coloured clouds. Danaeus did not see why the flower covered itself until the Bride explained that if they stared straight into it, they would be blinded forever.

"And that's no good for adventuring in the new place," interrupted the Hunter. In his mind, he was seeing the new world already, and his favourite tavern song was ringing in his head:

> *With a host of furious fancies*
> *Whereof I am commander*
> *With a burning spear and a horse of air*
> *To the wilderness I wander.*
> *By a knight of ghosts and shadows*
> *I summoned am to tourney*
> *Ten leagues beyond the wide world's end,*
> *Methinks it is no journey!*

The Bride looked up at him and smiled weakly. It hadn't escaped her that each of them was seeing something different at the centre of all that joy. Danaeus was seeing fields of flowers and she could actually just make out what he was talking about, the brilliance of blue and pink clouds and yellow light could give the impression they were also great fields of poppies and daffodils, sunflowers of course, and huge lilies, bright as the morning star. The Hunter laughed when she talked of impressions.

"Impressions? No use to us! A map maker is what we need. Can you not see the outline of it all? There are continents there, and great oceans, and lands lost, no, never lost, because they were never found to begin with. Don't tell me you can't see them!"

But the eyes of mortals, even those who have spent a while among the fey, are not strong enough to see such things. He tried to draw a map of the new lands that dazzled his imagination, but he stopped when he saw her head drooping and once again let her rest against his shoulder, forcing his thoughts away from the new beginning.

"Tell me what you see," he spoke gently, for he thought that concentration might keep her alive. She was so thin, so white, and her face was wet with the sweat of mortal illness, the veins on her arm distended, the hole where her hand had been was covered with dried blood. He tried not to look her in the eyes, for he did not want her to know what he knew. He did not want her to accept that she was dying. And he did not want her to feel the pity welling up in his unseelie soul. No weakness, he told himself, no weakness.

So instead, he listened. It was hard for the Bride to describe what she saw at the centre. Like the butterfly, she felt there was a face there, beaming with joy. It was indeed the face of a flower, but it was also the face of many other things: a reindeer, a mouse, a ball of gas, a man, a woman, a landscape, a shepherd, an angel . . . a star.

She was entering the smile of the great star, giver of life, and she was ready to become part of it, ready to leave the shades behind and never know sorrow again, when something wet sloshed into her mouth. The Hunter, in despair at her fading eyes, was emptying a wineskin down her throat. She spluttered. "How many of those things do you have?"

"I raided the Bridal suite. This one has woodruff in it, so it should keep you going—"

"AHOY THERE!"

The voice was tinny and small and came from far below. The Hunter and the Bride looked down towards the earth. Danaeus took no notice at all but carried on singing to himself as he headed towards the sun.

The Hunter swore.

"Dammit, Phynthoblin!" he roared. "Go away!" He could just make out the figure of Phynthoblin on a magpie. The magpie was wearing a nice bonnet. To the Hunter's perplexity, Phynthoblin was holding a small grey metal cone up to his mouth and shouted through the narrow end. It made his voice just about audible, up there above the wind.

"COME DOWN . . . " shouted the grasshopper. "YOU . . . GRAVE . . . DANGER . . . "

"He's a genius," snorted the Hunter, and sat back down in his place, determined not to listen.

"HUNTER!" Phynthoblin was nothing if not tenacious, "YOU . . . . RE . . . PON . . . IB. . . . KING!"

The Hunter couldn't resist the chance to mock, and imitated Phynthoblin's cone-enhanced tones: "STUFF . . . KING!"

The next words from Phynthoblin sounded very much like, "LAS . . . ANCE," but the Hunter couldn't be sure.

"We can go back and face the king or we can go on," he said. He already knew what the other two would say. Her face looked stronger, and Danaeus seemed supremely happy, bursting into the lepidopteral equivalent of an over-sky sprint.

Meanwhile, Phynthoblin directed Mrs Pyewacket to return him to the rendez-vouz. His policy had been well thought out. He had tried to stay true to his Prince; alas, the Prince was mad; more important, he was unlucky, and the only folk more unlucky than an unlucky king are his unlucky followers. Phynthoblin had worked so hard to give Hunter the advantage, Hunter who would also have been a mad king, but a lucky one. But Hunter wouldn't play the game. Sometimes policy must adapt, he thought, and shrugged. Oh well. Time for the ballista.

CHAPTER FIFTEEN
DAINTY AERIAL

———

THE PEOPLE OF DVALIN, ruminated PHYNTHOBLIN AS THE magpie landed, were handy allies, but hard to bargain with. They were strange stocky little beings, all hair and whiskers, huge arms and cats' eyes, who lived beneath the Iron Mountain in a very harsh part of the land, and had only gained the monarch's approval by promising to bring him all the iron they found there. But the Iron Mountain, like so many other areas of the Hedge, was a masterpiece of irony, in so much as the earth was rich in every other ore and jewel and crystal imaginable: rubies and emeralds and sapphires and certainly diamonds, white gold, red gold, yellow gold, some even spoke of black gold; silver and platinum and copper, marble and agate, gems and rare rocks some un-named and extraordinary, but not one scrap of iron, raw plain iron, had ever been found there. Sometimes Phynthoblin suspected they just weren't trying.

The Prince was not known for his patience, so they made the ballista for him. The ballista was a masterpiece of their craft, and the very sight of it made Phynthoblin wince. Oh, they had explained all clearly when it was first presented: it was a crossbow to be wielded by a giant. Unfortunately, all experiments with giants and weapons tended to end in disaster for everybody around them. They were not renowned for their learning ability or grasp of orders. The gift needed re-thinking. What was needed was a giant's weapon which could be used by the Folk, and for that to work, engineering was needed.

The ballista worked though a twisting wringing kind of magic called "torsion" in two skeins of sinew. An enormous wooden frame carried the ropes vertically, and a great spear would rest in a groove in the stock of the weapon. Two horizontal wooden arms passed through each skein and were linked by a bowstring that the dvalinsfolk swore came from the gut of the Fenris wolf itself. When the arms were pulled back, the rope twisted to become a powerful spring. Then the bowstring would be pulled back by a winch and retained by a curious kind of rotating trigger.

It had seemed a great deal of trouble when first shown to the Prince, and he had looked nonplussed, and even a little bored, until the people of Dvalin demonstrated its prowess to him: for when the bowstring was released, the huge spear shot forward with ferocity enough to strike through the bodies of even well armoured warriors in its path. It wreaked particular havoc with such soldiers as marched close in line, for it was strong enough to pierce several with one shot. The Red Duke's men had suffered gravely from the prowess of this weapon in the old wars. Phynthoblin had been worried about how many of these things the dvalinsfolk could make for their own use, but they had reassured the Prince that they had neither time nor need.

The only real flaw was that it took practice to use, and few of the folk could be relied upon to sit and learn about something so mechanical. There were a kind of folk in the Hedge often thought to be dvalinskin by those who knew no better. They were smaller, with broader smiles, brighter non-feline eyes, and even more hair than their mountain relatives. They had many names for themselves, but among the hedgefolk they were called the Gnom. They tended to prefer tiny, clever artifacts to huge clumping machines, but they had the touch and the smartness of mind to understand anything with cogs and wheels, pulleys and pressures, and their strength was great in proportion to their size. There were some of these here now, setting up the ballista at the grasshopper's bidding, and there were others too, not so usual in the Hedge, and certainly new to the keen eyes of Mrs Pyewacket. These were tiny creatures with pallid skins and bulging sightless eyes, though their ears were sharp and keen. Their spines were knobbled and curved like bows and they bore spears. It took eight of them to hold one spear aloft, for the spears were huge, with flint tips dipped dark in the blood of mortal miners who strayed into their underground homes.

There was one other there who carried nothing but a small pouch at its belt. This was taller than the others and very lithe. Its skin was blue and its eyes were blue and its hair was white, flowing down below its waist. The skin was studded with tiny gems of every colour in a kind of repeating diamond pattern, from below its neck to its feet. It was beautiful until it smiled, for then the mouth would open in a slit far too wide for its head revealing many rows of sharp, serrated teeth, like the jaws of a shark. It was one of the Svartaelfar, an old race apart from the others of the land. Some said they were more directly related to the nobles than the ordinary hedgefolk, others that they had been cast out for some great breach of the old ways. Phynthoblin didn't know, but his instinct told him that anyone who shunned the light of sun and moon could not be quite right. Still, if there was ever a time for darkness to be useful, this was it. They had already loaded the ballista with one of the flint tipped spears.

"No, no!" Phynthoblin shouted. "Did you not hear me before? What *he* said, what *he* said!"

And he pointed to the swartaelfar, who nodded with a kind of mocking courtesy.

"My apologies," it spoke softly with a lilting gentle voice. "They do not listen to me. They will not let me near it. It seems I make them nervous."

Them and me both, thought Phynthoblin, reckless in his grammar. He could understand their qualms every time it opened its jagged mouth. Even the ever cheerful gnom kept their distance from the swartaelfar.

Phynthoblin had no time for their misgivings. "Do it now," he said, and they winched the bowstring tight while the swartaelfar moved to the waiting spear. It spoke some unknown musical words that made one shudder to hear them, for all their sweetness, and it sprinkled the contents of the pouch—a dark nondescript powder—all over the spearhead.

"Now!" cried Phynthoblin, as the swartaelfar moved back, the bowstring released and the great spear shot straight towards a miniscule black dot in the sky, a butterfly headed for the centre of the sun.

THE CENTRE OF THE SUN WAS CLOSE NOW, MUCH CLOSER, smiled the Hunter, than it had ever been to any mortal or immortal. He could feel the sweat trickling through his hair

and over his collar, Danaeus was singing, and as for the Bride
. . . he had never seen her look so radiant, so beautiful. In fact,
he was beginning to suspect that she was as beautiful as the
sun in her own way, when taken away from the grey slate of her
world and the white lace of his. He resolved that the moment
they reached the new land, he was going to steal some of the
colours dancing across its surface, and ask her to wear them.
He had the feeling that all those wonderful reds and pinks
and blues would really suit her. Happiness really suited her,
in fact, happiness suited all of them. He was going to grab
that happiness and build a great galleon out of it, from clouds
and dreams and sunlight he would form bulwarks and sails,
a galley, a prow, a mast, a ship, the first of many. He could see
how easy it would be to create intricate maps and telescopes
just from the light itself, and then he would be able to see and
explore everything. And he kissed her head, though she was
too delirious to notice it, and moved up towards Danaeus'
ears to speak, when he poked his head out between the butterfly's left shoulder and wing, and saw something.

It was very far below, but from a speck it became a dot and
from a dot it grew to a shape and from a shape it grew with
a sound that was louder, louder, filling the air, and Danaeus
screamed, as his wing burst in pain, splintering across the
wind, ribbons and shreds parting, falling away from his body,
and blood and tears streaming into darkness. Danaeus's agony
was loud and incoherent, his body prepared to shatter with
his lost wing, when the spear turned in mid air and aimed
at them again. Even as they fell, they held on to Danaeus, the
Hunter cursing, his eyes red with the fury, and she . . . all she
could do was be ready to put her arms around Danaeus's neck

and kiss him, tell him that she was ready to go, that he hadn't failed, that he was still beautiful . . .

But she couldn't say anything. All she could do was look upwards at the great flower and speak from her heart to its heart, as they plummeted earthwards. She seemed to have done nothing but fall since she came to the Hedge: from the toad's pantry into the pond, from the tree and the pink man, from the crow's grasp and now. But this was the worst because of what she was losing, and the ruin of Danaeus' wings.

"Please," she whispered upwards, "You called us towards you. Help us. Help him. Please."

As the spear shot forward again, the Hunter jumped through the air towards it, changing his shape to grab his prey with eight strong limbs, and using his mandibles to snap off the flint head. The spear shaft sank away back towards the far earth, but the flint head fought to get out of his grip. He took it out of his mouth and roared an old and uncouth geas:

Ut, lytel spere, gif hit her inne sy!
if hit wære esa gescot
oððe hit wære ylfa gescot
oððe hit wære hægtessan gescot,
nu ic wille ðin helpan!

By the Howling of the Wind
And the Roaring of the Sea
By the Laws of the Vanir
And the Power of the Sidhe
I am Son of the Old Ones

From the Lost Country
I am Aelf-son, your kinsman,
Now you serve me."

And he spat his venom upon the flint, and placed it back in his mouth, pointing it at the butterfly and Bride. It sped towards them, faster by far than they, and when it reached them, they clasped on to the great grey spider as he sped on: beneath them the tracks of the sun rolled out east and south from the Hedge, towards a place none of them had ever seen before, a vast yellow land with a great glittering snake coiling through it, blue in the light. It occurred to the Bride that the blue and yellow reminded her of the smile of the sun as it blazed in the sky. She was still remembering that smile when they crashed into the sands.

CHAPTER SIXTEEN
THE RED SEA

———

WHEN SHE WOKE, SHE COULD NOT MOVE AT ALL. AT FIRST, SHE thought she must have broken her neck or back, so complete was her paralysis. Then she saw a terrible face, scaled and long and crimson staring down at her, and realized she must be in hell.

"No," said the red face, "you are on the shores of blood."

Her head burned and she tasted salt on her lips, but whether it was blood or sweat, she could not tell. *The red sea isn't red*, she remembered from school, it got that name from mistranslation . . . it's *the reed sea, the sea of reeds . . .*

"It is the red sea, the sea of blood," said the face. "Don't you remember?

> *"And they rode on and further on*
> *Further and swifter than the wind*
> *Until they came to a desert wide*
> *And living land was left behind"*
>
> *O they rode on, and farther on,*
> *And they waded red blood to the knee,*
> *beyond the sun, beyond the moon,*
> *Beyond the roaring of the sea.*

Beyond the night, beyond star light,
They waded red blood to the knee;
For all the blood that's shed on earth
Runs off the shores of that country . . . "

"That's nonsense," she tried to say weakly, but there her words died, for the great red face (*Draconic,* she thought, *that's what it is . . .*) opened its mouth, and slid its lower jaw under her back. Then the upper jaw closed upon her torso, and with the gentlest of pressures, she found herself lifted and carried over the rocks, down to the water's edge. From there to the horizon lay the red sea, as smooth as glass under the colours of the setting sun. She could almost make out an island of glinting yellow sands far beyond the scarlet lagoon.

The beast waddled out into the shallows and then swam. In the crimson light, it almost seemed to dissolve into the water itself, but she could feel its jaws on her back and chest. The sea flowed around her and into her, and her hair whipped like the fronds of an anemone fanning out from white coral . Then the sea covered her face and her lips and her eyes, and she realised that it was indeed blood, and she was drowning in it. Despite her sense of dying, she felt stronger, and choked out, "Am I drinking the blood of the sun?" even as she realised that no answer could be forthcoming while the creature held her in its mouth. So she waited in the warmth and the wet and the salt until the creature swam back with her to shore. When it put her down, she realised that not one part of her attire was white any more. She was a red woman from head to toe. The other thing she realised was that she was somehow not dying at all, that the pain was receding from her body, that she could stand up without wanting to faint. The creature looked at her for a while before it spoke again.

"Not the sun's blood," it said, bowing. "Mine."

It looked at the darkening tide and then back at her. "Others' as well. But mostly mine." She could tell by its expression that it felt it was explaining itself very clearly.

"Mine was the most important for you." Of course it was. She felt she began to understand the law of stories and the land of which the Hedge was part.

"Because you are the dragon?"

"Because I am a newt."

She accepted that she understood nothing. The land made as little sense now as when she first entered it, and she was sick of trying.

"You are a newt."

"Yes."

"Not a dragon."

"No."

"You seem very big for a newt."

"You and I both exist in both our worlds. In your world, I am a newt and you are much bigger than me. In my world, I am . . . many things . . . and you are quite small."

"Am I a sort of newt-vampire then?"

"That is a very silly idea. I am the guardian you were meant to find."

"Because I needed newt blood?"

"Yes." The beast sounded as though it was being very patient. "The blood is my geas, the magic of myself."

"Newt magic?" The Bride had never heard anything so gross and ridiculous. "What does that do?"

For answer, the newt swished its tail towards her. It was a long red tail with spots on it. She let her eyes wander up its length to the base of its back, where she saw a faint scar, ever so slightly paler than the skin around it. Then she really did understand. "Newts grow their tails back," she said softly. "And limbs . . ." it was then that she realised.

When she looked down at her wrist, five tiny stumps were growing out of it, like tubers out of a potato.

"It will take time," said the newt. "But it will grow again, and there will only be a little scar."

The Bride's eyes filled with tears and forgetting everything she had learned, she thanked the newt. The newt just bowed and said that there was nothing to thank. To help her was its pleasure.

"Is the sea where you keep your geas?" She asked.

"Yes," said the newt, "I bleed into it every now and then. Otherwise I should be taking bites out of myself every time someone needed help. I am afraid I don't like that much. It feels funny to have mammals sucking from me."

"Well yes," she turned and looked at the red sea. "How much you have given, to turn the sea red!"

The newt looked embarrassed. If it had not been scarlet already, she would have sworn it was blushing. "The sea is not just the place of my geas," it said. "There is more to it than that," and it fell silent.

The Bride would have pursued further, but she suddenly remembered the others, and taking her leave, ran along the sands to find them. By the time she did, the sun had fallen below the horizon, and bright stars she could not name were climbing the sky. The Hunter was the easiest to discover, for he had found a large whetstone and was using it to sharpen his sword, loudly. When she first saw him, she hung back, recalling the great baleful spider form he had assumed, but as he showed no sign of spinning a web or eating the tiny flies buzzing among the reeds, she reckoned she was safe enough, and approached him.

He was in a foul temper, and barely acknowledged her. The light at the back of his eyes told her how close he was to giving in to his rage. He did not even seem to notice her hand, and when she tried to thank him for bringing her to the newt he just glared at her. "I am not in the mood for company," he growled. "If you must chatter, make yourself useful and go talk to Danaeus. He needs it." And with that, the Hunter returned to cleaning his sword.

Danaeus needed something, certainly. He was huddled in the sand curled up, his remaining wing stuck out awkwardly to one side. There were tears down his face as he watched the sun melting into the night. When it had gone, he hid his head in his arms. She could not get one word out of him. So she stayed silent nearby, and then went back to speak to the newt. Later, she returned to the Hunter, armed with one of Sycorax's needles she had found still sticking in her hem.

"I want you to use your geas," she said. "I would ask you to make the rose-knight's gift grow back to the size it was when we found it."

The Hunter looked at her curiously.

"You know it will die quickly if I do this?" he said.

The Bride nodded. She did not need it to last. He spoke the

charm, and the rose grew, and the scent of it grew too, light and sweet and pink. She looked at the rose, its petals now half the size of parachutes. She pulled two away from the flower, and tweaked three hairs off her head to use as thread, and began to sew.

In fact, it took five large petals before her creation was complete. She was quite proud of it: it was a new wing for the Butterfly, and all it lacked were the black dots. She brought it to him expecting him to smile, but he didn't.

"What is this for?" His voice and his face were equally empty.

She shrugged. "Well, this is the rose knight's gift, made with the Bride's hair and new hand on the edge of the red sea, where the newt's remaking magic is strong, so I thought . . . "

"Take it away!" His voice was harsh and cracked, like something out of tune. "Take it away!"

"But don't you see—"

"See what? What is there to see?"

"When I talked to the newt, he told me that—"

"Newts eat butterflies, you stupid mortal!"

She had to bite back the tears. He had never called her stupid before.

"This one is not like that, Danaeus, just trust it, trust me—"

"Like I trusted the great flower?"

She was shocked into silence by the pain in his face.

'I believed the great flower and it lied to me! All I did was try my best and trust . . . I was so stupid, and now I'm a cripple and I can't fly. I can't fly! And you think you are going to make it right with your stupid ugly pretend wing.

It doesn't even match the other one, you stupid woman . . . stupid, stupid . . . "

And he ran away.

And the Bride cried.

Later, he came back and apologised, but her face was hard and cold as the ladies of the court. "You gave me a gift," she said. "Now you must let me give you a gift back."

He of course, had no idea what she was talking about.

"You gave me a gift of three insults," she said with all the hauteur of the Beloved. "Now you must let me give you a gift of three back."

He looked hurt. "Doesn't my apology count?" he asked, and when she didn't answer he said, "I thought we were better friends than this, my Lady Bride. But very well. I accept your three gifts, whatever they may be. What do you wish to give me?"

She handed him the wing she had made.

"If you let me push it against your shoulders and back, it should stick. The newt and I made a paste from his spit and some red sea . . . water . . . that he said would work."

The butterfly was silent, but let her paste the wing to his back.

"Next, you will go down to the sea and watch east until tomorrow."

"How will I know when tomorrow is?" It was not a foolish question. He had been born into the twilight of the Hedge and time was different there.

"You will know," she said.

"And the third?" His voice was calm but his eyes were tired and full of sorrow.

"The third is for us to be friends again when tomorrow comes."

She wondered if she was asking too much with her last demand. There was no conversation between them as they walked down to the water's edge, where she left him standing between the reeds and the stars.

When she sought him after sunrise, he had gone.

CHAPTER SEVENTEEN
PRESENTS OF MIND

———

IT WAS STILL A BEAUTIFUL DRESSING TABLE.

She may have lost the mortal who made it, but still, it was proof, if any was needed, that she, and not the Prince, found true dreams and fostered them. Her slave had carved it so intricately that she wanted to make stories for the little heads and faces, the nymphs and satyrs and winged cherubs. She brought them to life and tried to think of things for them to say and do, but nothing occurred to her. She was a controller, not a creator, and controllers were every bit as important, she told herself. So she ordered the little creatures to make her beautiful, and watched their progress in her mirror. They were tiny, even by the standards of the Hedge, and so ethereal you could slice their tiny bodies in two with a pin, and they would just close together again. It took a lot of them to open her powder box, and two to wrestle with the powder puff and dust her skin until it was cool and shimmering. One touched her lips with the deep red cochineal of enchanted poppy; this was how she would make her lover dream, with one slow kiss out of the quiet realm, she would draw him back to her, and he would never wish to go home again. The perfume was her own, gathered by herself, and the little creatures flutteringly applied it to her neck and ears, below her bosom, at her wrists, and in her hair. Four of them worked upon brightening her nails until they were exactly the same shade of scarlet as her lips. Two of them took the potion of love-in-idleness and aconite, and darkened her eyelids with it. The rest of the army worked upon her hair, swooping those long black locks up into charmingly improbable styles on top of her head and kept there by an extraordinary array of ribbons, pins and combs of tortoise-shell and ivory.

On the dresser was a most charming billet-doux, a box made from mother of pearl and corals of fine pinks and oranges, and the letter "P" picked out on the top in shining pearls. It was so charming, she would have been disappointed to find it full of anything as banal as chocolates. As her nymphs opened it, her smile widened. It was far from banal. The box opened out into a small chessboard, again, of mother of pearl and coral. Upon it, ready for battle, were tiny creatures from the deep, kept alive out of the water by a powerful geas, until such time as she would be bored of playing and wanted to eat them. Two miniscule crab kings faced each other with claws upraised, and calamari queens oozed and flowed between sea-horse knights. Sea-urchin pawns, their spikes tipped with silver or jet, waited for her command. It was a delightful gift, and all the more so considering who it came from. She read the card that came with it and laughed aloud, for reading the message made sense of the gift. No wonder it came from the sea; the tide had turned.

She put the card and the box to one side. There was another box too, larger and much more plain, and it also had a card with it. This time, she read the card before looking at the present. It made her frown.

The giver could be charming as she well remembered, but the message was the least charming request she had ever

THE SPIDER'S BRIDE

had the misfortune to receive. To put it bluntly, he wanted a powerful gift in return for the present in the box. A pity he had not come himself, so that she could laugh in his face. The fool had been more generous than he had planned, for now she knew he was alive and that information had to be worth something. And yet . . .

She bit her bottom lip, trying to decide. For if that information was deliberately given as a part of the present, then he was being generous indeed. Possibly. It would all come down to the quality of the cadeau, for the Beloved was a sound believer that there is no truth except in *things*.

When she opened the box, she almost slammed it shut again in irritation. There, wrapped in plain white tissue, was a plain white columbine mask, which, though delicate in its form, was deeply dull to look at. How could he possibly expect her to be impressed by this?

Almost as a reflex action, she put it up against her face and looked in the mirror. The mask instantly turned purple, checkered with black diamonds and dancing with daintily cut jet filigree above the brows and over the eyes. She focused and thought for a moment, and the mask grew white feathers. Part of the black filigree pulled itself away from the rest and formed a long snow coloured neck, and the Beloved found herself gazing at a swan's shape. She focused again, and the mask changed to a whirlwind of blossoms and feathers, again and it changed to a huge pink and purple orchid covering her head, again and it became an emerald hummingbird across her eyes, again and it became a crow, again, again, again . . .

She put it down, out of breath, astonished. This changed matters somewhat.

Her bower had changed too. Now it was pillared by huge croci, resplenent in purple and yellow, white and blue. Between them grew anemones, behind them daffodils. She considered her situation, and that of the kingdom, and the gift.

The Prince had made a fool of her, but he had used a great deal of his power doing it. Yes, she had been hoodwinked into losing Richard, but she had learned from her mistake. The Prince had no intention of wedding her, or of making her his equal on the throne, and perhaps it was just as well. If he was a fading star it was better if she seemed independent of him. The Hedge needed monarchs of summer and winter, and maybe there was even more to it than that, she ruminated, stroking the mask. A new way was needed, and the Hedge was ready.

Perhaps the Hedge was not the only kingdom at stake. She had pondered the words of the dolls: "He has stretched the old ways for season upon season, until the web has broken on the face of mortals and folk alike . . . " Obviously the Prince had prolonged the winter to keep the crown on his head. She could not see how doing this could make a difference to the world of mortals until she recalled their infatuation with the linear, their desperate need to measure time and space. She shrugged. If they insisted on being so dull, they deserved what they got, and she troubled herself no more about them. Home, after all, was all that mattered.

The seelie had no leader, and the unseelie Prince was losing his grip on the land. She had understood, as Phynthoblin had not, the point of all those sacrifices and why despite each one, he continued to look for something perfect to offer the old ones, some true love or great art willing to surrender itself to oblivion for him; the returning gift might be overwhelming, might be eternal rulership, night and winter always. A daring plan for a little king. How unfortunate for him that he was so loveless and horrible. And how fortunate for her that she was not, that finding the right blood to spill for the land would become as easily to her as to the greatest leanan-sidhe. After all, who had loved her as Richard the mortal had? And she had loved him in return. Oh, she had not always been kind, but kindness was over-rated. A little cruelty in love kept matters interesting. He was soft, that mortal, and unlike her Prince, she knew exactly how to reach him. She could get him back, and it seemed he was not the only soft touch beneath her pretty fingers. She had not forgotten the sea-shell box in her delight at the Hunter's gift. Power wears many masks.

Winter and summer, time and love and politics, all were games she played, for she was a true daughter of the crossroads, queen of the changing face, and the moving season, and she was ready to take what the Hunter was offering. She would say whatever she had to say, give whatever she had to give, and do whatever she had to do, for the chance to rule.

CHAPTER EIGHTEEN
THESE YELLOW SANDS

THEY HAD BEEN RESTING IN THE SUNLIGHT SINCE THE butterfly had gone. The Bride had to assume that Danaeus' wing was cured, because, as the Hunter pointed out, his footprints led down from sand to sea's edge, and no further. Wherever he went, he flew. The Bride's immediate fear was that Danaeus might have thrown himself into the sea in despair, and she was wondering if the newt could trawl for broken butterfly wings in case the worst had happened. The Hunter stopped her. "It's a big sea," he said. "And we have other things to think about."

He looked at her hand, which was now perfectly healed. She had grown so used to it not being there, she kept forgetting to use it. *Or maybe not so much forgetting*, she told herself, *as afraid in case it breaks off, shatters, or develops its own personality and demands payment for usage*. It was hard for her to trust the magic of the Hedge.

But was this still the Hedge? She could not be sure, for there was little here but red rocks and sand and the sea. Then she saw reeds fringing much of the shoreline and she remembered the bulrushes that sang on her way to her wedding. The Hedge had many shapes.

The Hunter had bathed himself. His golden coat, gifted from the Prince, was now in tatters and any charm he possessed was more savage than elegant. Still, his eyes shone again, and his sword rested in its scabbard looking fine and ready for adventure. *He's enjoying this*, she realised, and decided that it was a good time to talk, while he was pulling his boots on. She sat on the sand next to him.

"So," she said, "where do we go from here?"

He gestured at the desert around them. "We are surrounded by choices," he said. "But I have carried out the plan as much as I can remember. Your hand is back—my debt to you paid, I hope—" He raised his hat, and though his smile was wry, his voice sounded sincere. "And you are free to go back to your world or stay in the land, or do whatever you want."

She looked at the ground, and drew little swirls in the sand. Then she wiped them away with her fingers.

"Now that we have time," she said, casually, "why don't you tell me what the plan was?"

There was a pause as his brow furrowed. "The plan," he said, "Yes, well . . . it was a good plan, from what I recall. Part one was to stop the wedding. Part two was to get you out of the Hedge and into your own world. Part three . . . well, I don't remember it clearly . . . ."

> *"Come unto these yellow sands*
> *And then take hands . . . "'*

The voice was tuneless and masculine, and boomed from above and beyond them like rolling thunder. The Bride was expecting a genie or some such fantastical creature, for the voice belonged to something huge, and the ground beneath them shook.

"Courtsied when you have, and kissed—
The wild waves whist—
Foot it featly here and there,
And sweet sprites the burdens bear . . . "

"Foot it featly?" said the Hunter almost to himself as he ran to the rise of a dune. "What drivel is this?"

The Bride joined him in time to see the cause of the commotion; colossal sand-coloured creatures, stick-legged, long-necked and hump-backed, with bright-striped yarn rugs all over them. They were being ridden by what were clearly humans, albeit giant ones. Some were swathed in long pale robes, while others wore trousers, waistcoats and hats of a kind the Bride recognised, but not well; she knew such clothing had been worn many years before she was born.

"This is in my world," she whispered to the Hunter.

"Part two is a success," the Hunter whispered back. "Aren't you happy?"

"Happy? I'm the size of a pea and unless this is a film set, I'm thousands of miles from my home, and hundreds of years from my ti—" She stopped when she saw the Hunter dive behind a rock, placing a finger in front of his lips, and then gesturing to the back of the camel train, where the singing voice came from. There, swaying gently on his mount was a dark haired pale-eyed man they both knew. His expression was far from everything around him, the shadows under his eyes were deep, and swinging from his camel's belly, as it wandered closer to the dune, was the feeding form of a great yellow spider.

When the Bride saw it, she covered her mouth and ducked down behind another rock. The camel walked by, the singing continued. Neither Hunter nor Bride said anything until the beasts had wandered off into the distance. Then, she sat down in the sand as though the air had been knocked right out of her. The Hunter watched her. It was the first time she had seen the Prince since the wedding, and he did not know what she would do, or what he should say. He was expecting her to cry, but she didn't. After a long silence, she said, "What? What do you think he—"

"I'm no Phynthoblin," he told her. "I can't gauge him. He needs a mortal sacrifice, an artist, lunatic or dreamer. Now, I'll bet anything you like he doesn't have a clue where you are, and poor Palawinkes would never have worked as a sacrifice. Too level headed. When Richard belonged to the Beloved, he was her claim to the throne. But Richard got out, so he's free now . . . "

"So he's not the Beloved's thrall, anymore."

"No. He belongs to whichever of the Folk can take him and keep him. And he is a powerful prize, with his iron axe and his art, but he is still a second-hand discovery, an inadequate sacrifice, like . . . " His voice drifted as he tried to think of a human comparison. "Like you offering the meat of a deer someone else had hunted, prepared and cooked. It's all very well, but all you have done is bought it. You see?"

"And is that against the old ways?"

"It is against the spirit of the old ways. He must be desperate indeed." The Hunter couldn't help laughing. "Well, I'm sure they will be very happy together. Now we need to work out what to do about you."

"I don't understand. If he needed blood, why didn't he come to the red sea?"

"Because the old ways are specific? Because the blood's all mingled here and he doesn't know what he's getting? Because the sand irritates him? I don't know. He's never been much of a traveller before. Like I said, he's desperate."

"He is going to sacrifice Richard to keep his grip on the Hedge, isn't he?" She said, and as she spoke, she knew she could not let it happen. The Hunter looked noncommital. The Bride felt something waking in her, as though she finally understood some part of why she had come into the Land.

"Richard saved me from Sycorax, you see . . . and I made a promise to the fox woman." She tried to explain. The Hunter listened, distinctly unimpressed. She seemed to use a lot of air to say a very little thing.

She wanted to try and rescue the mortal Richard from the Prince. She knew it was the right thing to do, she was certain there had to be a way, she hoped that the Hunter would be very kind and help her. As tracking a dozen camels over sand was actually easier for the Hunter than standing still and listening to her, he agreed quickly and started off in pursuit. She followed him as he chased after their quarry and even in the hot turquoise of the day he never stopped. The directness of his hunt surprised her; after all, the Prince had only to look back and he would see them leaping down dunes, like dragonflies sparkling over the reeds. The Hunter dismissed her worries. He reckoned the Prince would be too busy slowly eating his way through camel entrails to look. "He will eat that thing until he is too stuffed to move, and then he will drop off," laughed the Hunter. It was then that another thought occurred to the Bride but she didn't dare express it, and if he guessed he never spoke.

You know what part three of the plan was, she thought at him, *and you have always known it. You've carried on for Pala-winkes' sake, but your heart's not in it. You can finish it, but you're stalling because you don't like what happens next.*

The camel train stopped soon after, with a yell from the man next to Richard, as one of the guides spotted the spider beneath his camel. Shouting occurred, sticks were brought out, and though the Hunter would very much like to have watched his royal cousin being stunned with staves or igno-miniously chased round and round the camp, he had to be practical. He bid her cling round his neck and then leapt upwards, grabbing a tassel that dangled from the saddle, and swinging them both into one of Richard's saddle bags. It was full of papers and pencils (the size and thickness of telegraph poles to the Bride and the Hunter) and smelled of paints.

"Behold!" He smiled as they fell into the leather pouch. "We have arrived!"

She disengaged herself from him. "What about the Prince?" she said. He shrugged.

"I think he'll hide himself. My cousin has used a lot of power and magic to get as far as this. I think he will wait until he is back in the part of the Hedge he calls home before he tries anything."

"Or maybe they'll kill him." She looked sideways at her companion. "That would be a very good thing I think. I don't know why someone hasn't tried it so far."

His eyes met her, and there was a strange maroon colour, an ugly light at the back of them.

"Ever killed anyone, Lady Bride?"

"No, but—"

"Ever killed a relative, Lady Bride?"

"Well, no, but if I had a relative so evil—"

"What would you do? Tell me all about it."

He stooped a little, within the confines of the bag, and his eyes stared down into hers with an expression of steel, cold and bright.

"Don't try to bully me," she said. "That's your cousin's way. And what about Palawinkes? Don't you care about that?"

His eyes flashed now, with an expression she had never seen before, and when he came close, she wanted to back away. When he spoke, his voice was soft.

"I. Do not. Kill my kinsmen. For mortals. Whoever they are."

"Then you should kill him for the land."

"What do you know of the land?" He sneered.

"That there should be a seelie ruler to follow in the summer, that's what he's trying to stop, isn't it? And later there would be an unseelie ruler in the winter, a new one. If you killed him, it would be you, and that's the problem. That was the plan you worked out with Palawinkes, only now you're bottling it. Because if it works, there will be no exploring and no new lands, no new hunting. So you're afraid, you're afraid of being stuck, you're afraid." Her voice rang as did his sword, drawn from its sheath and hurtling towards her. "Afraid of being king."

The sword struck through one of the massive pencils and cracked it neatly in half.

"The last bride I took from him," he said through gritted

teeth, "I ate, because she was no artist, and she never shut up. I have not seen much art out of you, and your dreams have all the banal stupidity of a little girl's. I am not afraid of kingship, or the Prince, and I am certainly not afraid of you. I am *bored* with you."

With that, he sliced the side of the saddle bag and the sunlight flooded in through the slash. He pulled the leather apart, stepped through it and was gone.

And they all lived happily ever after came the words floating through her head, as she watched him leave. It was amazing how little she had learnt since she came to the Hedge.

CHAPTER NINETEEN
REAL

———

IT WAS NOT AN EASY VOYAGE HOME FOR SIR THOMAS. HE WAS worried about Richard, whose breakdown had been diagnosed as a severe attack of brain fever, to be blamed on excess heat and exciteability of the kind famous for attacking the nerves of artists. It was a malady to which Richard was particularly prone, and the night in the temple seemed to have brought him down completely. Sir Thomas blamed himself. Richard blamed no-one, indeed he barely spoke. Corfu and Greece and all the glories of the Levant lay forgotten in his notebook. His eyes were as wild and melancholy as the seas and his sleep was haunted by dreams. He knew there was someone else in his cabin with him, he was certain of it, despite reassurances to the contrary. Once, he dreamt he saw a shadow sitting on his chest. It wore a crown and held a golden banner, and all it did was nod at him. When he tried to shake it off, he woke to find himself dank with sweat.

But a dream is not the same as a waking truth and he knew there was someone in that room with him, someone watching him. He tried to sneak glimpses of them out of the corners of his eyes but they were always just out of sight. Occasionally, he would take out his notebook and try to sketch what he had seen, but instead, he found himself gazing at the sketches and watercolours. There was one he kept returning to, because he did not remember painting it at all. It was a very delicate pastel of a tiny lady, her face refreshingly different to the others. She was not one of them clearly, though she was dressed in their clothes, and her skin was so pale that she must have been among them for some time. But her expression was kind and she was looking up at him so eloquently, he almost expected her to step off the page and speak. He very much wanted her to speak. He very much wanted her to be the same size as him. On the page she looked like a sweet little doll; and in real life?

He passed his hands very softly over the sketch. What was he thinking of? Pygmalion? Galatea? He shook his head. He had enough humility to realise that she was not his creation, she was too fine and real for that. No, he must have seen her somewhere and the moment that thought came into his head, he knew it was absolutely true. Three times his hands passed over the lines of her face and three times he spoke quiet words. Then he went to bed and he dreamt.

In his dream, the phantasy woman stepped out of his sketchbook and grew tall and beautiful as she moved towards the bed. From under his eyelids, he watched, all the time pretending to be asleep. The garments she wore were outlandish and yet familiar. They revealed much of her, more perhaps than she realised, for there were great rips and tears and blood upon them too. In his dream, she opened her mouth and spoke, but he could hear nothing. Then he dismissed the dream for the imposter it was, opened his eyes, and stood up. She stopped moving, like a mouse under owl-shadow. Perhaps she thought he would continue to believe he was dreaming, but he was only mad, not a fool. This was real, and he pulled her towards him. Perhaps he was a little insistent. He wanted her to be warm skin and soft hair, to be ready for him, he wanted her to *be*. Sylvia he had loved, but she was nowhere now, and the Beloved . . . but he was not going to think of the Beloved.

He focused instead on the woman in front of him, for once clear in his intention; he was going to touch her. His fingers moved gently beneath her chin and down over her breast-bone, until the base of her neck flushed and he felt the far-away drum of her heart thudding out a challenge to him. And then he knew, for all her rigidity and his doubt. Her face grew pink while his hand refused to move from the new discovery, even at the pleading of her eyes, her very human eyes. And all the while she sang in his head, a tiny plea of fieldmouse fury:

> *And if ye dare to kiss my lips,*
> *sure of your body I shall be.*

Too well he knew the verse that answered:

> *Betide me weal, betide me woe,*
> *That threat shall never frighten me . . .*

Then he brushed the song from him, like cobwebs from the corners of a long locked room. *No more songs. You are real. Like me . . .* she must have known it was true, for she stood motionless, while he bent his head down to her. *Let me,* he thought at her, *let me do this, it will be so sweet . . .* and covered her mouth with his own. She did not resist.

She does not know what she wants, he told himself, but he knew, as he touched her neck and shoulders and his hand travelled down to the small of her back. He knew because she was growing warm, even as she tried to pull away from the intimacy fluttering between them, he knew because he could almost feel her lips part to meet his, like silk, like ribbons in warm rain . . . He could hear the patter of drops against the glass. Richard glanced in the mirror behind her, as his hand gently tore away the back of the dress. He expected to see her naked shoulders revealed, the small of her waist and the curve of her hips. Instead, the mirror clouded dark grey, and out of it stared baleful yellow eyes in a face, a terrible bestial face, snarling at him.

He screamed, and released her for a moment, only to grab her again, as she ran towards the notebook. "It's a lie!" He screamed, "I am not the wolf!" And he forced himself to look away from the mirror, holding her wrist, as he wrested her towards the bed, saying, "No more dreams, no, no. I know how to make you real, I know . . . " But this time when he touched the warm skin it turned to paper, rustled and crumpling, and the sweet mortal scent of her was nothing more than the smell of acquarelle and water colours. And whether she pulled away or the apparition in the mirror cursed him, or whether the tides of dream washed her out of his arms, he could not tell, only that she became tiny and somehow stepped back into the book. He wanted to call out after her that he intended her no dishonour, his intention had been to let her lie on the bed where he would watch her and sketch her perhaps; the kiss, he admitted, had been a little forward, but he was no wolf, no wolf . . .

The woman was gone and the beast in the mirror had disappeared. Only the Beloved remained dancing in his head. "If that had been me," he heard the dulcet chime of her voice, "I would have stayed." And she laughed at him.

Richard knew he should have smashed the mirror, but he didn't. Instead he slept with his notebook next to him on the pillow. Nestling above his heart, yellow by the light of mirror and candle, a great spider sat and dreamed its own dreams.

SHE, IN THE MEANTIME, CONTINUED TO SHUDDER, SAFE between the pages of his notebook. The Prince was asleep, she could see that, and only when Richard had tried to kiss her had his eyes opened, a flicker, a leer, waiting for something horrible to happen. She had terrible visions of lying close to Richard, and that thing lying between them, clambering over her breasts and nuzzling her hair. In those dreams, it even made soft baby sounds. She felt it feed until it was replete, and then the spider bit her again and again.

The mirror went dark, the room filled with the sound of rain and the slow pad of paws that became the creak of leather boots. She sighed with relief to know who it must be. She would thank him, the moment he was close enough to hear her whisper, but to her surprise, he did not come over to the notebook. Instead, he sat on Richard's bed, and opened the mortal's shirt a little wider, drawing his sword silently. For a brief, terrifying moment, she thought he was going to slit Richard's throat, but instead he lay the blade across the belly of the great spider. The Prince's eyes opened.

"Hello, cousin," said the Hunter to the Prince.

The Prince laughed, a low creaking sound. "I looked for you everywhere," he said. "I should have known to let you come to me. Are you going to kill me, Hunter?"

The Hunter paused for a long time before withdrawing his blade. "Yes," he said, "But not here." There was a long silence.

"Was this your doing?" The Hunter made a gesture to the torn material still clutched in the sleeper's hands.

The Prince chuckled. "Oh no. All his own work. He would have finished, too, had you not spoilt everything . . . ." He wheezed in his laughter. "Personally, I was quite enjoying it."

"You know she cannot be your Bride any more."

"I don't want her. She disgusts me."

"So it is time, cousin, for you to abdicate. You cannot stay. It is over."

"Once more unto the—"

"No. No more." The Bride was awed by the simplicity of his voice, the sanity of his eyes. There was no sardonic wit, no cruelty. He looked calm and sorry.

"You are not the rightful king. Perhaps you never were. There is no blood you can shed which can regain you the right to the crown; Richard belongs to the Beloved, the Bride belongs to me."

She had to clap her hands over her mouth to stop herself from being heard.

"But you are my cousin, and before I shed your blood, I grant you the right to go into exile. Which will you choose?"

The great yellow spider backed away a little. "Obviously, Hunter, if you force me at knife point, I will abdicate, but . . . "

"But if you lie to me about this, we know I am freed from the bond between kinsmen, do we not? And you are going to lie, because you cannot bear not to be king. And then I will kill you." The Hunter sighed. "You are making me sane, cousin, and I do not know what wrong I did you to deserve it . . . "

The spider scuttled down Richard's chest and legs, over the bed and towards the mirror. "One more chance," he said. "As we are of the blood, Hunter, I ask it and in return, I promise . . . " His eyes darted round the room. "I promise to force no-one, mortal or of the Folk. Any who help me do so because they wish it. Agreed?"

"Don't be a fool, cousin, no-one will help you unless their veins are full of your poison, like that idiot on the bed."

"I cannot undo what I have done," said the wily Prince, "but I can promise not to add more venom to the wound. Agreed?"

The Hunter did not look at him. "I offer you the chance of life," he said.

"I take the chance of power," said the spider. The Hunter nodded. And the Prince, hardly believing his luck, scuttled through the mirror. His back legs had hardly disappeared when the Bride stuck her head out over the top of the bag.

"The Bride belongs to me," she imitated him, waggling her head. "How dare you! And what was that all about? You let him live!"

"You let him live!" He imitated in return, his voice a squeaky falsetto. "You let him live!" He looked at Richard's face for a moment, and his sword was slow to return to its scabbard. "Do you still want to help your groping satyr here?"

She nodded and waited for the rest.

"My cousin goes back to the land, to regain his strength and every geas he has at his command—and he has many. When next we enter the Hedge, we will either depose him or die ourselves."

"I don't understand. What was the point of giving him so much advantage?" She was trying not to sound exasperated, but it was hard. The Hunter looked at her and once again, she was struck by the inhuman kindness of his face.

"We have gained your friend time away from the Prince. Time to get over the poison, time to decide what he wants to be, which world he belongs in. You can try to speak to him in dreams. But it would be charity to let him sleep, without magic or complexity, like an ordinary mortal. And he may find his own strength."

He was no liar, and she knew, by looking at his face, how unlikely he thought that was. But in giving the spider prince a chance, he had given Richard hope. He gestured to the mirror.

"No," she said. "I will stay here with him—not to talk," she added. "Just to watch him."

The Hunter looked at her with a curious expression she could not quite make out. "As you wish," he said. "I go to rally our friends. Be careful now," and with that, he almost kissed her. She watched him leave through the ripples of the mirror, and turned her attention to the sleeping artist. She clambered back on to the bed, and made herself comfortable with him. Then they both slept and neither dreamt at all.

The ship moved out, beyond the blue of the Mediterranean, to stormy seas, where rain lashed the decks and darkened skies. In that time, Richard did not leave his room much. The fever came and went, and often, when he was not listening to Sir Thomas trying to cheer him up, or the doctor's admonitions, he was left alone for hours in his cabin.

It was in those hours that he could make her out. Sometimes she was tiny, a mote, ("*in size no bigger than an agate stone . . .* "). But sometimes she stood there and grew until she was the size of a real woman. The fairy light glimmered around her, in her ruined dress, but still her face was beautiful and mortal. She was wary of approaching him, but he knew that if he closed his eyes and made little moans like a man in nightmare, she would touch his forehead. Usually her touch rustled like the paper of his book, but now and then, she felt real and he longed for her hands to stay upon him.

But the Bride was more canny now. She had mastered the geas of shrinking and growing, but she was not yet quick enough to be sure of escape should Richard ever try to catch her again. She never tried to speak to him either. He was so locked into his dreams that the Hunter's advice seemed completely appropriate. The poor man needed peace, and a lack of magic.

He seemed to grow stronger night by night. Sometimes she sat by the porthole and read his journal, meandering through strange memories of Sylvia and Sycorax, understanding what must have happened in the temple. Sometimes she watched the moon rise over the sea, when its beams would strike him softly, with such beauty that she could not resist going over to have a look at his face. He lay there, pale with his dark hair, his shirt unbuttoned to reveal a slim throat and smooth chest. He was not entirely without muscle or strength, but compared to the power of the Hunter—but she tried to push the Hunter out of her thoughts. Where was the point of thinking about the Hunter? He never thought about her.

Power struck her as an interesting idea, as she sat thinking in the moonlight. She would look across at the ravaged face of the artist, and it occurred to her that he had never known power in his own hands, except perhaps when he painted. She looked at his hands, ("*Long and white are my fingers, as the ninth wave on the sea . . .* ") The nails were pitifully broken.

"Not even then," she told herself. "He has power over nothing. He is always serving some muse or other."

She wondered if that was so terrible a thing. Not every man is a commander, she mused as she stroked his face, pale and thin as the moon in sickle. It occurred to her that after all this, perhaps he was Lord Lune, the man in the moon, and he had indeed fallen to earth way too soon. The thought made her laugh; she had always loved nursery rhymes. His hair was very soft and fine, and she ran her hands through it. Her thoughts ran to witches and old wives' tales: stories of stables haunted at midnight, where grooms would throw their lanterns to the ground and flee, and the horses would tremble and snort, for the witch was coming to ensorcel the finest beast and make it ride far into the storm, whiplashed over clouds and through briar thickets, over ditches and banks of sea-holly, away, deep into the dark. She could see its sides flanked with sweat and blood, its mouth flecked with foam, its head becoming the head of a man.

Richard cried out in his sleep. She looked again and realised how easily she could straddle his chest and ride him like the witch's nightmare, far away until dawn broke. He would break, too, she felt, one more great enchantment would shatter him. But he was going to break anyway, so what was there to lose? She let her hands travel over his flesh, as he had intended to do with her, from the ridge of his collar bone to the hollow beneath his ribs. He had not succeeded because, in the end, it was his place to serve, not to take. Her place, however, had not been decided. Her hands travelled the breadth of his shoulders and down his arms, down to the soft trail of hair beneath his navel. He was breathing more rapidly. She suddenly feared the mirror, and looked back, half expecting to see the Beloved laughing at her. She saw nothing, but recalled the Hunter, and backed away from the bed.

The sleeping man sighed, as did she, and she touched him no more. But she never slept either through all the days and nights of the journey, while sometimes he dozed and sometimes he burned and sometimes he seemed more aware, and then weaker. Her eyes never left him through all his changes, until vigil's end when the ship docked at Southampton. A dark man dressed in the quaint garb of a cavalier waited for her on the quay, and Richard, too sick to walk, was brought home.

CHAPTER TWENTY
SPRING THUNDER

———

THE SOUTH OF ENGLAND IS BEAUTIFUL IN SPRING. THERE could be no better place to get well. Walter Potter's cottage had been rented by Robert Dadd because the place was perfect for his son, especially now when all the country was bloom and blossom. Flowers were everywhere, trees were verdant and the woods flourished under the growing dominion of the sun. The little hedge surrounding the cottage had not suffered too much from the ravages of winter. If anything, Robert observed, it could do with cutting back.

It was a beautiful day, the first that his son would be spending out in the open air since his return. Enforced bed rest and the efforts of the finest physicians had done as much as possible for Richard's nerves. Things from the old nursery had been brought to the cottage to reassure him, though Robert was not comfortable with that. A man should not look to the things of childhood to make him strong, he had to join the world and add his own efforts to become truly well. Nature in all its joyous abundance seemed ready to help, and Robert had high hopes. His son after all, was highly strung, but a rational man.

He was waiting in the tiny drawing room, once filled by Potter's curious taxidermical creations, now tamed by crockery in the dresser and tea on the table, when someone knocked at the door.

He opened it to see a woman there. Her clothes were not altogether common, but Robert was not an observant man. She told him in some distress that her dog had got free and was roaming the woods, and recommended care to walkers until she had retrieved the errant animal. "I would not have troubled you, sir," she said. "But I hear you have a person here whose health has caused concern, and I would not have you bothered."

As if to punctuate her words, a huge romping beast jumped over the wall, made a growling sound and jumped away again, despite all her calls and chidings. Robert was shaken; it was a very big dog, grey and grim as a wolf, and he could not help but feel irritated with the woman. What was she doing with a pet she couldn't control? He told her as much, warned her that he personally was not going to delay his walk by one second because of her animal, that that the police would soon hear of it, and finally promised to shoot the brute if it came anywhere near him or his delicate son. Cobham was full of idiots who couldn't control their dogs. The intimidating specimen even now loping through the woods (almost as though it was trying to look fierce) was obviously unsuitable for a lady, indeed, why women couldn't just stick to children, cats and spaniels, he would never know. And with that, he slammed the door in her face.

The shimmering of a geas later, only a hawk's eye could have seen the wolf spider clambering up the outer wall of the cottage, with something white and shining on its back. They were extraordinarily quick for such tiny things but then they knew exactly where they were going. Despite their speed, by the time they had made their way through the window into Richard's bedroom, both patient and father had started their walk.

"I told you it wouldn't work," said the Hunter. "Today is the day, and the battle will be soon. For the life of me, I can't see what we're going to achieve here."

She looked around the room. There were his sketches and here too, were dolls, alarmingly huge from the current perspective of the Bride. She was surprised to see so many in the room. Some wore long pinafores, some had squeezed-in little waists and surprisingly adult figures. Some were bald babies, others were clearly little women. Petticoats and bonnets were abundant. One was a strange painted wooden thing in billowing petticoats, one wore a little gypsy outfit, and there was one doll with wild hair, big furrowed brows, and a gouge across its neck. When she looked at it, she saw the name, "Sylvia," sewn into a label on its collar. A large pair of scissors lay nearby. It was then that she remembered where she had seen all these dresses before, and she ran across to the sketch book, pulling the pages across with as much strength as she had. Every variety of dress had found its way into the sketch book, but every face was identical. The colours changed but above each intricate costume, the thin nose and huge eyes were exactly the same: it was all *him*. She and the Hunter looked at each other, finally understanding. And then there was no time to stay.

Now the Hedge roared with the winds of March, and a certain young hare boxed his rivals in the fields and tore through daisy chains thrown by the folk, to tell the seelie that the time had come.

Now came the Red Duke and his armies marching through the spring grass, accompanied by the smooth smiles of svartaelfar, and the great siege engines of the dvalinsfolk. Above them clustered crows, chattering and waiting. Now the shadow thorns unhooked themselves from the Hedge, donned tatters and rags for armour and wheeled into battle, ever hungry. The huntsmen came, and the knucklavee who wore no skin and the red-caps whose faces were bloody from hat to chin. Now came the *bucca dhu*, with his long ears and goat face, and the thirsty blind folk from under the hills. Here also came the water hags and stranglers of children, green teeth and long claws ready and sharp. Behind them walked another army whom none could as yet see, but the shade of them made the land grow cold as they passed.

To face them came the summer folk, golden and green. Here came the bright elves and the insects that love the land in bloom. Here, too, came Adscita's folk and their kindred, the fluttering people of the day and the honey gatherers and those who hover among the river reeds, and those who live under thistledown. Among them flew a warrior, black and shining, with mighty wings the colour of fire and roses. Here came the nymphs and the oakmen, the curly-horned urisk and the wuduaelfen and the fair family from under the water. Here came the gentle shellycoat, whose looks were drab under all the shells he stuck on his skin, but whose healing was strong and well learned. Here came Phynthoblin's people, though he was not among them, with harp and drum and pipes; the ladybird with the arquebus was there with some friends of her own, and here too came the Gnom, smiling and passing good beer out to share. Here even came the Newt, and today of all days, he looked ready to breathe fire. Many of the soldiers of summer were prepared in glittering array to fight to the death, and fine and brave they were, but there was no denying that they were fewer in number than before. They were waiting for someone, and when he arrived, they let out a cheer, for here to lead them came the madman himself, the Hunter, and if he was ready to die, so were they. And the day shone very bright.

The Red Duke's herald, a cockroach of great size and shining purple armour, stepped forward.

"Be it known," he called out, "that his majesty the Prince of Spiders commands all loyal subjects to bend the knee to him now, in the name of the old ways. Renegades and traitors will be killed, but those genuinely remorseful will be pardoned. He gives this last chance to avoid bloodshed in his already tragically-torn kingdom. Who will take it? Who will accept the mercy of the King?"

Banners of red and gold and green fluttered. No voice answered. The herald looked over to the third party in the field. Standing back, wearing embroidered clothes and ribbons stood the followers of the Beloved. Some wore the yellows and blues of Spring, to show their allegiance, but everyone of them was masked, for they were people of the changing time. Among them stood a grasshopper in a wig. She who led them nodded to the herald, and that was all. The herald stood back.

The great butterfly of orange and black flew forward, and his voice was rich and lilting.

"Be it known to all," he cried out, "that the Prince of Spiders is no true prince. That he does not follow the old ways but clings to power, to the shame of summer and winter alike. His day has passed, his crimes are many, and we shall end them all. We offer truce and peace to those who are ready to face the coming of the sun. To those who would harm us, we offer none.

Speak, any who seek mercy." And Phynthoblin saw, even from behind the Beloved's mask, that the black warrior held a great flint tipped spear. It looked familiar to him. For no reason he could comprehend, it made him shudder.

There was silence. Then the horns of elfland sounded, echoing across the day. The Red Duke lifted his sword. The Hunter lifted his own, very high. And the armies charged.

ROBERT AND RICHARD WANDERED THROUGH THE WOOD, WHILE a tiny figure sprinted through the undergrowth trying to find them. Richard's eyes, fatigued with deserts, were cheered by the weeds and the green, morning glory and woodbine clambering all over the hedge. He swore that the longer they travelled along it the taller it became, until the shrubs grew like trees, young and fresh.

"Look at this fellow here!" Richard's father pointed down at a web which ambitiously covered the gap between two bushes. At its centre sat a fat tawny spider with darker markings on its back. "Unusual ain't he?" Richard's first instinct was to back away. The web was huge, and of very unusual shape, though he could not deny its symmetry. How could his father not see it? In its loops and lines, he knew who was speaking to him. With a fine touch he unhooked the web, and gently laid it over his face. He breathed in the final freedom of letting the spider win. It was not Richard the eater of cobwebs who recovered eighteen-forty-three from her hiding place beneath the hedge; it was not Richard the wearer of masks who ended his father's exclamations by striking his head clean off his shoulders. It was Richard, the face of Osiris; Richard the powerful; Richard the artist.

———

AND THE ARMIES CLASHED, WITH SWARMS OF THE DUKE'S red-and-blacks storming the forward ranks of the Summer folk. The Duke had made it clear to all his men that none were to touch the Hunter except himself, that this prize was to be his and his alone. In the meantime the siege engines pushed forwards and those with wings soared into action: the need was to cut the bow ropes on the bollistas without being shot out of the skies. The catapults were also a problem. Given time, the Gnom would have been able to work out a clever solution but as it was, they just employed drop-the-rock tactics, courtesy of a squadron of red squirrels, whose attempts to treat the battle like a bowling alley proved very useful. Their enthusiastic avalanche of hazelnuts, chestnuts, crocus bulbs and other heavy artillery smashed most the missile launchers into oblivion; the ones that could be loaded fast enough to retaliate aimed deadly showers of nuts and bolts, which were just caught by the squirrels and thrown back. They at least were enjoying themselves. Meanwhile the acid bite of the Red Duke's men proved powerful in hand-to-hand combat, and blood was beginning to flow.

When the Bride caught up with Richard, he was alone, his eyes glowing with a fervour that suited him but made her feel shy. The ground beneath her feet was wet and slick with a smell she knew too well. *Blood*, she thought, *it must have started already. I wonder where they've gone?* But she did not think about the battle for long. Richard was staring at her tiny form as she stumbled through the grass. He smiled as though he had been expecting her. "Will you come up to me?" he said, "Or shall I come down to you?"

When she said nothing, he smiled again, as though greatly amused, and shrank himself down to her size. Once they were of almost equal height, his face changed, and he was more gentle, more like the man she remembered on the boat. *He is not well*, she tried to remind herself, *he needs help . . .*

"You should not stay here," she said to Richard. "You know the Prince will try to use you. Where is your father?"

"My father has gone home," said Richard. "And we don't have to be afraid of the Prince of Spiders any more. The fairy tale is almost ended. Shall we join the others?"

The Bride did not know what to say, but let him take her hand as he seemed so gallant and confident, and lead her towards the battlefield. Hidden by the high daisies lay the body of a man, with his sundered head nearby, rolled like a nut from a hazel tree. The crows were settling to feed even as the two mortals walked away.

THE RED DUKE BIT DEEP INTO THE THROAT OF THE HUNTER, even as all around, Summer and Winter fought. For so long he had wanted this. In his dreams he had said many things, rehearsed many speeches, asked many questions. Now he realised that the only important thing was the Hunter's death, and if he felt anything other than that, it was perhaps a little pride that his famous enemy, who had fought many legions single handed, was having to concentrate solely on him. Adscita's folk were already being thinned by the svartaelfar and unseelie court, and the rest of Summer would not be long to follow. He drew close to the face of his foe, and bared his mighty jaws for the final attack. "Pay attention!" smiled the Hunter, and brought his sword round, cleaving one of the Duke's back legs clean off. The Duke almost laughed. A leg? He had several more, and his troops were winning; all this before the dark ones joined them. It was going to be a massacre.

Phynthoblin watched with an appalled fascination, as the ladybird brought down a throttling hag with her arquebus, and turned to face two great shadows looming above her, all thorns and smiles. "We are going to need more of those things," he murmured to himself, not knowing if he meant guns or shadows. His own folk were fighting with the gallantry that made them such proud summer bards, but their bravery was greater than their strength. They were dying and Phynthoblin knew it. He turned away before tears could gather in his eyes, and found himself face to face with the orange winged black warrior. There was something in its face that reminded him of the deadliest of the seelie, for summer is not always gentle. Sometimes it blinds, sometimes it strikes down. Beauty can be glittering and fierce.

"I do not know you," faltered Phynthoblin.

"Do you not?" smiled the being. There was a silence.

"And yet you know this weapon, I believe." And Phynthoblin stared at the great spear and remembered where he had seen it before. He sank to his knees.

"I did all this for the crown," he pleaded. "Mercy!"

"Mercy?" said the voice, ringing like poetry, like the spires of the sun. "Yes, Mercy. But not for you," and the spear flashed straight into Phynthoblin's stomach. It was withdrawn as quickly and the butterfly flew away. It occurred to the grasshopper, as he fell sideways and watched his blood soak into the grass, that he was a member of the Court of the Changing Season, the new neutral court, and this was surely a great insult to them and to her. Right in front of them, too. Strange that none had come to help him. He wondered what the cost of the court's safety might have been. Then, he wondered no more, and died alone.

The Red Duke wondered where the other army was. He could smell them on the wind, as could the seelie court, and he knew it was making them nervous. But the reinforcements were nowhere to be seen, and this was surely not part of his majesty's plan. A delay then, or maybe they were waiting for twilight, he thought, as the sword of the Hunter came whirling through, and left him no head for pondering.

"RICHARD—MR DADD—I'M SORRY TO ASK SO MANY QUESTIONS but I hear no battle at all. Are we anywhere near the others?" asked the Bride. She was pleased to see him so happy, but her thoughts returned to the Hunter and the battle. It was odd that she couldn't hear them, and there was a strange smell all around them.

"The others? Of course, come with me." He laughed lightly. "I know a bank where the wild thyme grows . . . " and led her into a clearing, soft with nettles and ragwort towering above them.

There, sat all around the clearing, were Richard's dolls, curls and ringlets all perfect. They stared at her out of porcelain eyes and china faces, and in their hands they held little prizes from an ordinary house: pins and bodkins and kitchen knives. They turned to look at the Bride, and lifted their arms in perfect salute. They were the source of the scent, which was definitely not wild thyme. The Bride had smelled it once before, from a dead man at a cross roads.

"My last game of shadows and toys," said Richard. "Before I leave all this forever."

THE THUNDER ROLLED UNDER GATHERING CLOUDS, THOUGH the wise might call it the roaring of a dragon, shrunk to the size of a newt. The svartaelfar magics caused great havoc, for after two blasts of fire from the mouth of their red sea foe, they started aiming all their spells at him. Lightning made the newt laugh, and no magics pierced his powerful hide, until one among the svartaelfar (some said it was the same one who had enchanted the bollista spear) sang a cold dark song and made a shard appear in its hand, curling into the shape of a small spiked spiral. The svartaelfar flung it towards the newt, who was, from the unseelie scale at least, too big to miss. As the weapon span straight into the newt's side, he let out a terrible roar which scalded the grass around him. Where the weapon struck, his skin burst like a squashed grape, flesh spilling out between his scales, and blood pouring from him faster and thicker than ever he let it flood into the sea. There was a moment's triumph for the unseelie as the poor beast grew pale. He staggered for a moment, then fell, and the shadow thorns and pallid ones from beneath the mines crawled all over his body.

The clouds were dark now, with white livid edges, and the air roared of storm. Even the first raindrops could not turn away the scent of the others; they were nearby and very strong. It made no sense to the Hunter. The battle was slowing turning against the unseelie. Why was the Prince sacrificing his court if he had another army?

"Save the newt!" he roared at Danaeus. "And offer them surrender!" And he ran towards the smell, over metal, under thunder. The first bolt of lightning struck the trees under which a masked woman kept her court. In the flash, she saw the Hunter looking across at her. She nodded and ran after him.

Rain was falling all around them. Leaves rustled in the water music, and the Bride tried to feel at ease. It was impossible. She stared at the surrounding dolls, who stared back.

"These things are horrible," she whispered to Richard. "Why have you brought them here?"

His eyes gazed into hers and for the first time since she had known him, he seemed without fear.

"They will keep my enemy away from me," he said. She thought she understood.

"He has done you great harm," she told him. "But he never will, again. I sat with you all through your voyage home, and I promise you he never came back."

"These," he nodded at the dolls as they stared glacially at her, "these are from a time before him."

"So they make you feel safe?"

He permitted himself a little laughter. "They make us both safe. None can get in . . . "

And none get out, she wanted to finish for him, but she realised how paranoid that sounded. The rain grew heavier, and nearby she heard the low growl of thunder. It reminded her of something just out of her mind's reach.

He turned his entire attention upon her. "You have been my guardian angel," he said. "I have you to thank for everything."

The dolls turned away for a moment, paying attention elsewhere.

He let his hands touch her face. This time she was no dream. "I remember a great many things about the voyage," he said, and watched as a blush stole over her cheeks. He touched her again. "Sweet," he said softly, and kissed her. The Bride was too confused to know what to do. His kiss was hungry and she realised how lonely she had been—a second's irritation flew towards the Hunter—and then she concentrated enough to realise that she liked being kissed, only for a strange unsettled feeling in her mouth. It was as though something was moving, or perhaps he was laughing, right under his tongue, just as their lips met. Whether it was that or the memory of the Hunter, she pulled away.

He looked, not unhappy but a little reproachful. "You do not like—you would rather I did not—"

"No, no," she said, "It's just that . . . " He looked at her and she found herself captivated by his wisdom and beauty. She also noticed something wispy crossing his face, thistledown perhaps. It seemed odd to her that she had not tasted it when they kissed.

He took her hand in his. "He is very attractive, I know," said Richard. "And far more strong and powerful than I am. Nonetheless, he loves as they love, not as we love. Their love is a flame, brilliant but insubstantial. It is easy to get caught in the glamour of it, as I was," and he looked very sad.

Years of servitude, she thought. *And if I waited for the Hunter, I could waste my life and my heart just as easily.* Her suitor fell to one knee.

"Marry me, Lady Bride," he said. "I know I should speak

more graciously, but marry me, and save my mind, save my life. Only your pity has kept me going. And it has not all been pity, no, not all of it. Not every night you watched me. There was something else. Is that not so?"

It had to be so. Whenever he mentioned it she turned a shade of salmon. At any other time he would have laughed, but he dared not take his eyes from hers. Neither of them noticed the swift exchange of blades behind them.

"Richard—"

"My dear!" He clasped her hand more tightly, while the scent of wet flowers surrounded them like a gift. Little thunder, less lightning, and the storm ending: the Hedge was becoming beautiful, as was he. He looked so happy she could barely lift her eyes to meet his gaze.

"I am not from your time at all. I would be as unhappy in your time as I would be in servitude in the Hedge. I belong in another place, far from here . . . "

"I will go wherever you wish, if I have you beside me for eternity. Marry me, lady, and love me as best you can. In return I will give you—"

"What? What will you give me?" Her eyes were sparkling, her lashes fluttering. Around the glade, heads were popping off and limbs were flailing, but this was so romantic and she was only human.

"All of myself," he finished, and waited, head bowed. She lifted him to his feet.

"Richard," she said, "I do not know if I can be a proper wife to you. I do not know if I can love you as you wish, as you deserve." He sighed.

"But I can try. I am ready to try, if I can save you from all this sorrow." There was noise around them both, but neither were paying attention.

"And can you love me enough to give me your trust?"

"I will do my very best, as well as I possibly can."

"And do you love me enough to trust me with your life? Your life and your heart?" The air quivered with coloured light and water, and now, from the very depths of his soul he kissed her and the mask of Osiris moved, and she tried to speak. He released her enough for that; it was the most important thing he was ever likely to hear.

"I love you enough to trust you with my life and my h—"

His kiss smothered her words passionately, and then he stood back, as the knife pierced her from between her shoulder blades. She watched as the iron tip glinted through her chest, and she bled, under a tremulous rainbow. Richard looked past her with shining eyes, as the mask fell from him.

"Sylvia," he smiled. "Thank you my dear."

And as the Bride crumpled to the ground, Richard fell, too, discarded like a shell. He was weeping as Osiris forsook him, weeping too, when he saw her put her hands on the wound, astonished at how much blood she had in her. She was trying to mop it up with her clothes, trying to stop it from reaching the soil, the roots of the Hedge, as the great spider crawled out of Richard's mouth to cry aloud:

"Hear me, old ones! Hear me, people of the Hedge! Hear me, all witnesses of the Land . . . "

Sylvia's head popped off while he was speaking. The Bride could only be marginally less surprised than Sylvia herself. The spider ranted on, and Richard sobbed.

"I have followed the ways!"

The Bride heard a whisper behind her saying, "Tie this around the wound!" as an object she recognised fell to the ground yards from her. Mottled and dark, it was a muzzle made of toadskin, used to tame Richard long ago. When she looked back, she saw the Beloved nodding at her from between the trees and heard the muttering geas:

> *Toad I bid thee once again,*
> *Now to keep my treasures in*
> *Round the bothy with thy skin*
> *Do it lest I give thee pain!*

Round the bothy . . . the Bride had no idea what a bothy was. She wound the skin around her chest, binding her breasts and the wound beneath. The doll had not pierced her heart or she doubted anything could work, but, short of the heart, she knew the toadskin's power of stilling and containment. It had worked on the mind of a madman, now it worked on the blood of the Bride. The skin grew slick and wet, and the pain grew less intense.

"I have given you dreams!" danced the Spider Prince. "And now I give you—"

Then the great grey wolf leapt out from between the dolls, straight towards the Prince. "Kill him!" screamed the Prince at his dolls, noticing too late that every doll had its limbs torn off, its head criss-crossed, its body mutilated. Nearby on the grass lay a mighty iron axe, still smiling at the Hunter's arrival.

"Obey me!" screamed the Prince. "Somebody kill him!"—as the great beast caught his fat body and threw it up into the air with a fine lupine abandon, catching him as he fell.

"No!" screamed the Prince. "I have done it! She gave me her vow—"

The grey wolf grabbed the spider and smashed it against a tree. Three of its legs crumpled beneath it. It slid to the ground. "Hunter," it said. "Be reasonable. I kept to our agreement. I didn't make her agree, and I didn't force him."

"You did! You did!" screamed the Bride. "Or how . . . he would never . . . you did this . . . "

"No," said the Spider Prince. "No, come, let us change back to our true shapes, Hunter, listen to me. I did not force him, I did not," as the beast picked him up in its jaws and walked casually over to eighteen-forty-three, who turned her iron edge upwards just for him. "It was a fairy gift! You know it's true, cousin. Perfectly fair! You know about fairy gifts! He took a fairy gift!"

And the wolf swiped him down the edge of the blade, clean, quick and straight.

"It may be true and fair," said the wolf to the shrivelling king, "but I am bored with hearing it." And he dropped the corpse to the earth.

CHAPTER TWENTY-ONE
THE GATES OF SUMMER

———

It was some time later, when the wound had healed, and the Beloved had taken her geas back without a word of thanks or explanation on either side, that the Bride had her first conversation with the new monarch of summer.

"I thought I had lost you," she told Danaeus, who laughed and shook his head.

"I am so embarrassed about that," he said. "In fact, I am embarrassed about all of it. The newt helped of course."

"I see the rose wing is just as good as the other." She looked at it with wonder and delight. "I'm sure you know better, but to me they look exactly the same."

"They are. They're just much stronger." He could not help extending them high above her head. She asked about the newt and the battle, and it transpired that the valiant beast had been saved by the ladybird with the arquebus. The shadowthorns and pale drinkers had been smothering him four deep, digging themselves into his wound, when she blasted the whole wretched cabal into pieces and nearly took him with them. The shellycoat was nearby with healing to spare, but it had been a close call.

"The Prince ruined his army and betrayed his general—I almost feel sorry for the Red Duke—and instead of crushing us on the field, kept the deadly ones to guard you and make sure you didn't leave. Admittedly, their numbers were much greater than ours, after that terrible battle at the wedding." His radiance dimmed just for a moment. "But the prince was a fool to count on that: he should know that Summer is invincible. And of course, he didn't know our new-crowned winter king was going to storm his elite troops all by himself . . . . Well," Danaeus admitted as an afterthought, "the Beloved was there too, but she barely counts," and he grinned, as the Hunter stomped towards them with a lopsided crown of holly and ivy dangling from his tricorn. He sat down, looking mutinous.

"I want nothing to do with any of this until the nights grow long," he said. "They are expecting me to be courtly already. I'll have none of it. What are you doing here anyway?" he said to the butterfly king. "They want to talk to you about your new palace, as if the coronation wasn't hellish enough. Why is everyone so excited? Don't they have homes to go to?"

Danaeus shrugged. "They're building me a mountain of flowers," he explained to the Bride. "I never asked them to, they're just very keen."

She laughed; of course they wanted to give flowers to the monarch of summer, if only to see them reflected in the spar-kling depths of his eyes. Her laughter had a slight hesitance that neither missed. They could not let it be, and so she told them that though she was happy for them and all the land, she could not be completely happy. She wanted to go home.

"You know," said the Hunter, "every human I have ever heard say that regrets it. Your home is probably here or you wouldn't have come."

"Like Richard?" she smiled ruefully. She had watched as men from the mortal world had taken him back. His eyes were grey and shone like the rain, the way he would shine among the mad and dreaming, in all the lost years to come.

"Not like Richard." The butterfly king touched her hand. "Things are changing. The Beloved will reign in spring, for this Richard of hers gave the land all he had; father's life and love, mind and all," Danaeus shook his head. The pity he felt for Richard could not cloud his joy.

"You could rule between my time and Hunter's. You can be our autumn queen, lady of harvests and home." Danaeus' eyes were faceted and brilliant, shining like the sun. "You know it could be wonderful."

She looked at the Hunter who said nothing. His eyes burned too, but she had never learned to read their flame.

"It sounds beautiful," she said. "And I know I will want to return here, to you both. But right now, I want the things I know, ordinary things. My home, where I make the rules." The Hunter raised one eyebrow, but still said nothing. The Summer Monarch and Winter King looked at each other and walked with the Bride. They led her away from the Hedge, until it seemed to shimmer and fade into a little grass verge, just where Church Lane joined the Park footpath . . .

. . . Then the butterfly lifted its wings, and somehow grew small to my sight. It fluttered upwards, landed on my hair for a moment, and flew away. The small grey spider wandered up the path with me towards the open front door of a house, where electric light still blazed bright, and it turned away among the cracks in the pavings. I thought I heard the word,

THE SPIDER'S BRIDE

"Remember," brush by my ears. On the doorstep lay a single finger, which I ignored.

Then I stepped in through the door and was home.

———

If we shadows have offended,
Think but this and all is mended,
That you have but slumbered here,
While these visions did appear.
And this weak and idle theme
No more yielding than a dream . . .
Gentles do not reprehend:
Give me your hands, if we be friends.

BIOGRAPHY

———

Debbie Gallagher works as a presenter for Cellcast TV where she features in regular appearances on Psychic TV, and also specialises in voice-overs for Sumo Television; her most famous work to date being an interview with a medium who claimed that Elvis had contacted her from beyond the grave to reveal his foot fetish. Debbie has written *Batman* for DC Comics, *Slaine* for 2000 AD, the *Ragnarok Book* and *Teeth of the Moon Sow* among others for Mongoose Publishing and *The Redeemer* Series for Games Workshop. She has also written various articles on alternative worlds and perspecitives, has been interviewed by *The Times* Newspaper on the subject of modern druidry, and has presented lectures on the Traditions of Fairy Legend in English Literature.

Debbie's interests include other worlds, dreams and lost memories, madness and art, and all of these feature in this, her first fantasy novel. But when she's not fantasising, she enjoys pointless travelling, eating sea-food, and playing with her cats.